EYE OF THE STORM

A GRAY GHOST NOVEL—BOOK TWO

AMY MCKINELY

ARROWSCOPE PRESS LLC

ISBN: 978-0-9994280-2-3

Publisher: Arrowscope Press, LLC; www.arrowscopepress.com

Editing—

Taylor Anhalt, Editor

Sara G., Content Editor, Red Adept Editing

Kate B., Line Editor, Red Adept Editing

Irene S., Proofreader, Red Adept Editing

Cover Design—T.E. Black Designs; www.teblackdesigns.com

Cover photo provided by: CJC Photography www.cjc-photography.com

Model: Alex Neff

Interior Formatting—T.E. Black Designs; www.teblackdesigns.com

In loving memory of my amazing cousin, Brian, who lives on in our minds and hearts.

*When someone you love becomes a memory,
the memory becomes a treasure.
~Anonymous*

CHAPTER 1

Tilting his head back, against gravity, proved too taxing. Pain lanced the side of his head and numerous other places, too many to count. With difficulty, he tensed his legs, testing for injury. Stirrings of alarm spiked through his blood at the slow rocking motion, and he refocused on controlling his breathing while he pieced all the information together.

He hung upside down.

Insects buzzed, and wind whispered through the trees. His foggy brain worked to sort through the noises and analyze the one that was out of place. The sounds clicked—some of them, anyway. He was outside, and everything hurt. His head throbbed as he fought to stay conscious. He dismissed the bugs, birds, the call of a monkey, and the croaking frogs, and was left with a sound that made him uneasy. The occasional slow creak stood out loudly and clearly. A gust of wind shifted his body and rattled the leaves around him. The groaning and creaking increased. He'd yet to open his eyes.

Something was definitely wrong.

The pounding in his head intensified, and his lethargic mind balked as he tried to connect the dots. Every part of his body throbbed with discomfort, but pain was one thing he could block out. What he couldn't ignore was his bewilderment at how he'd gotten there.

The agony lessened. A small, smooth, repetitive touch bumped against his cheek, filtering into his awareness. He sensed no threat. With great effort, he peeled open one eyelid and tried his best to focus his blurry vision on what it was. *A strand of tiny metal beads?* A sense of familiarity teased the edges of his mind, and his pulse increased as he tried to remember the strand's significance. Shapes and images danced around the edge of his mind, but every time he attempted to concentrate, to draw them in, they dissipated. His efforts brought blinding agony, because nothing was there. Where his memory should be, a void existed.

Blood pounded in his head, and when he tensed his muscles again, the tether around his legs, arms, and back filtered in. *What did I do last? Why would I be here?* At each question, his mind drew a complete blank. He ruthlessly shoved away the hysteria that tried to overtake him and instead concentrated on his breathing, inhaling slowly and lengthening his exhales. As his body somewhat relaxed, he mentally rehearsed what he needed to do—figure out where he was, why he was there, and how to get to safety. He observed what was around him with the small amount of focus he could gather. Leaves. Lots and lots of leaves.

Something dripped down his face and quietly plopped on the leaves below him. *Sweat?* His mouth was swollen and as dry as the desert. He tried to clear his throat, but the pounding and dizziness that swept through him stopped him. The humidity suffocated and sucked him dry at the same time. *Where am I?* Confusion sent zings of panic through his densely cloudy mind.

Still, he pushed past the nausea and impending darkness that pressed against the edges of his consciousness.

He pried open his other eye and instantly regretted it when shards of pain sliced through his skull. With several measured breaths, he forced both of them wide. Greens and browns swam in front of his blurry vision. As he rocked back and forth from the wind, the object that had bumped his cheek swung from his neck. The small silver beads tugged at his memory once more, but what they were escaped him. Whatever the chain symbolized would be there for him to investigate later. The immediate problem was the predicament he was in. He hung upside down in a tree and couldn't remember how the hell he'd gotten there or anything from the moment he'd opened his eyes. And if that wasn't bad enough, he couldn't even remember his name.

MARI

Branches slapped and battered Mari, stinging her arms and face. Her heart thudded against her breastbone as she gasped, dragging thick, sticky air into her lungs. Damn this jungle, and the stupid transporter who'd swindled her out of her weapons. She needed a gun, a blade, anything. Then she'd turn the tables and show what an armed Colombian woman was capable of.

Her breath sawed in and out with each slap of her feet against the slick leaves, twigs, and branches that caught at her pants legs. The last months of her freedom looped through her mind. She'd been so close, having fled Colombia before they'd realized she was gone. She'd sought shelter in rented rooms until the day the Ramirez cartel marched through the streets, leaving destruction in their wake. She knew who sent them—her childhood friend turned worst nightmare. Defying him would enact retribution from the cartel. It was inevitable unless she could manage to escape.

Against all odds, she would. Her life would be her own.

Roots snagged her feet, seemingly determined to capture her. She ran for her life through a dangerous and hostile jungle that teemed with insurgent guerrillas, drug-traffickers, and kidnappers. But none of that mattered. Her options for escape had been limited before and had grown even more so.

A Colombian guerrilla chased her, closing in fast. Wiry, quick, and used to the conditions and terrain, he stood a good chance of outrunning, outmaneuvering, and overtaking her. A new surge of adrenaline pumped through her veins, probably the last of it, so she took advantage of the rush.

The heat sapped her strength. *Must make it.* Her desperate fingers grabbed roots that stuck out in the slippery, mud-coated incline, as she fought to stay ahead.

Her thighs convulsed, and the stitch in her side threatened to take her down. She sweated by the bucket load, and dehydration was inevitable. She wondered how much longer she could really go at this pace, in this environment. Beautiful but deadly, the jungle had her at a disadvantage. Nausea cramped her stomach. Thick foliage trapped her and slowed her down. Without a machete, she had no choice but to dive through the mass of green, praying for a trail on the other side. Maybe going it alone in the wild wasn't the best of ideas. But she hadn't had another means, or anyone to help her.

Cruel fingers scraped along her head, yanking out some hair. *Bastard.* Her fury spiked, and she whirled around, her arm extended. Using the momentum, she flung her arm against the side of his face. His head snapped back, and he stumbled. Spinning around, she pushed herself to run, to take advantage of the small gain. If he touched her again, she'd make him pay.

She forced her body to move faster, harder. It was more a

mental challenge than a physical one, and she could do it. An opening loomed ahead, and she dashed forward. The freedom of movement gave her false hope. She'd pushed too hard and too fast in the heat, and her energy stores were depleted. Her body slowed, and she pressed her mouth into a tight line. *I can do this.* Even with an iron-willed determination to live, she knew she couldn't outrun him. The tangled branches and leaves had worked against her. He did too. It wouldn't be long. He'd be on her in a matter of minutes, if not seconds.

The small pack on her back felt as though it weighed ten times what it had when she'd left her last hiding place. It thwacked her back in rhythm while her feet pounding across the slippery forest floor. Twice, she'd fallen and dropped to a knee as the slick ground worked against her.

The sound of his boots slapping behind her shifted along her side—he was trying to force her to turn, to head down a narrow path that begun at the base of a muddy incline.

In a split-second decision, she lunged to the left, avoiding the steep hill she knew he wanted her to travel in exchange for a thicket of spindly trees, heavy with green leaves. She was smaller and thinner than he was, so she could slip through them more easily. There, she could maintain her speed for a while longer. The incline would have sapped her strength. It would have been her end.

She'd escaped from the town she'd grown up in, working her way to cross the border and to start a new life. Knowledge of her imminent fate counteracted the optimistic hope she'd once had. He continued to pound along behind her, closing in once again. After running and hiding, she'd thought she was almost free, but it wasn't meant to be. She'd found a new enemy.

She did have one weapon, sort of, the pack that slammed into her back. If he caught her—and he would—she'd go down swinging.

As she sucked in each breath, she almost faltered, and something changed. The odor of foul decay permeated the stifling air, and she tried to veer away, stifling a cry. The sight that greeted her was gruesome. The stench took residence in her nostrils. Five decapitated heads rotted on spikes. *This is not good.*

He was too close, and she had no choice but to sprint past the putrid heads on pikes. *Shit. Cartel territory.*

He was herding her.

Her adrenaline reached uncharted heights when she risked a glance over her shoulder and saw his arms pumping, a gun gripped tightly in his fist, and his gaunt face, which held cruel lips and cold, dead eyes. Another few inches, and he'd have her. Why he didn't simply shoot spoke volumes. She'd be his toy before he killed her.

The muddy ground sabotaged her again, and she fell to a knee. Jumping up, she cursed at the lost time. More than anything, she wished she had her knives. She'd bury one in his throat and dance in his blood as he died.

A pop echoed in the dense jungle, and she felt the displacement of air by her left ear. Mari jolted right. A dull thunk hit its mark behind her—*the man*—and then she heard the thwap of a body hitting the forest floor. She sprinted to take cover behind a tree, then she stopped to rest with her hands on her knees, panting in a desperate attempt to slow her breathing. Squinting, Mari searched for the safest way out. *Who shot him?*

With a new enemy somewhere out there, she feared taking the risk of moving, but the danger of staying still in one place while he advanced on her was great, too. Like a rabbit caught in an impossible trap, she waited, calculating her next move.

Trading one pursuer for another wasn't good. It might be preferable to other alternatives, but freedom—safety—was the ultimate goal.

"Come out." The quiet command of a female voice cut through the dense foliage.

Mari was immobile with shock while her rescuer came into view, training a gun on her head. *Maybe she's not a rescuer.* The woman had steady, pale-blue eyes and blond hair pulled back into a ponytail. The woman's voice and coloring made her stand out—she obviously wasn't a Colombia native. *Odd. Why is she here?* She was dressed in ill-fitting clothes, wearing the same style of the guerrilla insurgent who'd chased her. She'd spoken English. *Is she with his group?*

"What do you want?" Even though this woman had helped, Mari wouldn't trust her blindly.

Her lips pressed into a hard slash, the woman jerked her head at the prone body. "Check the body." She kept the gun trained on Mari's chest.

Digging her fingernails into the tree's rough bark, she attempted to put it in between her and the mystery woman. She lifted her chin and snapped, "You shot him, you find out."

Brows raised, the woman lowered her gun a notch. "You're not really in a position to argue. Check the body, and I won't shoot you in the leg."

She had a point.

Seconds ticked by, and Mari took a step away from the safety of the tree. When no bullet came, she moved to the man sprawled on the ground. A single hole bloomed crimson in the center of his forehead. The woman was a good shot.

Unwilling to turn her back on the blond woman, Mari squatted beside him, her fingers finding the spot by his neck where a pulse would flutter if he was alive. She felt around to be sure then pulled her hand away when nothing moved beneath her touch. "He's dead."

"What are you doing here?"

"Running." Willing to risk being shot, she searched the man

for his weapons. The gun had flown to where it rested on his other side. If he had other weapons, she needed to find them—and take them.

"In the Darian Gap, the most dangerous place in the Western Hemisphere? So close to a guerrilla camp? You do realize people who come here usually die, right?"

Mari took a breath, feeling her temper rise, and counted to five before she stated the obvious. "This was my best option to get out of Colombia undetected. As for the guerrilla camp, I didn't plan to cross into it. He chased me." Maybe it was just apparent to her what'd happened. She didn't know who the woman was.

"Drove you, more likely."

No kidding. Mari stopped herself from rolling her eyes. She knew the man had been attempting to corral her in the camp, but what choice did she have at the time? The additional rush from the shooting seemed to bring out the worst in her. "It hasn't really been a good day for me. At least tell me your name." Her words slurred, and she bit her swollen tongue in an attempt to curb her runaway mouth. God, she needed water.

The woman gave a tight nod. "Hannah."

"Look, Hannah, I appreciate you saving my life, but this isn't really the time to have a chat, considering where we are."

"No, it isn't, is it?" A few seconds passed, and Hannah's head tilted to the side and her shoulders relaxed. "I need a little more information before I decide if I want to kill you or not."

CHAPTER 2

MARI

Mari remained in a squat next to the body of the man Hannah had shot. Even with Hannah watching her every move and deciding whether to kill her or not, Mari risked looking over his prone form. His gun wasn't close, but his knife was. She leaned back on her heels a tad, her fingers itching to circle the metal. The gun would have been preferable. She was a good shot, too. But any weapon would do.

The blonde's eyes narrowed, and Mari froze, not willing to make the woman's decision for her. A loud thumping echoed through Mari's head, and she worried it was the sound of feet pounding the dirt until she realized it was the amplified cadence of her pulse.

Hannah tilted her head and pursed her lips. A beat passed between them in silence. "Are you connected to any of the factions in this area?"

Mari couldn't answer that question without her bitchiness

waving its red flag. The effects of exhaustion, running for her life, and dehydration had a hold of her. "You're kidding, right? He was chasing me. It would not have ended well. There's no way I'd have anything to do with drug trafficking or the guerrillas who're probably on their way to kill us right now."

Hannah lowered her weapon to the side of her leg, and the corner of her mouth twitched. "That's the most likely scenario." She took a few steps closer, reached into the pack at her back, and tossed Mari a thin plastic packet before she bent and swiped the guerrilla's gun from the ground then tucked it into the waistband of her pants. She moved the man's canteen over to Mari with her foot.

Relief rushed through Mari as she tore the packet open and poured it into the half-empty canteen. The powdered electrolytes would aid her focus and clear some of the fogginess from her brain.

"I think we can come to a mutually beneficial agreement—a fair trade. I need help with something, and clearly so do you. But let's start with the obvious. I saved your life." Hannah paused until Mari gave a curt nod. "And it seems you want to get safely across the border. I have a way to get you through here and across, without being killed, but I need a favor."

The reality of their situation whispered through her mind, telling her there would be no guarantee this woman would keep her safe. But no matter what, her odds were better with someone who also knew how to shoot a gun. "What's the favor?"

"A life for a life. I saved yours, now there's someone I want you to do the same for."

"That's pretty broad. How do I know that what, or who, you're trying to saddle me with won't bring me down and keep me here indefinitely? Or kill me?" Mari frowned. "Why don't *you* save them?"

"I have somewhere I need to be, and you'll be going the opposite direction, since you're planning to get out of Colombia. If we don't get to him soon, others who are searching for him will. That wouldn't be good. You can help this person get far away from here, too."

Lovely. Are more guerrillas on their way? "Fine." *Maybe, but only once I know who and what the person I'm supposed to save is.* The goal here was to keep Hannah's damn gun pointed elsewhere. If her cold gaze and unhurried demeanor were any indication, ice pumped through her veins.

If Mari got shot in the leg, there wouldn't be anywhere she could go. She'd be a sitting duck, ripe for enemy plucking. "Who *are* you?"

"Hannah. I told you that." The woman's gun lowered completely.

Not exactly what I meant. "I'm Mari. And who's the person you want me to help?"

"I'm going to show you."

Mari dropped her pack from her back then fell to her knees and riffled through it. "Okay, I guess." She didn't really have a choice. If she ran from Hannah, there was a high probability she'd get shot, so she'd have to go along with a new adventure as her next move. With a hard yank, she unzipped her pack and rooted around for her own canteen, which she'd stowed inside. When her hands clamped on the smooth plastic and she brought it to her lips, she almost cried. Almost. She doubted she had any tears left in her dry husk of a body.

Water poured down Mari's throat in a warm stream, and she instantly felt better, less likely to drop to the ground, never to get up again. It helped to restore a little energy to her flagging will and would keep her going. Swiping a hand over her brow, she stopped the sweat from dripping into her eyes. What she wouldn't give for a fan, an ice-cold drink, or a freezing shower.

With careful movements, she re-capped the container and put it back in her backpack before slinging the heavy thing on her back with a groan. She shifted it to a more comfortable spot on her shoulder.

Hannah waved her gun in front of Mari, and she pushed out a breath as she got to her feet. "Okay, I'm ready. Where is this mysterious person who needs my assistance?" If she could see the humor of the situation, she would have laughed. How she was going to help anyone else when it seemed like she went from one crisis to the next was beyond her.

Reaching up, Hannah tugged on her high ponytail until it was tighter. Mari couldn't understand how the eye-catching platinum blonde survived out here. Being a woman was dangerous enough, but she didn't blend in at all with that light hair. She probably made it because she was a damn good shot. Looking her up and down, Mari wondered how much ammo Hannah had on her. Once that ran out, she'd be a sitting duck—just like Mari.

Out of one terrible situation and into the next. What has my life become? After her aunt had passed away, she'd felt so alone. She'd hated the isolation, but would welcome it in the predicament she was in.

For the first several months after her aunt had died, Mari had struggled with an unwavering loneliness because she had no one left. As she'd left the relative safety of her last hovel, she'd realized she would die if she didn't try to make it out of South America. Either from the emptiness inside her, those in authority, or the man she ran from. None of the options were pleasant.

She took a quick glance at Hannah, and a part of her relaxed. Traveling with a woman through this hellhole might be nice. At least she'd have someone to talk to.

With her brows scrunched together, Hannah turned behind her, obviously contemplating something about their direction. "I wonder." She motioned for them to head deeper into guerrilla territory.

"Wait." Mari stood her ground and spoke through her teeth. "That's suicide. You want us to go closer to their camp? We just got rid of one of them. Why would we go into a nest? How is that not insane?"

Hannah turned back to look at Mari, and her cold gaze latched onto her. Mari bristled. The woman was intense, and something about her penetrated Mari's exhausted mind. She was powerful, confident, and cunning. *Yeah, I'd do well to stick close to the scary woman. At least for now, it'll up my odds of survival until I can get out of this godforsaken nightmare.*

"We need a few things. What better way to get them than from their camp?"

"How the hell are we going to do that *and* stay alive?" Mari swatted away a bug, wanting to smack Hannah as well.

A half smile curved Hannah's lips. "As long as you're quiet, it shouldn't be too difficult."

Dios mio, this woman is crazy. Realizing she didn't have much of a choice, she fell into line with Hannah, trudging through the brush. Pressing her lips together, she restrained the string of insults that she longed to hurl at Hannah about her new idea.

Their progress quickened as the terrain became easier to traverse. Unlike the rest of the vegetation Mari had traveled through, there was a narrow path where someone had hacked a trail with a machete. With each step her feet weighed more, her legs burned, and her mouth leeched of all moisture. At least she didn't have to fight through leaves, trees, and bushes.

"Be quiet," Hannah snapped, her voice a whip-like whisper. "Do you hear that?" She stopped and waited for Mari's tight-lipped nod. "They'll be close to the river. You need to be quieter, or we'll have company we don't want."

That's for sure. Mari took care to step where Hannah did,

falling directly behind her. The woman glided like a ghost through the harsh environment, very unlike Mari, who struggled to pick up each foot and move it forward.

A hand clamped down on her forearm, and Hannah leaned close. "They're right up there. See them moving through the trees?"

Squinting, Mari jerked her arm away from Hannah. Fear doused her exhaustion. They were outnumbered. Many bodies moved around a fire, getting their rations of lunch. Her stomach growled. She watched through a break in the leaves as each got a bowl, ladled something—probably stew of some sort—into it, and found a place to sit. Tan camouflage hats, shirts, and pants identified them as belonging to the same unit as the man who'd chased her. Sick dread churned in her empty stomach. This was the camp he'd been driving her toward.

"Follow me."

She trailed behind Hannah as they skirted around the base with enough distance to avoid detection. The sounds increased the closer they came to the river.

"Stay here. I'll be right back." Hannah held her gaze, waiting a beat until she got the reassurance she sought in Mari's expression.

Bossy much? She fought from rolling her eyes. *Really, where am I going to go right now?* Mari sank to the ground at the edge of the river, cupped the water, and with care not to make noise, splashed it on her face and over her head. Sticking her face in and drinking her fill was tempting, but the water was most likely contaminated by the men, given how close she was to their camp. Fresh water sloshed around in one of her canteens. She could wait to refill the empty one when they located a stream, which tended to have cleaner water, or so she'd heard growing up near the Darien Gap. If it wasn't rainwater, she would prefer to use the few iodine pills she'd brought or to boil it, if given the opportunity.

By the time she sat back up from leaning over the water, Hannah was nowhere in sight. *Wow, she moves quietly.* She hadn't even heard Hannah leave. Mari leaned against a tree, inches from the water, wanting to plunge herself in. Fatigued, she eased her head against the bark and tried to make herself as small as possible so as not to be seen from the other side of the trunk. Her nerves leapt in fear of being so close to the enemy. Their grueling pace was exhausting, and her fight-or-flight reaction to the guerrilla who had chased her had sapped precious energy. She fought to remain awake and aware, but her eyelids fluttered closed.

Something woke Mari from a light doze. *Holy hell, I passed out.* She wasn't sure how long she'd been asleep. A prod on her shoulder sent white-hot fear through her nonresponsive limbs, and she fell over. Her body jerked, and she reacted, pushing to her feet and swiveling, ready to take on who'd found her.

A shit-eating grin split Hannah's serious features. The woman's silent chuckle made Mari see red, and she took an adrenaline-fueled step forward, tempted to slap that expression from Hannah's face.

Hannah shoved a palm flat into Mari's chest, stopping her in her tracks. "Let's go."

Cursing under her breath, Mari pushed aside the confusion that swirled following Hannah's command and quick change of mood. Mari fell in line behind the taller woman and glanced over at the river. *Thank the heavens.* A long, narrow canoe, tethered to a branch, bobbed in the water. On Hannah's back rested two of the guerrillas' packs, complete with sheathed machetes.

They had a way out.

CHAPTER 3

MARI

The sky darkened with angry clouds as she and Hannah traveled down the Atrato River at a pace too quick for Mari's liking. While she wanted to get out of the area, she would rather not capsize and risk the loss of their dugout canoe.

She'd seen it all when it came to makeshift boats—tied logs, inflatable kayaks, and long, narrow canoes such as what they were in. Some had motors. She considered them lucky to have one of the dugouts, even if it lacked power. The thought of being on a log vessel made her edgy. There were crocodiles in the river.

Hannah had stolen the canoe farthest from the rest, the one the guerrillas would be least likely to notice if it went missing, or so they hoped. With one of the hand-carved paddles, Hannah guided them close to the overhanging trees, which offered some coverage from the beating sun. Mari, tired and sore from her trek through the harsh jungle, was grateful for the break. They'd traveled through the hottest part of the day. A nap, or even lying in a stream, would've been preferable to any type of movement just then.

A scuffling sound came from the underbrush not far from them, causing Mari to look over her shoulder. *Are we being followed?* With narrowed eyes, she searched the bank of the river for any indication that someone was there. When nothing emerged from the cover of the trees, she dismissed it, assuming it was an animal. Mari pressed her lips into a stubborn line as she turned back to Hannah. "Where are we going?"

Hannah spared her a cursory glance. "I told you." The dominant tone she used set Mari's nerves on edge.

"Yeah, yeah." She swept her arm out, gesturing to the vast jungle. "To find someone. And when we find this mysterious person?" Her patience was drawing to an end. They hadn't stopped to eat, assuming there was food in the packs, or even to hunt. Ever since they left the outskirts of the guerrilla camp with the wafting smell of stew, her stomach had felt as though it was eating itself. She'd even settle for munching on a few leaves if it would ease the cramping.

Hannah's miraculous presence when she most needed aid still sat askew in her gut, as did her fair complexion, which screamed "foreigner." "Why are you here?"

"Why are you?" Hannah countered. "Just be glad I was in the right place at the right time. If I hadn't been, that man would have caught you. Do you think he would have outright killed you, or perhaps he had other plans? Then where would you be?"

Thinking of the terror she'd narrowly missed caused a shudder to wrack her body. Hannah's quiet, measured words reminded Mari of the debt she owed her and of the reluctant promise she'd given—one she had no doubt Hannah would still collect. She just hoped it wasn't something she'd regret more than taking her chances alone.

Mari pulled on her ponytail, tightening it even more and wishing her long hair wasn't so thick. Her shoulders slumped, as she swallowed what little pride she had. She had to admit that she would be in a world of hurt if it hadn't been for this woman. "I never said it earlier, because, you know." Her annoyance with Hannah—in addition to the threats, running, and all they'd already been through—had stopped her from expressing her gratitude. "Thank you for helping me."

With a nod, Hannah accepted her poorly offered words of gratitude. Scanning the trees and horizon, she paddled them to the bank. She must've made a decision and figured out where this mysterious stranger would be.

Even though she'd yet to meet him, she felt a small kinship with him. From what Hannah had said, someone with ill intent was after him, and they needed to get to him first, maybe to save his life. She considered how she needed to leave before she was captured and returned. Maybe they could help each other and form a mutually beneficial relationship.

She and Hannah jumped into the shallow water. Sloshing around in the roots and mud that tried to keep them as payment for their passage, they tied the canoe to a tree. Hannah pursed her lips. "We may need this."

"The canoe? Of course we will. That's our transportation out of here."

"No." Hannah's ice-blue gaze swung her way. "To bring with us."

"Ah, it looks pretty awkward and heavy. I don't think that'd be a good idea."

With her brows furrowed, Hannah looked around the dense jungle ahead of them. "You're right. We'll figure something else out."

What? "Can you give me a little more information? I don't understand what you're talking about." Her irritation at the situation flared. There was a reason she'd entered the jungle where she had—there had been less chance of being stopped by the cartel that searched for her. "We need to get out of here, and from what it looks like, you've maneuvered us very close to where I started in Turbo, Colombia!" Alarm spread through her as, once again, the direction they were heading in registered in her tired brain. After all she'd been through, trust wasn't easily given. They were going farther into the swamps she'd already traveled, not out and toward the mountainous Panama border that she'd planned to cross.

Hannah's face was suddenly an inch from hers, a snarl curling her lips. "You ask too many questions."

Mari held her ground and tilted up her chin. With her heart pounding, she straightened, balling her hands into fists at her sides. "Tell me why we're going deeper in the swamplands, and why I should trust you." She swiped away the sweat that trickled too close to the corner of her eye. "How am I supposed to know if you're leading me to some other pack of wolves?"

"You don't. But would it make sense for me to save your life only to end it?"

She frowned. "No." *God, I want to lie down and sleep for a week.* "Look, I'm having trouble with this whole situation. I mean, look at you. You're obviously not from here, so what are you doing?" When Mari felt Hannah press the unyielding point of a knife against her throat, she went silent.

"We're done with the questions. We had a deal. Now, hold up your end of the bargain." Hannah waited a moment then slowly lowered the blade.

Dammit. Who is this woman? Annoyance crawled through Mari's tired mind.

Hannah turned and pressed on through the dense vegetation, and Mari trudged behind her. She'd play the complacent follower, at least for a time. The fact remained that Hannah needed her help, which meant she was most likely safe for the moment. As long as the arrangement benefited Mari in the long run, she'd go along with it.

Hannah alternated from looking around them as they walked to scanning all the way up into the trees.

"What are you doing?" Mari cringed, hearing the panic in her own voice as she considered who might be lying in wait. If they had to contend with armed lookouts in the branches, their journey would become outright hellish. "Seriously, why are you looking up there?"

"The man we're searching for could be anywhere. Just look for anything unusual."

Why did I agree to this? She should have just run, as fast and as far away as she could. Maybe she would have been close to crossing the border, instead of on a crazy hunt in the opposite direction. She should have called Hannah's bluff and risked being shot in the leg. *God knows whose territory we're in now. We're asking for trouble.*

Swatting at mosquitos, Mari struggled to put one foot in front of the other. Hannah was like a freak of nature or a robot —she seemed never to get thirsty, hungry, or tired. If Mari had the strength, she'd yank that swinging blond ponytail until Hannah fell. Then she'd sit and rest.

Mari's gaze was trained on the ground as she carefully stepped over a dead branch. She slammed into Hannah's back and stumbled back a step before she hit the ground. "What is your problem? Why did you stop?"

Too fast, Hannah turned around and shushed her. "Look at the trees."

Mari huffed before she looked to where Hannah indicated. At first, she didn't understand what she was looking for, but then she saw a diagonal line of broken branches, damaged and angling downward until the breaks disappeared behind a large tree.

"He may not be the only one here. Follow me. No talking."

Mari nodded, and took Hannah's hand when the other woman offered to help her up. *Things just got real.* Adrenaline pumped through her veins at the thought of who they could encounter. One crazy run from a guerrilla was enough for her.

They picked their way through the plants, saplings, and roots. An unfamiliar creaking sounded in the jungle's symphony of insects and animals.

As they approached with caution, Hannah bent to the ground twice, once right in front of Mari. The second time, she'd veered off course, checking beneath the vegetation around a larger tree. Both times, she'd straightened with a long, fairly thick, and almost-straight branch in her hand.

Mari's brows rose when Hannah turned and pressed one of them into her hand. She waited, wanting an explanation.

"For a stretcher."

No way. We have to carry someone? In these conditions?

The wind continued to increase, and tiny hairs that'd escaped her ponytail tickled her face. It was October, and the wet season was in full swing. Soon, the rain would come. She practically tasted the water in the air.

Mari picked her way over the raised roots of the huge tree, their destination. When they arrived under it, her mouth dropped open. *This is the favor Hannah wants?*

Several feet off the ground, a fairly undistinguishable man twisted upside down, strung up by a torn and tangled parachute. From their vantage point, she couldn't make out his features, just that he looked to be large, which meant he'd be heavy. Blood dripped from a wound, and something dangled from a chain around his neck. What worried her the most was the dark camouflage that he wore.

"Oh, God." Mari took a step back. Her warring emotions churned inside of her at the sight above them. "No." *I'm not getting involved in this.* "I won't."

Hannah's hand clamped over Mari's mouth, and her eyes went wide. "Yes, you will. Get him well, and he will get you out. Safely."

Her muscles locked from the shock and tension, and she stood rooted to the spot. *Out. Safe.* Those little words meant everything. They snared her, and she didn't run. More than anything, Mari wanted out. That'd been her plan all along. All the fire and pent-up agitation inside her deflated. She tilted her head back and looked up at the man once more. If there was the slightest chance he was her answer, maybe she could do it.

Her past was catching up with her in more ways than one. "He's... military." She skimmed over the dark-green camouflage. She didn't quite recognize the specific uniform, but its meaning —what she'd experienced over the years—held. Without meaning to, she'd solidified her fear of all and any people of power in South America in that simple statement.

More often than not, the police were on the take from the drug lords, and they chose to look the other way when it benefited them. The cartels ruled the streets, and the guerrillas, who opposed the government, worked in tandem with the cartels. Then there were the border police she planned to avoid when she neared Panama. Even though there were good people on the police force and in the military, she had witnessed too much bloodshed to blindly trust anyone in a uniform. Her experiences told her it wouldn't bode well for her.

Hannah's face softened, and once more Mari had a fleeting thought of how it was a miracle this woman was alive. A woman alone out there was a prime target for every powerful man in the area. If they could stick together, even with Hannah's cold, often clipped tone and standoffish nature, her company was preferable to a man she didn't know.

"He won't hurt you. I'm sure of it." Glancing back at the tree, Hannah motioned for Mari to stand beneath it. "We don't have a lot of time. In fact, I'm surprised he's still here." With the thick branch she held, she indicated for Mari to remove her bag. "We need to make a stretcher."

A sick feeling swirled in Mari's stomach. She was serious. She dropped her branch, removed her pack, and tossed it near Hannah's crouched form. "What are you doing with these?" All three packs were piled up around her.

"Making a stretcher. It's the best way I can come up with to carry him out. Help me. Just feed the straps through the branches and loop them once to secure them. It won't be great, but it's better than dragging him through the brush to the river."

It wasn't a bad idea. Mari bent and helped Hannah with the awkwardness of the long sticks as she situated the bags evenly down the two poles. The man would be cradled, hopefully, with the backpacks and wood supporting him. *We'll have to grip the ends of the poles to transport him. That will suck.* She glanced up at him and tried to determine how heavy he was. No matter how she looked at it, he'd be difficult to carry.

Hannah gripped the base of the tree with one hand and a low branch with the other, hoisting herself up. The rough bark looked to Mari as though it scratched her palms.

"I'm going to have to cut him down. You'll need to be lower so you can slow his fall. Leave the stretcher on the ground and climb up behind me."

Leaves rustled as the hot wind continued to pick up in intensity. There would be a storm, not just the typical afternoon rain. Hannah managed to get halfway up, and Mari stood below, weighing her option to run back to the canoe and try to get out on her own. *Could I make it?* Being alone in the jungle had proved to be equally dangerous for her as this, if not more so. Traveling alone was no longer her best option.

Shit, I should have called Hannah's bluff and grabbed a weapon from the guerrilla she had killed.

Hannah looked down. "Hurry up."

Mari shifted from foot to foot. That was a long way up to climb, and she didn't see how they were supposed to get him out of there without falling themselves.

"I know you're tired. We both are. But there are worse things out there that'll surely find us if you don't climb up here. Trust me, he's your best chance."

"Are you sure he's alive?" She peered at the dark-haired soldier, whose blood fell in a steady drip. Flies and other winged insects buzzed around his wounds. Even if he was alive, he would have an infection for sure, and quite possibly botfly larva in that gash. She shuddered at the thought.

"He's breathing. Looks like the blood is mainly coming from a head wound. We won't know if anything's broken until we get somewhere safe."

Pushing out a breath in resignation, Mari rose to her tiptoes and grasped the lowest branch. Scraping her exposed skin on the bark, she climbed until Hannah told her to stop. *Why am I doing this?*

"Move under him and wait for me to toss one of the lines from his parachute." Hannah edged over to the mess of tangled cords, tested them, then selected two to cut. She dropped them down to Mari. "Tie these tightly to the branch you're on. Make sure it's secure, or he'll fall all the way, and that won't help you. Trust me."

With a glance above, Mari scrutinized the parachute caught among the branches. The tears were expected, but what looked like several sprays of bullets were not. Then again, they were in the Darien Gap, and she probably shouldn't have been surprised at his—or his equipment's—condition.

Mari curled her hands around the ropes, inched closer to the base, and squatted down so she could lean against it for leverage while she secured the ends to the branch she stood on. Her fingers ached from pulling the rope taut, testing the knot she tied.

"Ready?" Hannah whispered from overhead.

"As much as I'll ever be." Mari wrapped her arms around the tree while Hannah cut through the tangled parachute lines. With each one that fell her heart thudded. There weren't many left, and the man's body jerked, putting even more strain on the last couple tethers.

"Here goes," Hannah warned as her knife sawed through the last one.

Dead weight, he dropped. He crashed into the branch above her head, and Mari winced. She pressed as flat as she could against the base of the tree, staying out of the way of his drop. *Holy hell, this is bad.*

A deep male groan sent a tremor through her tense body. She looked down. The ropes she'd tied held. A few feet from the ground, he dangled, twisting and bleeding, with his face obscured from her view.

"Go."

The harsh command kick-started Mari into moving, and she mimicked Hannah's frantic descent. Once her feet were back on solid ground, she looked up to Hannah, who perched on the limb she'd just vacated.

"Reach up and grab his shoulders. I'm going to cut him down. Try to slow his drop so we don't add to his injuries."

"Right." Her queasy stomach rolled and cramped once more.

Hannah shimmied along the branch until she was in position. Grabbing the first rope, she looked down at Mari. "Hold him steady."

On her toes, Mari strained to stop him from swinging, which was brought on from his descent and the wind. Twisting the rough material of his camouflage jacket in her fingers, she steadied him as best as she could. She pushed the heels of her hands into him and prepared for the impact of his weight once Hannah cut him loose.

"All set?"

"I think so."

Hannah leaned over enough to get a good view of what Mari was doing to prepare. "You might want to turn so that you're facing out. That way, when he drops he can sort of roll onto your back and ease his landing. Pull him forward a little so he doesn't drop straight down on you, but angles instead. Less impact for both of you."

She did as Hannah advised, worrying about getting hurt but doing it anyway. His body jerked as Hannah sawed through the ropes. With each millimeter Hannah severed, the threads stretched, and her body strained and shook as she took on the burden of some of his weight.

Mari grunted when he slammed into her. Her knees gave out, and she fell to the ground. Then his weight shifted—he rolled off of her, and she followed, landing partly on top of him.

Shit! Scrambling away, she sucked in air and froze when she took her first good look at his camo-paint-and-blood-covered face. The coppery tang of blood hit her, and she inched away, pushing up onto her heels. In a crouch, she waited for Hannah to drop to the ground.

Doing this—helping him—will cost me more than I can probably give.

Hannah dropped with a light thump, but Mari never shifted. *Can he really help me, and how do I return the favor?* His condition would mean her stay would be elongated. His dog tags captured her focus. "I can't do this." Intense fear rolled through her coiled body along with an instinctive need to survive. Lying at her feet, he represented one of the people from whom she'd been running, and the whole scene caused her to question her past mistakes, even though his identification and uniform told her he wasn't from here. Her stomach churned the more she took in every *military* inch of him.

CHAPTER 4

MARI

"No way, Hannah." Mari's heart pounded while Hannah bent to inspect his injuries. She paced back and forth, her obsessive gaze straying to him time and again. His features were nearly indistinguishable through the blood and camo paint. His short brown hair was matted and filthy. Even so, a trail of worry burned through her when she contemplated who he was, especially given that there were still men after her, bent on returning her against her will—or killing her. "He'll kill me. Why'd you save me, only to set me up for certain death?"

Lifting her gaze from the man's prone figure, Hannah pinched her features into an annoyed grimace. "*He* is your best bet to stay safe and get out. I can't help you, and you obviously need it."

Wow, just wow. Hannah was right, but it still aggravated Mari to hear it. She pushed herself to her feet then peered at what

Hannah was doing. She poked at his cut then moved on to his eyes, pulling back one of the lids and looking. She did the same with the other.

"He most likely has a concussion." Hannah waved her hand at the blood on his head. "The head injury will need to be cleaned and bandaged. It doesn't look too bad."

"You're kidding, right?" Crimson seeped from the ugly wound, and a rainbow of bruising bloomed around it and spread across his forehead. Part of her worried deeply for him, but the part that wanted to flee—on her own and for survival— couldn't afford to.

"Could have been much worse." Jumping up, Hannah rushed over to the makeshift stretcher. "Give me a hand. We need to prop this branch under him and roll him onto the wide part."

Mari shifted her weight from one foot to the other. A question burned on the edge of her tongue, something she could not ignore. "How do you know him?" It could cost her to show interest, but she'd fought to keep the menace from her question.

"Hurry up. There's no time for questions. We've got to move!"

Reacting to the urgency ringing through her voice, Mari bent and helped Hannah roll him. Hannah had mentioned that someone was searching for him, and that was enough to force Mari's hand. Once they had him situated as best as they could, Hannah squatted down, faced away, and took the front ends of the stretcher in her hands. With her gaze glued on Hannah's back, and not on *him*, Mari grasped the other end of the stretcher.

Every muscle in her body screamed as they pushed off the ground and rose with him supported between them. Even with his weight distributed relatively evenly, he was incredibly large and heavy. His body was cradled well enough from his head to his knees, which bent to allow his lower legs to dangle from the DIY gurney. Mari hoped that his thick hiking boots wouldn't slow them down by catching along the ground.

Hannah glanced back. "Ready?"

Her body shook, but Mari gave a quick nod. They took a slow step forward. Hannah increased the pace, and Mari worked to stay with her, taking care not to trip on any exposed roots or rotting vegetation in their way.

They made it a good distance from the tree when Mari's arms, shoulders, and back began to burn from the strain. "We've got to stop."

"No, not yet. Keep pushing yourself. If we stop, it'll be even harder to pick him up again and get to the river." Hannah's hoarse voice cut through the birds calling to each other. Both sounds competed with the internal screaming of her fatigued mind.

Fine. I can do this. The loose hairs around her face stuck to her like spiderwebs. The buzz of insects was as loud as the pounding of her heart. She panted as she strained her lungs to suck in more oxygen. *No, I can't do it.* "I need to take a break."

"Fifty more steps and then we will. Count them in your head. Focus on the numbers."

The woman was relentless as she soldiered on. And Hannah was right about one thing: they did need to keep moving so Mari could reach her destination—out of the Darien Gap, out of Colombia, and far away from everything she was running from.

Mari's shoulders felt as if they were going to pop from their sockets, and her hands and elbows screamed in pain. Her back and legs were in agony. Channeling her focus, she worked to block everything out. With each painful movement forward, Mari did as Hannah suggested and counted her progress. Hannah was right. It helped a little. Anything to take her mind off how her body begged to collapse was worth a try. With single-minded concentration, Mari diligently counted, even when salty drops of sweat and black spots compromised her vision. "Fifty." She wheezed.

Hannah nodded, and they bent simultaneously, Mari falling down the last several inches and dropping him. Lying on the ground, she moaned. Faint shuffling sounds penetrated her exhausted state, and she forced her eyelids open when a shadow fell across her. Hannah stood over her, another slim plastic packet in her hand.

"You need more electrolytes. Dump it into your canteen. Suck it down. We move in two minutes." She tore the end open and handed it to Mari. "After you take this, you'll start to feel better."

After swirling the contents around in her canteen, she clamped her lips around the opening and sucked every last drop of the sweet concoction down. She kept her eyes closed as she waited for it to take effect, hoping it would give her a little clarity and relief from the exhaustion. It didn't take too long for her to begin to feel a bit more like herself.

"Sit up." Hannah grasped her hand and pulled. "Drink some more."

Mari took Hannah's canteen, put it to her mouth, and gulped down as much water as she dared. She replaced the cap then handed it back. Things seemed bad, but they could be a whole hell of a lot worse. If she'd been struck with heat exhaustion or severe dehydration, she'd have to take it easy and consume only a few sips at a time. She wasn't that badly off, though she was depleted. The fluid stayed down. "What else is in those bags?" she asked, trying anything to keep them from lifting the stretcher again. With shaky hands, she pushed the annoying, sweat-drenched hairs from her face.

"Everything from extra socks to antivenin injections for

snake bites." Hannah moved to the front and took her position as the lead. "Come on."

With effort, Mari got to her feet. She wrapped her hands around the two sticks then listened to Hannah count off when to lift. She grunted through it. *He must have gotten heavier. Seriously.*

They trudged on for twenty painful minutes, his prostrate body swaying between them as they made slow but steady progress. "Hear that?" Hannah asked quietly.

"The wind?" It was still gaining momentum. A storm would hit any minute now.

"No. The water. We're close."

That got her attention, and Mari perked up, moving a tiny bit faster. As soon as they were at the water, they could load their burden onto the canoe. It would carry his weight, and she could rest.

She refused to entertain any thoughts about him other than the next steps. When the time came, she'd deal with the rest. His head wound could mean quite a few things, especially if it was serious, and it looked that way to her. Maybe somehow, she could increase her odds of getting him to help her.

Both women pushed as hard as they could to get to the canoe. As they neared the water, the ground changed in consistency to mud, slicked with fallen vegetation and riddled with random roots, which made it harder to walk. Shifting leaves to the side offered peeks of churning water. *We made it.* At the bank, they set him down. Hannah turned to the water's edge and yanked on the rope that secured their bobbing canoe to bring it closer. Rolling her shoulders, Mari bent and hovered over him, appearing to check his injury. What she was really doing was not taking any chances, should she need an advantage with him. With deft fingers, she yanked the dog tags from his neck and shoved them deep in her pocket. She straightened then rushed to help Hannah pull the canoe as close as they could. They lodged it partway onto the bank before they returned to their heavy burden to load him on.

They lifted the stretcher one last time. Hannah sloshed into the water to get her end farther up into the canoe before releasing him. He shifted, but at the last second, they heaved him over the edge and he crashed in, his body awkwardly skewed along the bottom of the canoe. The packs were crushed beneath him, but he stayed put on his makeshift bed, so she didn't worry.

She scampered into the canoe with their unconscious patient and positioned herself by his head, well out of sight if he regained consciousness. She wasn't ready for that, or for the discussion that would follow.

Hannah took the space by his feet after she pushed them off. Once they were as steady as possible, she tried to keep them from capsizing by digging the paddle into the rough water.

Every now and then, Mari glanced up to check their surroundings, even though it didn't really matter where they were. Not at the moment. Instead, short, dark hair, spikey lashes that cast shadows on his angular cheeks, and a strong chin compelled her gaze.

She knew his name was Chris.

Why he was here, what he was doing, and how he and Hannah knew each other, remained a mystery for the time being.

Mari's fingers dug into the side of the wooden canoe in a desperate attempt to stay afloat amidst the rolling river water. Wind punished them. The sky opened up, jagged lightning sliced overhead, and thunder boomed. Heavy rain pounded down on them.

She stared at his face through the punishing weather and saw one of his eyelids twitch. Trying to make herself as small as possible, she shifted a tiny bit to stay out of his direct line of sight. She wasn't ready for him to see her. Hannah leaned forward at Mari's movements, and her focus shifted from the river to Mari before finally falling on Chris.

His hazel eyes opened and latched onto Hannah. Mari froze as his quick flash of confusion morphed into fury. Peeling his lips back, he roared. He lifted his powerful arms and lunged at Hannah. Mid-grab, his face clouded with disorientation, and he turned green. Vomit erupted from his mouth, and he dropped back from his impromptu rise, falling back into unconsciousness.

Ew. Mari met Hannah's grave expression. "What just happened?"

Hannah's lips pressed together, but her features remained emotionless. "He's confused. You saw his eyes. They were dilated from his head wound. Most likely a concussion, like I said before." She swiveled and scanned the tree line. "We'll travel a little farther down the river, then I'll help you get him off of this and to a relatively dry place."

A garbled noise came from Chris, and Mari shifted back some more, uncomfortable with his initial reaction. *What have I gotten myself into?* At least the rain continued to pour down on them, offering a little relief from the heat. As an added benefit, it helped to wash him off.

Hannah yanked on one of the exposed zippers and pulled a canteen from the closest of the packs. Taking a small funnel, she unscrewed the top, fit the little piece of plastic inside, and attempted to fill it back up with rainwater. Wedging the canteen between her legs, she freed her arms to paddle.

They moved downriver at a fast pace. Hannah used the paddle only to guide them, not needing to do anything to keep them moving forward—and away from where Mari had been trying to go. "Why are we going so far? It'll be that much harder to reach the border now." Unease pressed upon her, slicing through the exhaustion. "Hannah."

"We need to put distance between us and where he was. The farther away, the safer."

"Why?" *What had he gotten himself into?*

"You noticed the parachute, right?" Hannah's voice dropped a notch. "There were bullet holes in it." With a careful finger, she pointed to one of the oozing spots by his temple. "This was caused by a bullet. It just grazed him, but we don't really know if he was hit anywhere else."

The water continued to propel them further from where she wanted to go, and Mari had to work to contain her frustration and suspicion. "Was he with you? Were you two working together?"

With a shake of her head, Hannah clamped her lips tight, making it clear she was done with the conversation. "We'll stop just around that bend." She leaned over and dug the stick hard into the riverbed, struggling to turn them from the rush of the water to the edge.

They shot past the point she'd indicated, but eased closer to where Mari was able to grab a protruding branch. Digging her heels into the wood beneath her, she worked to keep them in place—and herself in the boat. Hannah used the paddle to aid her. Slowly, they got the canoe to the edge.

Mari kept hold of the branch while Hannah jumped out and landed on the soggy bank. With the rope in hand, Hannah leaned back and hauled them in, guiding the canoe closer and lodging it between mounds of tangled roots. Mari let go of the branch and stepped over the canoe's edge and into the slick mud. Bending, she tugged the canoe in farther, thoroughly wedging it between the trunk of a submerged tree and the cluster of roots. Hannah tied it up, then they both pulled and yanked until they got Chris off the canoe. Thankfully, he remained on the makeshift stretcher.

"Stay here. I'm going to look for a good place to rest that's relatively dry."

Mari lifted a shaky hand and almost caressed his cheek. When her sanity returned, she jerked her hand back and clutched her wet fingers together, annoyance rolling through her. *What am I doing?*

Not thrilled but lacking the energy to protest, Mari let Hannah go without complaining. Lying in the mud, she waited for her heart rate to subside and for Hannah to return. Time passed both slowly and quickly as she rested, with rain streaming down all around her. Sleep was a few seconds away. Her body relaxed in gradual increments.

"Found something."

Dammit. It felt as though Hannah's words slapped her awake and violently expelled her from the waiting arms of slumber. "Holy hell. You scared me." Mari pushed herself up. Thick mud oozed between her fingers, and she went to the river and washed them off. "Is it far?" she asked when she returned.

"Not too bad. A few feet from here, elevated, and safe if the river floods. Ready?"

"Yes." Mari bent, grabbed the ends of the stretcher, and lifted when Hannah counted them from three to one. It didn't get any easier. It was actually harder, with the ground slipping out from beneath them. Mari took several painful falls to a knee. It took longer than it should have, as they had to move with greater care.

"Over here." Hannah nodded to the right, and Mari followed her lead. A limb had fallen from a giant tree and was propped in a partial-teepee fashion against the trunk. The severed limb rested against the tree, its branches and leaves cascading down. The base spanned at least six feet in diameter. Its thick canopy of leaves splayed over the jungle floor in a mound at least as tall as Mari was.

Hannah led them over to the side where the arc of the limb was highest. A small gap in the branches was their way in. Inside, it was relatively dry, with the thickness of the leaves acting as a roof of sorts. Bending at the same time, they set the man down, and Mari dropped to the ground. Hannah did not. She tugged Chris off the stretcher, just enough to yank one of the packs free. His lower half still rested across the contraption. Reaching inside, she pulled out a rope hammock. "Help me secure this."

With great effort, Mari rose and did as Hannah asked. Once the hammock was up and off the ground, they grabbed Chris by the shoulders and legs then struggled to set him in it. It felt like the man weighed a ton, even with Hannah helping her. Once they got him into the hammock, Mari slumped against it, her limbs weak from everything she'd been through that miserable day.

Hannah bent and yanked another pack off their stretcher, slung it on her back, and in three quick strides, stopped at the spot where they'd entered the hideaway.

The blood drained from Mari's face. Hannah was leaving.

Looking over her shoulder, Hannah caught Mari's gaze. "Remember the debt. A life for a life."

CHAPTER 5

MARI

The sound of rain beat against the leaves in a heavy staccato, dulling Mari's senses and drowning out any possible commotion that could be caused by someone closing in on her. Thunder rumbled overhead, and the fine hair along her arms rose. There was a sharp crack, and wood exploded close by—for a full two minutes, Mari froze, her mouth hanging open. *Did lightning cause that, or is someone else out there?* She leaned against Chris's arm, his body cradled in the ropes of the hammock, and listened to the noises that surrounded them. *What did I agree to, an undetermined amount of time in the jungle?* Hannah had left, taken off after binding Mari with a promise to save him. It could work to her advantage, if Chris agreed to help and to protect her. With that thought, she made the decision to do whatever it took to secure his aid.

Every little noise felt amplified in Mari's overly sensitized mind. The Darien Gap was no place for a single traveler. She'd thought she could traverse it and had been desperate to—it was the one way out of Colombia where she was sure the cartel wouldn't have been tasked to search for her. Even her exit from the town of Turbo, across the Gulf of Uraba, and then into the jungle by the Atrato River delta seemed to be the safest. It was a path less traveled than the one edging along the port towns to Panama, where she would surely be found.

A twig snapped not too far from their shelter, and she cringed. Their camp wasn't terribly far from a full army of guerrilla soldiers. She began to realize she needed help in the moment the guerrilla soldier had tried to capture her.

Mari closed her mouth and looked at Chris. *Shit.*

For several moments, she warred with herself. She could leave. She doubted she'd run into Hannah again. It'd be fitting to run away, but it would not be in her best interests to wade through this dangerous place alone. She tugged at her dripping-wet shirt. If she did that, she'd be alone against thieves, guerrilla armed forces, and drug traffickers. It'd been so long—months—since she'd had to run and hide on her own… *No, I refuse to think of any of that, at least not until he wakes up.*

While her aunt was sick and after she'd died, Mari had been emotionally vulnerable. The shop needed attention and someone to manage it, and she'd done so. It kept her busy. Unfortunately, she'd stayed too long and had crossed paths with the one person who could drastically alter her life. In her state, it'd been easy for him to take advantage of her.

The clawing loneliness she'd been feeling since her aunt died still churned inside her. It was marginally better being with Hannah, if only to have a woman to talk with, even if they hadn't exactly hit it off. Part of her didn't trust the other woman. But out there, she too had to become something she wasn't. She needed to be tougher, stronger, and willing to do what it took to survive.

If Hannah hadn't come along when she had, things would have ended very badly. Suppressing a shudder, Mari shoved the events of the greater part of her day out of her head and turned. She took in the sheer size of Chris. A sense of déjà vu sifted through her at what she'd agreed to do for him. Not too long ago, she'd been in a similar situation with her aunt, trying desperately to nurse her back to health. She'd failed.

But she'd cared for her aunt and made her comfortable until the end. With Chris, things were different, and she knew that if he would help her then this delay in the jungle would be worth it. As long as she secured his protection, it wouldn't be a waste of time.

There was still the chance he could leave, and she'd be left to fend for herself. There was no telling how he'd react, especially with a head injury.

Doubt stabbed her repeatedly. She'd be at a disadvantage when he woke, when he was well. From his reaction to Hannah, she needed to protect herself just in case. Her gaze travelled over him, and she almost whimpered with relief at what she saw. He had weapons, and she quickly disarmed him, taking several knives and guns then sticking them in sheaths on her clothes or nearby for easy access.

Sleep called to her. Her body and mind screamed with exhaustion, both threatening to collapse at a moment's notice. But there were a few things she'd have to do before she could rest.

Riffling through her bag, she pulled out another hammock and went about setting it up. Sleeping on the ground only begged for trouble. Dropping a mosquito net on her hammock, she drew another from the guerrilla's pack and secured it over him. Chris's military bag hung from a sturdy branch inside their camp. She would look in there later.

She examined his head. The blood still seeped in a thin

stream from his wound. That would have to be taken care of before she passed out. Same with their wet clothes—at least their socks. There was no way she was removing his clothes. She pressed her lips into a tight line. *Damn you, Hannah.*

There was too much to do, and she had to stay awake for a little while longer. Scanning their shelter, she noticed all the places in between leaves and the branches that peeked through to the jungle beyond and exposed them to danger. She ducked under the canopy opening and went in search of some fallen limbs, thick with leaves. The wind tore at her hair and clothes, and she was able to find many twigs scattered across the uneven ground, not too far from their spot.

Hauling in a bunch, she made her way back, not worrying about the trail she was creating. The rain would wash away her footprints, and the gusts would scatter any crushed twigs or leaves she'd trampled. She shoved the sticks into the lean-to and worked them in securely, weaving them through the layers of branches, so as not to look obvious.

She stepped back and looked over her handiwork with a critical eye. It would do, so long as the wind didn't tear it apart. It was a huge and very full bough that'd fallen to create their shelter, so she was hopeful.

The next item that needed her immediate attention before she passed out was Chris. She dropped down next to him. For several seconds, her gaze roved restlessly over his imposing form. Even unconscious, he filled their small space to a point that made heart pound. *If he exudes this much presence and power in the state he's in, what will it be like when he opens his eyes and fixes them on me?*

Strong shoulders, stacked with muscle, tapered to a trim waist. His legs were long and toned, like the athletes she'd glimpsed on the rare occasions when she and her friends had watched sporting events. Her blood heated as the pads of her fingers tentatively brushed over his forehead. His carnal looks affected her more than she'd care to admit. He had a strong jaw, prominent cheekbones, and kissable lips… Her fingers tingled where their skin came into contact. She yanked her hand back and took a steadying breath.

Hannah had said he was her ticket out of the jungle and to safety. The enormity of her situation weighed heavily on her shoulders, and a flash of animosity for needing to rely on him burned inside of her. *I have to. It's life or death, and I choose life.*

He was a mess. Blood was caked down the side of his face. With a sigh, Mari moved to one of the packs and rummaged around until she found the medical supplies. For the time being, she'd honor her stupid promise. She knew she couldn't leave him like this, anyway, promise or not.

She opened the kit and looked through the contents. Nestled inside were bandages, alcohol wipes, a vial of antibiotics, several pain pills, and a few syringes. Carefully, she read the labels. Starting with the wipes, she worked at the blood on his face. The rain had washed most of it and the camouflage paint away, but the gashes needed to be scrubbed. Thank God he was knocked out, because it had to hurt like hell. With a wadded-up piece of gauze, she scraped deep in the cut, working to make sure no fly larvae lay inside. She doused it with an antiseptic then patted it as dry as she could before slathering on an antibiotic salve. She covered the wounds with bandages and pulled out an antibiotic shot she would give him after she finished her inspection.

She noted his lack of dog tags and remembered her reckless move from earlier, when she had slipped them off him and shoved them deep in one of her pockets, which held a tiny zipper. There they would stay. She'd sewn in two hidden pouches before she'd left on her journey, small enough that they wouldn't be detected, but big enough to carry money—and the military identification tags. Their meaning didn't sit well with her. Nothing good had come to her from anyone in authority, family aside. Those she'd come across with power in her life abused it. And her.

Wind howled outside, and a loud crash made her body seize up in fear. It had to be a branch breaking somewhere, not a person crashing through the jungle to drag her back to where she'd run away from. As time ticked by, she relaxed in slow degrees. Shoving aside her worry, she focused again on Chris.

They'd cut the parachute harness from his body, but she still needed to check for other injuries. With shaking hands, she unbuttoned his coat, deciding to work it off him to hang, hoping it would dry. The heavy rain was mostly blocked by the leaves overhead and around them.

She struggled to pull him up, her arms and stomach muscles burning in the process, and leaned his dead weight against her chest as she got the jacket off. Before laying him back, she pulled the back of his olive-green T-shirt up and checked his bruised back for bullet holes or gashes. Her fingers skimmed him, feeling, as she couldn't really see past his bulk. Broad, muscular shoulders dwarfed her. Everywhere she touched was toned and corded muscle. She had to push aside her concern over his build and trust in what Hannah had told her. Even with Hannah's assurances, he could turn on her, and she'd be at a severe disadvantage. She'd been there before, and the fear of returning to that place terrified her. He was an enigma.

It'll be okay. I'll make it out, safe and alive.

She pulled the back of his T-shirt down then carefully lowered him as much as she could. Picking up one arm, then the other, scrutinizing each of them. When she slid the front of his shirt up, she saw a rainbow of bruises, but no holes.

With nothing else to stich or clean, she yanked his shirt down and inspected his pants for any signs of injury to his skin beneath. Those, she refused to remove. His ankles and calves looked terrible. They'd been twisted in the ropes, but maybe they'd be okay after she doused them with antibacterial salve. It took a little bit of time, but she got his boots and socks off, then set them underneath his hammock to dry as much as they could.

The pack that'd been strapped to his chest, and which hung on the inside of their fort, drew her attention, and she opened it out of curiosity. She wondered what he had planned to do. Inside held C4 plastic explosives, what looked like detonators, some MREs—military food packets—and water. *Shit, Hannah and I tossed that around.*

Whipping out one of the MREs, she tore the end and swallowed down the unusual concoction. Food was food, and she planned to survive. Taking his full canteen and hers, she placed them in her pack too, just in case.

Her hands skimmed along his pants, looking for weapons. She'd already removed the ones strapped to his arm and calf and concealed in his boot—he was a walking arsenal. If she was smart, she'd leave him, taking everything she could use. But she wouldn't, not yet. The promise held her—*he* held her. *Damn this misplaced loyalty.* It'd landed her in a bad spot some time ago, too. She was fixing that, though. *Hopefully this won't prove to be another detrimental mistake.*

Without meaning to, she found herself staring at his face. He was beautiful—not in a sweet, boy-next-door way, but in a rugged, take-charge kind of way. His chin was strong and his features chiseled. *That's what got me in trouble before—a charming boy who was easy on the eyes.* Brows furrowing, she realized how stupid she was being. She had to maintain perspective. Sleep was what she needed.

There was nothing she could do but wait until he woke. Worried about his risk of infection, she didn't waste time before giving him antibiotics. She grabbed the shot she'd set aside earlier, tugged the waistband of his pants down a little, and gave him the shot in the top portion of his butt.

Done with everything she could think of doing, she grabbed her pack and hung it next to Chris's, along with the extra guerrilla pack they had. As soon as she woke up, she would search him further. She'd already taken two guns and several knives off him. One of the handguns rested securely in her palm, the other inside her bag.

As her eyes drifted closed to the chorus of rumbling thunder and raindrops, she pacified herself with the weapons she'd armed herself with. She wouldn't be used by anyone. If Chris made one single move against her, she'd shoot him.

CHAPTER 6

CHRIS

*V*ertigo spun the world in a crazy circle as he peeled his swollen tongue from the roof of his mouth. He blinked. A shaft of light shone through the dark—*is that the moon?*

His eyes were dry as sandpaper, and he struggled to see where he was, wondering why sweat trickled down his face. *Or is it blood?* Pain hammered his body with an equal-opportunity vendetta of torture.

Pressure on his thigh drew his unstable gaze, and he breathed through his queasiness. Clarity came, if only for a few seconds. In that miraculous gift, he registered the reason for the slight weight pressing against his leg. A woman leaned forward, and the light bathed her in its soft, silvery glow. He drank in what details he could. She had an exotic face, a small build, and large amber eyes that were wide with concern.

His stomach heaved, and his rollercoaster ride resumed,

taking him back under, where dark enveloped him and again freed him from the agony of being awake.

~

MARI

Every single noise stole sleep from Mari. For hours, she tried to shut her eyes, but each new sound, rustling, or twigs breaking had her lurching out of her hammock, gun in hand, peering through small gaps in the leaves for threats. Nothing eased her exhausted body and mind, which stayed in a state of constant vigilance. It was still the dark of night, maybe an hour or two before sunrise, when she decided rest was a lost cause.

She found herself studying Chris, looking for clues in every sharp angle and plane of him that might tell her why he was there. She must have risen to check on him several times already. Aside from a light fluttering of his eyelids, he hadn't fully regained consciousness. Eventually she succumbed to sleep, hypnotized by the rise and fall of his impressive chest.

Hours later, the rain had stopped, and the pressure on her bladder yanked her from her unconscious state. Her hands, one still tightly gripping the gun, rose above her head, and she stretched. It was for the best she got up, even though she knew everything had changed. She'd backtracked and taken on the added risk of nursing Chris back to health. The longer they remained tucked in their small hideaway, the more she would grow accustomed to his presence, and she'd want him to stay with her against what she very well might face—should he help her.

Still, there was a chance he wouldn't do what Hannah said he'd do. He might not help her. It was a risk. Hannah seemed to know him best—but Mari barely trusted the woman. And when

Chris had briefly woken, he'd reacted with violence at the sight of her. She might need to do or say something extreme in order to garner his protection to get her to safety. At this point, she'd do whatever she had to do.

With difficulty, she flopped onto her side in the hammock. She was done fighting the inevitable pull as she studied his face and the strong line of his jaw. *What are you doing here? He's from the States, so what reason did he have for going through the Darien Gap, quite possibly on his way to cross the Panamanian border?*

A thick growth of dark hair dusted over his angular features, as it must have been a day or two since he'd shaved. Maybe that was an indication of how long he'd been in the jungle.

Forcing herself to rest her eyes, she listened to the sounds of the forest and the man next to her breathing. They didn't have a lot of time.

Teeth clenched, she shoved her thoughts of impending danger away. The guerrillas could find them, and there were others after her—and apparently him, as well—but there was nothing she could do about it.

With a sigh, she opened her eyes, reached across the small space, and brushed a gentle hand over his forehead, which was still hot but not feverish. He was healing. The more time they could spare, the better he would be. When morning came, she'd check his wound and try to get him to drink some water.

A low growl sounded, and she was surprised it was from her stomach. Too tired to do anything about it, she shut her eyes, willing sleep to come again. Soon, he would wake, and then she'd have her answers.

~

CHRIS

Drawing strength from deep within himself, he forced his eyes open, blinking against the soft light that spilled from all around him. His fingers curled around the bed he lay in. *Rope.* Information filtered in, and he pieced it together to determine it must be a hammock of sorts. He wasn't restrained and knew no other type of rope bed.

A soft rustle sounded to his left, but he couldn't turn his head because the vertigo was too great. The gentle touch at his head made him want to sigh, and he would have, if he trusted himself not to throw up, given how his stomach cramped and rolled.

She leaned over him, and he was able to see her better this time. *Do I know her?* The edges of his vision were fuzzy, but he watched her closely as she gifted him with a soft smile.

"You're doing great. The bleeding has stopped. I'm just going to tape another bandage to your head to keep it clean."

He felt the pressure of her fingers on his forehead while she smoothed the edges of the gauze and tape she'd just put on him. Questions flooded his mind, but his grip on consciousness was precarious. Instead, he fought to pay attention to her and the kindness she showed him.

Something very bad must have happened.

Her small hand slipped behind his head, and she helped him lean forward. The strange room he was in tilted, but the water she drizzled into his mouth centered him. With greed, he swallowed it down.

"Easy. We want to keep it down this time."

This time? He raised his gaze to hers, and everything in him stilled.

CHAPTER 7

CHRIS

Sounds echoed as if someone had cranked the volume all the way up. Chris's head ached and spun. Nausea hit him in waves. Intense heat and humidity pressed against him like a suffocating blanket. With great effort, he slitted his eyes open, wary of the light's effects on his out-of-control headache. *What did I do last night?*

The world slowly came into focus, inch by fuzzy inch. With a grunt, he tried to clear his throat as his eyes tracked the strange leaf canopy under which he lay. He heard a small intake of air to his side, which sent alarm through him. He wasn't alone. Instinctively, he reached for his gun. *Shit, nothing's there.* Taking a chance, he turned his head to where he sensed the noise came from.

The barrel of a gun pointed at him, and he reacted. Lurching forward, he grabbed the side of the weapon with one hand, the other slamming into a small wrist as he wrenched it away. Flipping it around just as fast, he aimed it at her.

Her?

He blinked. Her hand jerked back.

With his arms still straight out and the gun locked in his palm, his body swayed in the netting he reclined in. The only thing keeping him from tumbling to the ground was her shoulder, which he'd snaked a hand out to grasp. He waited for her features to clear before his swimming vision.

Silence fell between them. He stared into wide brown eyes framed by thick, sooty lashes. They were details he hadn't gotten quite right while he was so out of it. She was beautiful but deadly—not the impression he'd received the other times he'd woken.

Sparing a second, he swung his gaze away to make sure it was just the two of them and that his mind hadn't played any other tricks on him. That was a mistake, as his world teetered on a crazy carousel. When he looked back at her, he took a few steadying breaths but still drew a complete blank as to who she was. *Do I know her?*

His head pounded, driving home the other problem he faced—he was injured and had no idea what'd happened. Every inch of his being stilled as he sized up the situation and held her under the full weight of his stare. *Who is she?* She wore an unbuttoned long-sleeve tan shirt over a tight black tank top, and her dark, mahogany hair was pulled back from her face. Nothing about her clothes told him what he needed to know.

The scowl that took residence on her face was cute, but the knife in her hand, not so much.

He worked to puzzle out the details of his predicament. *Where the fuck am I?* Something was very wrong, and he needed to assess what to do. "Who are you?"

She pursed her lips, and a calculating gleam flashed in her eyes as she glared at him. "You don't know?"

The air between them was charged. She shifted, and he knew exactly what she was planning. There had to be another weapon close by, in addition to the knife. "Hands where I can see them," he growled.

In slow increments, she lifted her hands in front of her, palms up, knife pressed flat against one and held secure with her thumb. The blade clinked against the band of a ring on her right hand.

"I'm going to ask you one more time. Who are you?"

His gaze dropped to follow the movement in her neck as she notched her chin higher and swallowed. "You don't remember?"

"Obviously not. If I did, I wouldn't be asking you." Sweat ran down his face in rivulets, and it took all his strength to keep the gun steady.

A hard glint entered her expressive eyes just before she cleared her throat. "Maybe you should tell me why *you're* here?" Her words whipped out of her mouth, which she'd pressed into an angry little line. As her statement settled in, a flash of confusion washed over him at the direction of her question. Now that he was coherent, as opposed to before, she brought up the one point that'd been dancing through his paranoid state in a game of hide-and-seek. *Why am I here?* His mind frantically tried to jump back, but it was as if a thick, dark wall stood in his way. There was nothing, just a black void. *Holy hell.* Darting his gaze all around them, he again took in the sounds of a jungle and the intense heat. With determination, he clamped down hard on the panic that rose.

Soft morning light filtered through the leaves and played among the warm highlights of her hair. "You don't know, do you? Do you remember anything?"

He growled, and her face paled.

"I guess you don't remember anything." Her hands fluttered around her thighs, rubbing along the front of her pants. Seconds passed, and she seemed to come to a decision. "Mari. That's my name." She cleared her throat and stood taller. "And… I'm your wife."

Pretty. That'd been one of his first thoughts when he'd woken to the stunning brunette hovering over him. Her name fit. *Wait, what the hell had she said? His wife?*

His eyes narrowed on her as he racked his brain, while pain sliced through him like a knife. There was nothing, not a goddamn thing, where his memories, his past, should be. *I don't even know my name.* Alarm rolled through him in a hot wave.

Locking his gaze on hers, he forced his body to release some of the tension, and chose to rely on his gut instincts instead. "Why are you holding a gun on me if you're my wife?" Another image—but that of a blonde—swam into his mind, and he wondered who she was. Fury and betrayal swarmed to the forefront at the thought of that woman. Pushing the problem aside to revisit later, he paid attention to Mari. Then again, maybe it was a good time, after all. "Why aren't you blonde?"

Color flooded her face, and her hand shot out, smacking him in the shoulder. A string of Spanish followed, and she sneered. "Typical man."

No—he would prefer her, not the blonde. *But my wife?*

"The gun, I had that pointed on you because you reached for where you had it. *You* were going to pull it on me!" She slammed a hand on her jutted-out hip, irritation all over her face. "And I can't believe you don't remember me, Chris. Actually, I'm not surprised."

Chris. So that was his name. It felt right. "And why is that?"

"Why?" Again, a string of Spanish blasted through the air, so fast he struggled to keep up with it. What he did catch was her anger.

"Because you abandoned me. I was vulnerable." She crossed her arms over her chest and stuck her chin out. "One minute, you confessed you were leaving the military, and then you never returned. I had no idea if you were alive, or if you joined the guerrillas. There was no word from you."

He lowered the gun and ran a finger over where a wedding band would've sat. There was no indentation. Still, something about marriage and commitment seemed familiar and right, and it brought forth a swirl of memories that were just out of his reach. What seeped from the locked box of his past was a sense of longing, loss, and pain at the mere thought of marriage. *Something* rang true from her words. It could be that she told the truth. "Why is the ring on your right hand?"

"Because I assumed you were dead." Her voice fell flat. While he stared at her, she switched it over to her left ring finger. She moved close and then skimmed her fingers along his hairline.

He caught her wrist and pulled it down, eliminating the distraction of her touch. "Why are we here? Where are we?"

"I have no idea why you're here. The only reason I can think of is that you joined forces with the guerrillas. That would explain why you left me without a word. I've heard about that happening—loved ones leave their families all the time. Someone's husband or brother would disappear after getting into trouble, then no word back to the family, ever. No body found, either. It makes sense."

"I doubt that," he said roughly. Despite the nausea churning in his gut, he held still, studying her every movement and expression. The slight touch of their hands had singed and distracted him. "If we were married, there'd be no way I'd leave you unprotected." What looked like relief flashed in her eyes so quickly that he wasn't sure if he imagined it before she pinched her lips closed.

"*If* we were married?" She huffed. "I guess I shouldn't be surprised. It was a whirlwind— an impulse—our time together. And, I'm not sure why you're here. Well, maybe it's because of *her*. The woman who helped me, you recognized her. You know, the *blonde?* Is that why you left me—for her?"

The blonde. No. There was no way he would have skipped out on his wife to be with that woman. Something about the other woman evoked a deep rage. He shoved that aside to work with the only thing he knew—what Mari told him. "Where are we?"

She lifted a shoulder and let it drop, her features resolved. "I don't really know anymore. We're by the Atrato River. As to what territory we've crossed into, I'm not sure. It's probably still the guerrillas'."

The familiarity of the name she'd told him settled into his murky brain, and he placed it. "South America?"

She furrowed her brows. "Well, yeah. The Darien Gap, to be specific. Are you alright?"

"Fine," he said between clenched teeth. The gleam that again appeared in her eyes sent alarm bells screaming through his head.

"What were you doing here, Chris?"

His mouth opened, only to close again, because the answer he'd planned on giving her wasn't there. *Fuck!* He couldn't remember a thing. His head pounded. Beyond the two women screaming, he had no memories. He faced a terrifying thought: *amnesia. God willing, it'll be temporary.*

He scanned their surroundings, his clothes, and her face. Trying to recall what happened shot a volley of pain through his head. Either she'd done something to him—maybe drugged him —or he'd hit his head extremely hard. His entire body ached. "What did you give me?"

"Antibiotics. Keep your voice down." The color leached from her face, and her gaze darted around. "I swear I didn't give you anything else. But I had to give you that." She vaguely waved in the direction of his head. "You're injured, I guess from landing in the tree. We cut you down from it."

A tree? That sounded familiar. "'We' who?"

"Hannah." Again, her eyes flashed with irritation. "How do you know her?"

A face swam through his mind's eye, and a memory tugged at him, just out of grasp. *I do know her.* Although for the life of him, he couldn't place her. "The blonde—Hannah. Where is she?" He ignored her question, needing answers.

"Oh, she left." With one hand, she shoved at a few small strands that'd broken free of her hair tie, pushing them away from her face. "I'm… She made me promise to take care of you, get you well. If I did, you'd help me get out of here safely. Since you'd deserted me before, I hoped she knew you better than I supposedly did." She stressed the last words.

Interesting. The tension on the gun he held relaxed further, and he notched it all the way down. Whatever they really were to each other, she had stakes in his recovery. That eased his mind a great deal. If she was indeed his wife, she seemed to wish him no ill intent—he hoped. For now, he'd move forward with that theory in mind, despite her prickly attitude.

"So, are you going to?" Mari asked quietly as she shifted from one foot to the other.

Chris spared her a brief glance. "Going to what?"

"Get us safely out of here?"

"Seems that way." His distraction with why he was here bled into his half-hearted answer.

With a huff, she stepped away, and his hand fell from her shoulder to encircle her wrist. "I'm getting water." Twisting her wrist free of his hold, she leaned down and grabbed a canteen on the ground. After unscrewing the cap, she tilted it up and took a long drink before passing it to him.

Taking it, he sat up, swaying slightly in the hammock. Sucking in a few breaths, he willed the nausea away. He drank greedily, realizing he must be dehydrated. With regret, he lowered the empty canteen. She took it from him, and he raised a hand to his head, running his fingers over a bandage. "You did this?"

She nodded. A war seemed to ensue in her gaze and across her features until she dropped the attitude and again stepped close. Soft, feathery touches along his face transfixed him, and he stared at her lips. She leaned down and brushed them across his forehead, and something inside him stilled. *What the fuck?* Maybe she really was his wife.

"You're still a bit feverish. Do you want any more water?" Her hand dropped to his shoulder, and she pinched her brows, her concern seemingly overriding her agitation.

"In a minute." The loud grumble of his stomach echoed between them, and she laughed quietly.

"There's some jerky in your pack. Just a second." Unzipping one of the three packs that hung inside their fort, she pulled out the dried meat. She handed him a piece. "Let's see if you can keep this down first before you have any more."

Grateful for their small truce, he sampled the air and caught a faint rancid scent. "That's what that stench is, huh?"

She grimaced. "Yeah, you threw up all over yourself, twice. I can rinse out your clothes in the river, but you're too big for me to get them all off. You'll have to help me."

She was a tiny thing, and he could see how hard it would be for her to lift him to peel off his shirt or pants. At least it explained why he wasn't wearing any shoes or socks.

Chewing on the salty dried meat, he relaxed back, taking in more of their surroundings. There was netting above him. Part of it was moved to the side, probably so she could check on him, which could have been what she was doing when he woke. The faint smell was getting to him, and his stomach churned angrily. He really wanted to keep the beef down. "Yeah, it's probably a good idea to rinse out these clothes."

"It was really just your shirt that was doused. The rain washed most of it away. At least, until you got sick again here, but it wasn't too bad the second time."

"Great at attracting bugs, I'm sure." He eased himself up with the sides of the hammock and grasped the back of his T-shirt from over his head. With a yank, he pulled it off and swallowed several times, working hard to push the tidal wave of nausea down from his sudden movement.

Mari nibbled her lip, with her gaze locked on his chest, and her brow creased with worry lines. He looked down and noticed the marbled bruises she stared at. Grabbing the shirt without touching him, she shoved one of the branches aside and hurried out. *Interesting.* Dropping the netting back around him, he cut off a few insects that tried to gain access. He'd go to the river later, if he could stand by then. Dizziness circled through his head, and he eased to a reclining position once again on the hammock, where he continued to evaluate his situation.

Mari was a contradiction: she was agitated, snarky, seemingly mistrusting, possibly jealous in one moment, and then would do a complete one-eighty into care and concern over his health.

Whatever their story was, he'd go along with it for the time being.

CHAPTER 8

CHRIS

A rhythmic thumping stirred Chris from a light doze, and he pried his eyes open to be greeted by the fading, colorful rays of late afternoon. Pushing himself up into a sitting position, he slowly navigated out of the hammock and went in the direction of the noise. Parting some of the leaves to let in the fading daylight, he found the reason he was awakened.

Mari tossed a knife twice in a catch-and-release before she let it sail through the air, lodging it into the tree trunk with a satisfying *thunk*. She let two more fly before walking over and pulling them out, only to repeat the process again.

Damn, she's proficient at throwing knives. We have that in common.

She continued to throw with a steady, repetitive motion, and he wondered if it eased her mind about the situation she'd found herself in—it would comfort him. Whatever the case, he liked watching her, and extra practice never hurt, especially since they were in such a dangerous jungle.

A few more rounds, and she re-sheathed all three blades. Night was descending quickly. He parted the branches further, where he'd seen her do it earlier, and stepped out, wearing only his pants.

"Nice job." Chris's voice was quiet, but she startled and whipped around, her hand hovering over one of the sheathed knives.

Mari eased her hand back, her shoulders relaxed, and she flashed him a tentative smile. "Thanks. It's getting dark out." The sky was full of clouds, and she swatted at mosquitos. "I think it's going to rain again."

"Seems like it, but it'll be good to get more drinking water." He cataloged her every move, still trying to figure her out. *Why is she so skittish with me, if she's my wife?*

"It's good to finally see you up. Maybe we can head out on the river tonight?"

The thought of being away from solid ground, riding moving water, had his stomach cramping painfully. Still very weak, his body swayed. He needed a little more time to recover. "Maybe not tonight."

She took a few short steps and stood in front of him. She brushed her hand along his forehead in a light caress. "Okay. At least the rain will do your fever some good, too—maybe it'll help to break it." Heavy drops began to fall. It wasn't much, but enough to warn of what could come.

Rising on her toes, she laid her hand fully on his forehead and checked to make sure his temperature hadn't increased, which sent a volley of goosebumps along his exposed skin. He wasn't too worried because it was low grade and not terribly alarming, all things considered. What intrigued him was his own reaction to her.

"There aren't any more antibiotic shots. I used all three of them on you when you were unconscious."

None remained if they needed them, which could prove to be dangerous. "I'm fine." With care, he turned back inside their tree canopy as he clasped his hand around hers. The pounding in his head was relentless. He wasn't fine, but there was no point in causing her stress. What he needed was the return of his memory and more sleep. Grogginess still clung to him, and the ground undulated beneath his feet.

She'd washed his shirt and hung it on one of the branches inside. He lifted one section of the mosquito net, and with her hand still in his, pulled her under with him. The sense of loss with his past shook him more than he could admit. "Lie down with me for a while." The circles under Mari's eyes hadn't gone unnoticed by him. She needed to sleep, too—and he'd use that to his advantage as a way to keep tabs on her while he was unconscious. If she moved, he'd wake. As his wife, his request shouldn't be abnormal, and it would give him sensory information.

She tugged on his hand. "Oh, no. I'll lie down on my own hammock. There's not enough room."

"Humor me, please." Without meaning to, he swayed, and she reached out to try to steady him. She nibbled on her lower lip, and concern etched across her features just before she gave him a slight nod.

He settled into the hammock before he pulled her in and tucked her along his side, despite how tense she was. Seconds passed, and in slow increments, she relaxed, trapped against him. Soon, her eyelids fluttered closed, and the gentle rise and fall of her chest as she drifted further into sleep gave him a modicum of comfort. As he lay next to her, his mind turned over what Mari had told him, that Hannah swore he wouldn't leave her, or hurt her. *How does Hannah figure into my situation, and why don't I remember a life with Mari, even if it was an impulse relation-*

ship, which she'd hinted it was? With that in mind, am I an impulse type of guy? He didn't think so.

Her reluctance to be too close to him hadn't gone unnoticed. He knew Mari had some concerns. *Why is that? What could have possibly happened between the two of us to make her that wary?* Warning bells at this whole predicament—at his amnesia, and at being where he was, clanged through his mind. Something didn't add up.

Lightning flashed, and moments later, thunder rumbled. Hunger gnawed at him as he listened to the patter of rain against the leaves. They had a decent supply of dried meats, MREs, nutrition bars, and the rain, which they needed to refill the canteens. That, at least, was good. He'd prefer they supplement their meals with some game, but as it stood right now, he wouldn't be going very far. The dizziness and aversion to light would compromise his awareness of their surroundings and could possibly put them at greater risk. Instead of hunting, at least for the time being, he'd rest and recover as much as possible.

If he was able, he would build a Dakota fire when they were up. The underground fire would burn hot and emit very little smoke, keeping them well hidden from potential enemies. From what he could remember of this area—funny that he knew that, of all things—it was full of danger.

He was tired, so he closed his eyes, too. It would take some time to heal enough to move out. If they tried to leave right away, the dizziness and nausea from his head wound would hinder them too much. With a gun tucked into the holster on his waist, he let himself drift into sleep.

His body relaxed, and Chris hovered in peaceful slumber until the sky darkened to pitch black in his dreamscape and wind thrashed against his body. The whirl of helicopter blades overhead faded as he plummeted down.

He reached the designated altitude and deployed his parachute. It unfurled and caught air, jerking him to a slow descent in the inky sky. For a few moments, he floated in peace, with only the adrenaline of the mission as company. The peace didn't last. Light strobed below, and the flash and pop of gunfire sent a swirl of alarm through his tense muscles.

Heat burned on the side of his head. He gritted his teeth, cataloging what had just happened as a flesh wound. He'd been shot, and sticky warmth leaked from the wound. It was a mere scratch, and he wasn't terribly worried until his vision clouded.

Lethargy slowly leaked into his limbs and set a muted alarm that trilled through his head. *What coated that bullet?* He heard a gentle whirl approaching, and in a matter of seconds the parachute cords jerked. His projected descent seemed to shift. Even the wind's direction subtly changed.

He thrashed, mumbling garbled words under his frantic breath as he clawed his way to the surface. The dream still held him, but it shifted slightly forward in time. Again, he hung upside down, the gentle tap of his dog tags rhythmically brushing against his cheek. Soft words swirled and danced around him while he swayed amidst tangled branches. Too weak to cut himself down, he searched for where the sound came from.

"Shhh. It's just a dream."

His eyes popped open at the whispered words, but his mind fought the present, questioning his safety. The soft body pressing against his side sent confused signals flashing through him. *Friend or enemy?* Wrapping his arms around her waist, his viselike grip bit into her softness, and he pulled her on top of him, immobilizing her in his embrace.

His biting grip loosened as the gentle touch of her fingers moved across one side of his head, and she repeated that he'd been dreaming. He toggled back and forth between wakefulness, the too-real dream, and the possibility that an enemy had captured him.

"Stop."

The softly whispered command jerked him fully into the present and out of his foggy head. Her features swam into focus. The touch of her hand through his hair became a comfort, as well as her full lips, which were temptingly close.

"You were dreaming." Wariness swam through her dark eyes, and confusion knitted her brows.

His hold eased further as she continued to run her fingers through his hair. The gentleness of her touch brought him back, and he focused on what he'd done. "Shit, did I hurt you?"

After a moment, she shook her head. "No. But you had me worried. Your pupils were dilated, and you were mumbling something about a trap, and being drugged."

The fog cleared a little more, and he zeroed in on the remnants of the panic that pinched her features. "I'm sorry, babe. I didn't mean to scare you." The softness of her body pressing against the hardness of his continued to distract him, and the stirrings of desire spiked through his blood. All he could concentrate on was her, how she felt lying on top of him, and the sizzle of electricity everywhere their skin touched. Her mouth opened, and he grasped the back of her neck and pulled her close. *I'm wondering…*

Their breath intermingled, and she seemed to soften in his arms, even with the partial wall she kept up to shield him from the depth of her emotions. *But this is my wife. Right?* She would expect this—she would welcome his touch. At least he hoped she would.

His lips brushed hers in a slow caress. It felt as though flames leaped up his body as she molded to him. They went back and forth, his lips caressing and teasing hers to open further.

The soft little moan she made drove him wild. *My wife.* With reverence, he kissed her, fueling her desire and building it until she squirmed against him.

He groaned against the decadence of her mouth and the way she responded. Their kisses heated them both, until her body tensed and she pushed at his chest, breaking the connection. "Wait."

He lifted the heavy weight of his hands on her neck and back. Releasing her, he gave her space to breathe. She turned her head back and met his gaze. In the early rays of dawn, heat flooded her cheeks. From anger or passion, he couldn't tell.

"What are you doing?" Mari's question wedged between them, her words breathy and low.

He lifted his body into a sitting position, and she scurried out of their hammock, putting distance between them. *God, that woman can kiss.* He fought the urge to reach for her and pull her close. He held himself still, watching her.

She fidgeted against his stare, and a sigh pushed past his lips. He understood. They barely knew each other—or at least that's how it was for him. For her, it could be a bevy of reasons, most likely stemming from how she perceived that he'd abandoned her. The stress of their predicament had to be getting to her. It was getting to him, too. He couldn't remember a damn thing. But losing himself in her kisses and touchable body stole the worry and made it bearable.

"Look, I'm sorry for moving too fast. It's clear there are unresolved issues between us." He ran his hand over his face, avoiding the bandage on his forehead. "This whole situation is driving me crazy."

Mari relaxed her shoulders and gave him a small smile as she lowered herself to sit in her own hammock. "I'm sure it is. Staying here for so long is making me jumpy. We need to get moving, as soon as you're well enough." Her gaze traveled down his shirtless body and the myriad bruises that covered him.

Fuck. He scrubbed his stubbled jaw. "I can't for the life of me remember why I'm here. Where did you find me, again? In a tree?" He pushed himself up, and they sat across from each other, their hammocks lightly shifting from their movements.

"Yes, you were hanging upside down, maybe ten miles that way." She pointed in the direction they'd come from. "I'm not sure, actually, because we traveled here by the river, and it was storming, so it could be twice as much."

He knit his eyebrows together. "I remember something about water and the rotation of helicopter blades above, loud pops from a machine gun, and falling. But before being fired on, there was something else. I'm not sure what."

"Is that what you were dreaming about?" She shook her head. "Your reactions are a little unpredictable when you're sleeping."

"Right. Maybe that was a mistake, and you should stay in your own hammock. I'd never forgive myself if I hurt you."

Her shoulders moved in a nonchalant shrug, and he once again admired her strength.

Speaking of strength… "Exactly how did you manage to cut me down and bring me here? And, with that in mind, how did you know I would be where I was?"

"Hey, no suspicion cast my way. I didn't shoot you down. And if you'll recall, *you* left *me*. I thought you were dead." She huffed, pausing while she tempered her emotions. "I'm sure your memory will return, but for now? Just trust me. Remember Hannah?"

He gave a wary nod.

Her lips twitched. "I have no idea where she came from, but she saved me from being chased by one of the guerrillas. So what could I do when she gave me an ultimatum to return the favor? The alternative was getting shot. It wasn't ideal, but she assured me you would help me get out of this place safely. She knew your general location. Imagine my surprise when it was *you* hanging from the tree."

His gaze stayed riveted on her face, and he fought the urge to reach out to her. "She did, huh? What did she tell you about me?" His voice sounded harder than he would've liked. No matter what she told him, he still searched for the truth behind her words. He hunted for anything that would be the key to unlocking his past. As for being his wife, he'd trust in the reactions they had to each other, and in her word.

"Not much. Although, it's apparent you've met before, or at least you worked together. How else would she know where you were?"

Hannah had to be involved in why he was here and why he was injured. *Where does that place Mari?* "There is that. I don't think it's a coincidence that she knew where I *landed*."

Shrugging a shoulder, she remained stoic, her expression giving nothing away. "Yeah, well, that crossed my mind too, but I have no idea. All I know is that she told me to get you back to health, and you'd help me escape. As your wife, I'd hope you'll honor that." Under her breath, she whispered, "Unlike before."

At her words, his attention sharpened. *Did she tell me this before?* "Where was it you'd planned to go?"

"Across the border. Anywhere that's far away from here. I'm done with this place." Sadness and bitterness coated her words, even though it appeared that she tried to bite them back.

"Care to share why you're in the jungle, alone?"

"Care to share where you were?" Pressing her lips into a firm line, she glared at him. She slipped her hand around her back and raised an eyebrow at him.

Anger pricked him at her softly spoken question. He knew she had a gun there, where her hand was around her back. *Un-freaking-believable.* "Why would I threaten my *wife*? I have no intention of harming you in any way. Answers are the only thing I want right now, Mari."

She waited a moment before she nodded.

"I need to figure out how Hannah knew where to find me."

"I have no idea. I'd never met her before she helped me."

A dark cloud sailed into his thoughts and conjured a fierce frown on his face. Out of the corner of his eye, he saw Mari shift uneasily.

"If she'd told me anything about you, what reason would I have to hide that?" Mari challenged.

Silence fell around them. The only noise came from the incessant buzz of insects. She knew something else, and he could sense it.

The battle that waged across her features saddened him. *Am I one of the reasons she had originally fled her home?* It didn't add up. But still, badgering her with questions seemed too much of a gamble, at least just then. He chose to follow his instincts where she was concerned and trust in the awakening feelings he had for her, even if he didn't understand them. Because if they were married, he knew there was no way he'd willingly leave this woman, unless something had physically kept him away. Too much about her feisty personality appealed to him.

In contrast, nothing appealed to him about Hannah. He remembered the moment she hovered over him in the canoe. There was an animosity between them. There was history, possibly deadly history, given how he'd reacted. He'd have to figure out more about the connection between Hannah and Mari. With the way Mari spoke of her, he had to assume a connection existed. "Mari, I'm not upset with you. It's the thought of the danger you were in that bothers me."

A small smile touched her lips, and he watched the pulse in her neck speed up ever so slightly. He rubbed at his forehead in an attempt to ease the pounding pain that occurred when he tried to force himself to remember his past.

"Hey. Stop trying so hard. I'm sorry I can't fill in more blanks for you. I'm sure it'll come back, probably when you least expect it." She stood and closed the distance between them. "Are you feeling better?"

He grunted just before she lightly touched his forehead.

"Good, the fever is gone."

"What happened to make you want to run away?"

She flashed him a sad smile as she lightly traced the side of his face. "So much time had passed. If things hadn't gone south while I lived with my aunt... But that's what happened, and it was time to leave. There was nothing there for me anymore. After everything I'd been through, I just..." She shook her head. "My life became mine alone, not for a man to own."

"I'd never own you, Mari. Where're you getting that?" Unease made him lightheaded. There was a story behind her words, one he didn't think he'd known about during their time together. *What'd happened to her after they'd parted ways?*

"That's a story for another time. Are you hungry? We have some of that dried meat left, or MREs, and I can pick some berries." Rooting around in the pack, she pulled out the plastic bag that held the jerky.

Seconds passed while he debated pushing her, but instead he gave her space with the change in conversation. "I'm starving. But not for that." He shoved himself to his feet and swayed a little. Shock and fear rounded Mari's eyes as his action leached the color from her face. He knew his height and size were intimidating, and for some reason him looming over her set her fear loose. *Why?*

She inched back, her fingers grazing the hilt of a knife. "Easy." Cautious words stirred Mari from her near panic, and she blinked several times. In slow increments, the color returned to her features.

"I'm going to go out and get us something fresh to eat. Hand me that knife, will you?"

Curling her hand around the knife strapped to her thigh, she withdrew it and handed it to him hilt first.

His raised eyebrows were the only thing indicating he was aware it was his.

"Are you sure you're well enough to do this? Concussions aren't something to mess around with." She waved her hand at him. "And you're still black and blue."

He cast her a reassuring glance before he parted the branches and stepped out of their hiding place. The light rustling behind him indicated that she'd followed him. "You could build the fire pit while I'm hunting."

"Why would we risk a fire?"

He waited for her to stand by him before he walked over to the area he had in mind. "This is a little different. It's called a Dakota Fire Pit. It's what's used when in enemy territory, and it's relatively safe." He knelt not too far from the tree and waved her over. Once she joined him, he cut the top portion of the ground away and dug it out, placing it at the base of the tree so they could put it back when they wanted to hide the evidence of being there. The diameter was about ten inches. The air tunnel leading out would need to be ten inches from the pit.

As he talked to her, he dug the main hole for the fire pit. "It burns hotter than a regular fire. With it being under the tree, the leaves will disperse any smoke that's created. While I'm gone, if you can dig the air tunnel, starting from that point over there, that would be great. Fill the pit with some kindling, but not too full." Handing her a curved, wide stick, Chris showed her how to dig the air tunnel. Once she looked like she had it under control, he left their camp perimeter to hunt.

With his usual stealth, something he'd come to realize he did without conscious thought, he slipped back into the slight clearing by their fort. Dizziness and nausea still hounded him, but he could do it, if only for a short period of time.

It didn't take too long—maybe about an hour—for him to find game, kill it, and butcher it. As he made his way back to her, he slowed to a stop along the border of their camp near the river. Just for a moment, he paused to watch her.

Mari had her back to him, her long hair unbraided and falling to an inch or two above her waist. She'd combed it out, and it shimmered in the early light.

His gaze lingered on her as he made his way to the fire pit he'd partially dug. She was lovely. As she stood from the riverbed, turned, and made her way back to where they were camping, his muscles locked down from the expression on her face. She hadn't seen him. Because of that, he witnessed her unguarded demeanor. Fear pulled her features taut. A sixth sense told him there was more to the story she'd told him.

What surprises should I expect?

CHAPTER 9

CHRIS

Chris ran his hands over his face and tried to scrub the sleep away. Another night had passed, and he was feeling marginally better from his injuries. Not a hundred percent, but given the terrain, that wasn't to be expected. A sound of frustration from Mari had him looking over at her as she worked a knot out of her hair. With deft fingers, she braided the thick strands. He couldn't stop looking at her, every chance he got.

They'd shared a kiss. If he could remember any others, he'd swear it was unlike any he'd experienced before. Out from beneath the mosquito net, he waved away a few pesky insects. The heat was already unbearable, giving a clear sign that the afternoon would be brutal. At least their hiding place offered shade, and the nearby river was a modicum of relief if they chose to risk lying in it.

They munched on the bananas and berries they'd gathered

for breakfast. It wasn't enough, but it would have to do. He could only manage hunting once yesterday. The new day would be better.

"Do you think we can leave today? We have the canoe… It wouldn't be too difficult to ride in there for as far as we can." Mari tugged on her braid before flinging it over her shoulder and straightening her spine.

In two strides, he was at the small opening they used to go in and out of their shelter. Tension crackled as he checked the grounds he could see for any movement. Looking over his shoulder, he caught her studying him. The more he moved about, the more she'd stumble or her posture would stiffen. It didn't add up.

Rather than rub his aching forehead, he kept his hand at his side. She'd caught him doing that too often—it was his tell for attempting to remember. Even so, he tried over and over again to piece together who he was, why he was there, and what Mari and he had meant to each other once. An impenetrable wall blocked him, but determination shot through him. He'd break it down. As for the way he moved and the precautions he took, that came naturally. As did handling weapons— they were an extension of him. That told him something. It had to.

His lips twitched as he took in Mari's stance. She looked like a rabbit, frozen and trying not to attract attention. It was time to peel back some of her layers. "Tell me something about our past, about how we met."

The slight lift of her shoulders was the only movement she made. "I lived in Venezuela, and you were there on holiday, in Caracas. The moment I laid eyes on you, I knew my world was about to change." She grinned. "I was walking out of a restaurant where I'd eaten with friends. The city has changed. At night, past eight, the atmosphere shifts, and fear is almost a scent in the air. That night, I was in a hurry because it was getting late."

As she spoke, he drifted closer. "Why didn't you stay with your friends, leave together?" A vein pulsed along his neck at the thought of the risk she'd taken.

"I wasn't thinking, I guess. I had work in the morning and wanted to get home." A quiet, self-mocking laugh filled the space between them. "I wore a new pair of stilettos, and they were quite high."

He moved even closer, her voice hypnotic to his senses.

"My heel caught on the sidewalk and I would have face-planted."

With the pads of his fingers, he glided over the soft curve of her cheek. "Would have?"

"You were there, coming from the opposite direction. You caught me." Her voice took on a breathless quality, and her pupils dilated. "You swept me off my feet. For some reason, you always seem to be exactly where I need you, when I need you."

The spell broke as she took a step back, and his hand fell away. He would've done that—caught her—but it wasn't enough. He wanted the memories back—all of them.

"I'm going to go wash up." Mari tried to slip past him, but he stopped her with a hand on her arm.

"We'll go together. I want to check the perimeter to make sure there aren't any tracks."

At her nod, they brushed the leaves aside and went out into the open. His gaze tracked every place he would've lain in wait for an ambush. When he cleared them, he did another general sweep as they walked side by side to the river.

Curiosity poked him, and he plied her for more answers. "Did we live together in Venezuela?"

She shook her head. "No, not really." Her features hardened as she turned to him with the full weight of her stare. "It was a silly little fling, and we both got caught up in the possibilities of it. But the truth was, we were from different worlds." She swept her hand to indicate his clothes. "You were from the U.S., and I was not. We got drunk one night, and a friend convinced us to get married. There wasn't much needed beyond some easily acquired paperwork, and we went through with it. The problem was, we didn't really know each other."

Sitting back on his heels, he watched her as her face flushed with heat. Her posture and her tight lips told him she was done with the subject, but he had one more question. "And now?"

Her head jerked back. "Now, we're both trying to survive. This time, our paths are on the same trail—one that ultimately leads to the States."

He let it go, and they busied themselves with gathering wood for the fire, keeping their conversation light. Now and again, he rested, building his strength back up. They needed to leave, and he knew she was anxious for them to be on their way. Time moved swiftly, and before he knew it, lunch rolled around. The dizziness and nausea had decreased even more, so he went hunting, leaving Mari behind where it was relatively safe. If they were staying for even one more night, he needed to secure their area—to set up traps.

When he returned, he noticed her pinched features. Her hands were clenched on her weapons, and she had wide eyes. For all of her fierceness and bravado, her nerves got the best of her when he was away. The only thing he could do to ease her stress was to behave as if he didn't struggle constantly with his lost past. He acted as though he accepted they were in the jungle together, and he gave her the support as her husband that she obviously needed.

"I'm back." He grinned. "Check out what we're eating, probably for dinner, too."

Mari jumped. His voice caught her off guard, and her brows

furrowed in irritation. "How is it that such a big man moves without sound?"

He waited for her to get her racing pulse under control before she realized what he'd caught, carried, fileted, and wrapped inside several banana leaves.

Her mouth dropped open. "That's a lot of meat. What is that? Wild pig? Is that what that is?"

He laughed, and at his nod, she rushed forward to take a couple of the already-filleted pieces from his hands. "How did you catch it, and where did you butcher it?"

"No need to worry." Amusement colored his words at her concern. It seemed to go against his nature not to take precautions. "I fileted it down by the river a ways then buried the remains. We're good." He set the rest down so he could get the fire going.

After picking up several green sticks they'd debarked and sharpened at the ends, she pierced the filets in a kabob. They placed the spitted meat over the high-temperature fire to cook.

Chris lowered himself next to her and pressed a kiss on her cheek. He monitored the food, turning it every so often. "I checked for any signs of people and didn't notice anyone had come close to us. So far, we seem to be okay. But staying here too long is really risking detection. It's been four days, and I'm healed enough. We should head out, at most, by tomorrow."

Her smile stretched wide before she glanced behind her at the shelter they'd been living in. "I have no idea why I'm sad to leave this place. It's an inferno, and I do want to get out of here as fast as we can."

"Probably because it's been relatively quiet so far, and you're feeling safe."

She'd slowly let her guard down around him. They were making progress and establishing trust. He couldn't imagine what it was like for her to travel through this jungle alone, because it would test a seasoned soldier's resolve.

She leaned against him, heedless of the body heat they shared, which only amplified the high temperatures and humidity around them. Over the time they'd spent together, he noticed that his presence reduced her anxiety, and he liked it when she was close. That was all she'd give him, though. Maybe a kiss. If their intimacy went any further, she'd pull back with a guarded expression.

"I'm sure you're right. I want to get out of here, to cross the border. I think I'm just afraid of what we'll encounter."

With another turn of the spit, he faced her and tucked a stray piece of hair behind her ear. Something about her brought out a fierce protectiveness in him. Of course, she was his wife, and that was only natural. "I'll be by your side, Mari. We're in this together."

Lines appeared between her brows. "What's wrong?"

He shook his head. "Nothing, really. Just the usual—I'm trying to figure out why I'm here and what it was that I was doing."

She slipped her hand behind him and rubbed his back in a circular caress. "I've wondered that myself, many times, but whatever the reason, it's probably best left alone. This place is dangerous. We'll be lucky if we get out alive."

"Sweetheart, I'm dangerous."

"Well, yeah."

Her eyes widened, and Chris grimaced. "Not to you, only to anyone who tries to hurt you. Try not to worry too much. I'm always assessing our situation. We'll get out of here alive." He cupped her chin and turned her face toward him. "I promise."

Her gaze softened, and his need to protect her overwhelmed him. The short time they'd spent together in the jungle showed him who she was, even if he didn't remember their time together. The fierceness that blazed within her to take on and overcome challenges, her ease and skill with weaponry, and her concern were shown every time she took care of his injuries and worried over him—that all meant something. Their relationship hadn't been a long one, apparently, but he felt himself falling for her all over again, easily seeing why he would have in the first place.

If I remembered my past, would I have reason to challenge her? He pushed the contradictory thought away. Thinking like that was a fool's game, not to be entertained. A soft touch of Mari's hand against his chest brought him back to their conversation.

"I know you'll get us out of this place." Quiet sincerity rang through her words.

He pressed his lips to her cheek then turned back to move the skewered meat around on the fire. Soon, the mouthwatering smell of roasted pig sent his stomach into a cramping fit. He removed it and placed it on one of the leaves she had ready before placing the rest of the food over the fire. They let it cool for a few minutes before eating.

"Mmm… I can't remember the last time I ate this well. Wow." Chewing more, she swallowed. "I mean, before you got better, I don't think I had more than a few pieces of dried meat and one of your MREs. I was constantly starving, but too nauseous to really do anything about it."

The fierce frown he flashed her when she turned toward him caused her to falter and rush her speech. "Oh, it's okay. I'm fine now."

"That's not good, Mari. If something happens to me, you have to be able to go on, to hunt on your own. I need the assurance that you can and will. If you don't know how to do something, I want to know now, so I can teach you."

She waved away his concern. "No, it's not like that. I was worried about you and didn't like leaving your side for too long.

Hey, why don't we make some of this meat into a stew for dinner tonight? I completely forgot I brought along a light-weight bowl. It's small, but we can make two servings. That would taste so good with some bananas, and the rice-and-bean MRE from your pack."

He chuckled. "Sure. We can cube the last of the filets and prepare them to simmer, with a row of sticks acting as the grill over the pit."

"I'll get started on it." She left him to finish the rest of the cooked meat. Retrieving the knife she'd been using for cooking, she set to work at cubing the last of the wild pig. "Hey, Chris?"

"Mm-hm?" he murmured around a mouthful.

"You had another nightmare last night, or some sort of a dream." She glanced up, and her eyes widened when she caught his intense stare. "You were talking to someone named Trev in your sleep."

He winced when she said "Trev," but then his expression returned to a somber one. An avalanche of emotion slammed into him but without context—he had no idea why the name caused such an intense reaction. He could only shake his head in frustration. "No. I recognize that name like it's my own, but I just…" His teeth snapped together as he clenched his jaw in frustration.

"Don't worry about it." She flashed him a small smile. "I just thought I'd mention it. I'm sure it'll come back to you." Clearing her throat, she tried again. "Do you think he could have been your contact? Who you spoke with before joining the guerrillas?" Her eyes dashed to the task she worked on. It was as if she was worried about what she'd see in his eyes.

"Mari, come here." Still, she questioned his motives. It was confusing.

She glared at him, dark emotions swirling in her eyes. "I can't," she whispered. "My hands are dirty."

"There is no way I'd join an outfit like that. You've just got to trust me. I don't have any idea what would cause me to leave your side, but deep in my heart, I'm positive I'm not a part of them."

With a shrug, she mumbled an okay, then rose to go wash off her hands. The firm grip on her upper arm stopped her and gently turned her around. He tilted up her chin, and she met his sincere gaze. "It's just a concern I have."

"Put it to rest. I'm here now with you. Focus on what we have together, right now. And what we'll have in the future." *Because that's all I'm able to do.*

She nodded before she slipped away to clean up. When she came back, she started the stew and left it to cook slowly over the embers. By the time dinner rolled around, they would have a hearty meal.

The sky darkened, and clouds rolled in thick abandon. Some were dark, and some were a murky gray, but all told them rain would arrive soon.

Dusting off her hands, she stood, only to be pulled back against his chest. He preferred her fire, and he wanted it to return. She relaxed against him and seemed to let her worries scatter to the hot wind that stirred the leaves around them.

She reached a hand behind her and threaded her fingers through his hair at the nape. It'd grown a little, and it drove him crazy, but she liked it. With a gentle tug, she wiggled closer, and he complied by surrounding her with his arms, his presence, and his touch.

Small kisses peppered the curve of her neck, and she tilted her head to the side to give him greater access. When he felt her tense, he stopped rather than have her pull away. He could tell by her actions that she wasn't ready for more, and he didn't really blame her.

"You're so beautiful." His forehead dropped to hers, and he

shifted the hold he had on her to her waist. He puffed hot air against her cheek. She slipped her arms around him, rose up on her toes, and buried her face in his neck.

So much about her intrigued, amused, and pleased him. Something else had to be at play, because there was no way he could ever have left her.

～

MARI

Mari picked her way among a few broken twigs, jagged stones and pebbles, and a beetle inching over the soggy ground. Placing large banana leaves over the muddy bank, she sat down because she needed a few moments alone. He confused her, making her want things she hadn't thought would be possible. They were living a lie, and the guilt ate at her. It'd been a stressful few days, weeks—months, really. Chris helped her with that more than she'd like to admit. The more time she spent with him, the more comfortable she'd become. She'd left him resting in their hideout, needing a few minutes to think without his distracting presence.

She slipped off her boots, then her socks, before she rolled up the ends of her pants and dipped her toes in the slowly moving water. For a while, at least, the sky was clear. Several branches overhead helped to shield her from the brutal rays of the late-afternoon sun that peeked through the rolling rain clouds.

"Be careful of the crocs."

She shrieked, jerking her feet out and back to the leaf she sat on, where they were temporarily safe. The chuckle behind her had her seeing red, and she leapt to her feet, ready to deliver a piece of her mind. "You think that's funny?"

He wore a wicked grin, and his shoulders shook with restrained laughter.

Covering the ground between them in a few angry strides, she pounded her fist on his left shoulder, the only place she knew wasn't bruised. When his hand covered hers, her gaze flew to his. Their eyes locked, and some of her irritation fled. His bright hazel eyes captured hers, and her heart rate increased—and it wasn't from the scare he'd just delivered. Pulling her hand from his grasp, she took a step back.

What is he doing to me? She frowned, unsure of her softening feelings toward the soldier she'd tied her life to—at least for the next unforeseeable time. Or until they crossed the border.

"I hate crocs because they scare me out of my mind, with those huge, sharp teeth and the scaly skin." She shuddered, and he reached out and squeezed her shoulder.

"I'm sorry." His grin slipped a notch. "I didn't realize that would frighten you so much." His hand skimmed over her thigh, and she sucked in a breath. When he pulled a knife from the sheath in her pants, her frown only deepened. "What are you doing?"

"Target practice." He winked at her and turned on semi-unsteady feet. His health had improved, but there were moments she knew his head injury caused him to weaken, the dizziness too great to contain.

Over his shoulder, he glanced at her feet. "Put your boots back on. I don't want you to injure the bottom of your feet."

She shrugged. He was right, and she retrieved her socks and boots. Bending, she slipped them back on, taking a moment longer to tie the laces. By the time she straightened, he'd set up a few makeshift targets with some flat pieces of bark and wood from the forest floor. Intrigued, she joined him, pulling another knife from its sleeve.

About a half-inch-long piece of medical tape was in the

center of each target. He flipped the knife he'd taken from her in a catch and release before he threw it at the farthest target. It happened faster than she could blink, and her mouth dropped open.

"We can warm up a little first then make things interesting." He winked, and her curiosity—and the stirrings of desire—grew.

This man, and the things she was learning he could do... There was nothing hotter.

They took turns, and with each one, her giddiness increased. It was fun. It was something she loved to do. Apparently, so did he, judging from the wide grin he wore.

It was nice to have something in common, and it made her see possibilities she knew she shouldn't really entertain. Since she was in the role she was, she allowed herself to go with it. But as she did, the guard around her heart slipped another notch, inviting Chris in.

"Can you hit a moving target?" His eyes sparkled with mischief as he held her gaze.

She nodded with determination, stomping down on her urge to laugh with sheer enjoyment. He tossed one of the targets in the air, and it soared high in a circular whirl. On an exhale, she let her knife fly. She hit the target dead center, grinning at him as it plummeted faster with the weight of the blade in the center.

"Not bad." Admiration flashed over his handsome face. "Try two."

In fast succession, he tossed two targets, one of them smaller than the other. She flung her knives, one after the next. Both hit home, but the second was slightly off-center. He jogged over to her and pressed a quick kiss on her cheek before he retrieved her knives. "Wait, let me throw them." He paused, and she met him by the targets then took them from his hands.

He turned so his back was to her. She was confused for half a second, and her pulse increased its pace as she realized what he meant to do. Trying not to make a sound, she hurled first one then the other target high.

A slight scuffing was all she heard when she released the wood. He whirled around and, with lightning reflexes, struck both targets, in the air, dead center. *Oh my God.* She'd never witnessed anything hotter. Her kaleidoscope of emotions confused her, and she made an excuse to leave, saying she needed to go to the bathroom. Afterwards, she reentered their small space with care. Chris sat with his back to the tree and his eyes closed, and she took the reprieve given to her by his impromptu nap to go back to sitting by the river, where she mulled over her growing feelings for him.

CHAPTER 10

CHRIS

Chris stood and left Mari's side. She'd been quiet, which was unusual for her. For most of the day she'd been at the water's edge, seemingly lost in thought. Tilting his head, he skimmed the back of her form as she sat on the bank of the river, with the cool water running over her toes. His fingers twitched—he wanted to hold her and to brush the strands of hair that he knew drove her crazy from her face. But there were things to take care of, and he wanted to be ready to leave quickly, should the need arise. He didn't doubt that it would.

We need to move out. Very soon.

Several days had passed since they were reunited. Chris stirred the embers, making sure the fire from their dinner was out, then lifted the clump of earth to cover their fire pit so it looked as if nothing was there. As he knelt, he checked on her again. Her shoulders slumped forward, and a twinge of worry hit him. "You alright?"

Over her shoulder, she glanced at him, a ready smile in place. "Yeah, just tired. Need help?"

He didn't buy it. "Nah, I've got this."

She seemed to get more and more restless the longer they remained in one spot. She'd done a lot for him, standing by his side while he was injured, and for that he would give her the benefit of the doubt regarding their marriage.

He stretched, pulling his arms up over his head. Most of his symptoms had diminished, and the wound on his head had scabbed over. He needed to talk to her about heading out.

Chris paused when a succession of plops along the water disturbed the cadence of the sounds in their small space. "What are you doing? Skipping rocks?"

Her throaty laugh mingled with the chatter of two bickering birds in a nearby tree. "If you call tossing pebbles into the river skipping rocks, then sure."

With a chuckle, he gripped a leafy branch and brushed away the majority of their footprints. Mari seemed content to sit where she was, and he didn't mind—he felt compelled to check and double check everything anyway. Inside their makeshift home, he made sure their belongings were always packed up in their bags, so they could flee at a moment's notice.

So far, everything had gone smoothly. No longer did he have issues with light causing dizziness or nausea. The concussion wasn't entirely gone, nor was the bruising, but the week's rest had done wonders for him—and for them, too. Each day brought them a little closer together.

Now, he could tell she was itching to leave. She could barely contain her desire to do so. He wanted to go, too, but they'd held out because the stronger he was, the safer they would be.

"Hey, how long does it take to throw some dirt over our fire?" she teased.

A grin stretched across his mouth. He had been lost in

thought. "Point taken." Scrutinizing her stiff posture and too-bright smile, he narrowed in on her red, puffy eyes. *Is she upset? Have I done something, or is the situation taking a toll?*

Her gaze found his, and she rolled her eyes, so he let it go. He finished banking the fire then went over and sat beside her. His arm brushed against hers, sending tingles of awareness through him where they touched.

"This sounds bad," she said, "considering that we're safe and actually have food to eat from what you've caught, but I'm sick of fish. The wild pig was fantastic. Wish we could find some more of that."

"You have no idea how good we have it. I've gone on much less for a lot longer. This is paradise."

She sat up straighter, her breath hitching. There was a slight pucker to her lips. "You remember?"

Is she worried that I remember something? A dark cloud swept over his face. "No." Several beats passed before a look of pain flashed across his face and drew his features taut. "I don't know where that came from. I couldn't tell you where or what that statement was about."

She ran her hand along his biceps, her own features visibly relaxing. "It probably came to you because you weren't trying."

Chris dropped his head into his hands, overwhelmed by the many things that plagued him.

"Stop putting so much pressure on yourself. I know what you're doing, and it'll only cause pain." She brushed her fingers along his jaw.

When her hand dropped away, he thrust his fingers through his hair before he turned her way, frustrated and not wanting her to see the conflicting desire her simple touch evoked—one that brought about the stirrings of a memory that flashed deep within him. The intensity of both the present and past burned bright before his brain extinguished the elusive information. With it went the possibility of learning more.

Unwilling to dwell on what he couldn't access, he brushed a finger along the curve of her cheek. *This woman.* Her body reacted to his energy, softening as she pressed against him, which she often did. When her gaze dropped to his lips, he leaned close, wanting her.

Leaves rustled, and Chris jerked away. Before Mari had time to react, he was on his feet, racing toward the noise. *Shit.*

They'd been discovered.

It wasn't an animal, but a flash of tan camouflage peeking through the foliage. Separated by a few trees that were spaced a good distance apart, the guy hadn't noticed him just yet. Chris leapt through the dense coverage and surprised the threat with a fist to his face.

The soldier crashed to the ground, and Chris straddled him, raining punches onto his face. The satisfying crunch as he broke the guy's nose, and the spray of blood that arced from it, only fueled him.

Out of the corner of his eye, he caught another soldier quickly closing the distance between them. He saw a flash of metal—the guy's gun was trained on him. *Dammit!* He knew better. The thought of these guys anywhere near Mari had spurred his base instincts. He shifted enough to pull his gun out as he heard footsteps stomping near.

Mari. Out of the corner of his eye, he saw her yank the gun she kept on her free while she ran toward him. On the ground, Chris eased back from the unconscious man and aimed to shoot the new guy first.

Time slowed as fear for her crawled through him. The other guerrilla's strides lengthened. His pinched eyes stopped on Mari, and Chris's heart leapt in his throat. Determination tensed Mari's jaw. Her focus was locked on the soldier. He'd die. Chris would make sure of it, and he would kill the man *before* Mari was hurt.

Panic painted Mari's features pale. She locked her arms out in front of her, and her finger tensed on the trigger. Pounding feet slapped the ground as the guy raced their way. Shots rang out, and Chris dropped to the side, partially shielded from the man he'd beaten. Bullets whizzed by his head.

At the flash of tan and green clearing two trees, Mari shifted and got off two shots at the same time Chris did. The loud pops echoed through the forest. The man dropped first to his knees, then flat on his face.

He was dead. But he was a member of the guerrilla force, and Chris wondered how quickly others would arrive.

Time moved slowly. Chris got to his feet and edged over to her then pushed her gun down and snapped the safety back into place. Her eyes were glazed. As he spoke to her, she made no response, his words failing to penetrate as a shiver shook her body. With practiced movements, he slipped the gun from her hands. She swayed, and he wrapped an arm around her and maneuvered her out of sight of the dead man.

Over and over, he talked to her. He reassured her that it was all right, she was safe, and they were okay. She gave several slow blinks then flinched. It seemed as if the world came back to her full force in that second, and he breathed a sigh of relief.

"I killed him."

"It was self-defense. He planned on shooting me. You did the right thing."

"I know." Her dull voice alarmed him.

"Are you okay?"

"No. It's just… They found me—us." Mari's eyes widened as she shook her head. "Killing isn't what terrifies me. It's what's coming next."

"Shhh, Mari." *What's coming next?* Her cryptic words alerted him to a problem. She was withholding information.

Her unfocused gaze pulled at him, and he coaxed her back. "Come back to me." His hand brushed against her cheek, and the dampness of the ground seeped into their clothes. She lifted a hand, brushing it against her leg. It seemed as though her awareness of the moisture was another step in grounding her. In slow increments, her color returned.

Leaning into him, she shuddered. "I-I-I—"

"Shhh. You did what you had to do. Don't beat yourself up. Later, we can talk. Right now, I need you to snap out of it." He shoved the lighter of the three packs into her hands. Absently, Mari slung the bag over her shoulders.

Part of him would have preferred that the man's death was what freaked her out. Instead, she feared something else—*but what?* Despite her despondent attitude, as long as she was walking, he'd give her space, at least for the time being. They'd revisit whatever was causing her so much anxiety once they were relatively safe.

Chris emerged from their fort, and she followed him. He went to one man then the other, relieving them of any gear or weapons they could use and stowing what he found in his pack. He picked up the man he'd beaten. He then slung him over his shoulder and headed to the river. Rather than standing by the guy she'd shot, Mari followed, stopping when they reached the bank and he launched the guy into the water. Mouth hanging open, she stood there while he went back and repeated the process with the other man.

"Why?"

He turned to her fully, understanding that her sluggish mind refused to make the connections—she was in shock. The manhunt, or woman-hunt, she assumed they'd face most likely ran through her brain on a mind-numbing loop.

"Crocodiles. They'll get rid of the bodies and buy us a little more time."

Gagging, she lurched after him, revulsion etched across her features.

"This extra pack we've been using is from their camp, isn't it?" He turned and leveled a look at her. At her nod, he continued. "And the canoe you have partially hidden?"

"Do you think that's how they found us?"

He shrugged. "Could have been, but they didn't come from the direction of the river. My guess is they've been combing the area, looking for the two women who raided their camp for a pack and transportation. Someone could have seen you both, or when you killed the guy who chased you. Either way, we need to move out of here."

Her expression turned hopeful. "Are we?"

"Going for the border?" He met her questioning gaze with a distracted one of his own. "We'll head that way."

She cleared her throat. "Hannah was right."

"What are you talking about?"

"Ah… I… It's just this hellhole. It messes with your head. Everything is uncertain, and I've been submerged in this jungle for too long. You're so good to me. I just—" She shook her head. "Nothing. Forget what I said. I'm just trying to process right now."

Mari took Chris's proffered hand and stepped onto the canoe, which bobbed in the gentle current. When they were settled in their seats, he pulled out a map from his pack, studied it, then shoved it back inside. Without the looming storm, the water wasn't as insistent in pushing them where it wanted them to go. Their packs rested in the bed of the skiff, and he dislodged them from the bank and used the paddle to manipulate their path.

"Why are we going this way?" Mari's voice sounded shrill and laced with anxiety.

He cast his gaze to her and noticed she was fighting tears, which was very unlike the woman he was coming to know.

"Why are we going away from the border?" Mari reached forward and gripped his arm. "Or is my sense of direction off?"

They were still headed farther away from where she wanted to go. "Just a bit farther down the river, there should be a stream we can access. After we make our way a few miles down that, we can set up a new camp. It'd be best if we travel at night as much as possible. The moon is still full enough to give us some light."

Rolling her lips, she pressed them into a firm line. His sympathy for her stirred as he watched emotions play across her features. Even though she'd taken time to ensure he was healthy, he'd noticed her agitation growing with every day that passed. And he hadn't forgotten that she was crossing the jungle to the border before they were reunited. He'd like to think she was searching for him. But she'd told him that she was making the trek on her own, that she had to. He knew that her need to get out of Colombia and away from the jungles of the Darien Gap was a desperate flame that burned hot inside her.

"Eyes here, Mari."

She didn't listen. A shudder coursed through her body as they caught up to one of the dead men floating and bobbing in the water. The other was nowhere to be found. Maybe his lungs had filled with water and he'd sunk, or the crocs had already gotten to him. They continued down the river in silence, each listening to the sounds of nature and searching for those that didn't belong. Out in the open like that, they were taking a risk.

Oppressive heat blanketed him from all sides. The late afternoon sunlight blasted them, and temperatures rose to extreme discomfort. Yet, he saw her shivering. As they coasted along the rolling river, his unease at her pensive silence ate at him. "Are you okay?"

"No. They're coming."

"Come here, Mari. Move the packs to help balance where you were and sit in front of me."

She did as he asked and settled back down, leaning against his chest. "We can handle whatever we come across. Trust me." They'd be fine. With her close to him, their skin brushing against one another, he felt her tension ease ever so slightly. Each time they'd touched, kissed, and held one another, she let down her guard more. No matter what scared her so, he'd catch her. They'd developed a fragile trust, which blossomed in the daily chores, in her nursing him back to health, and in the desire that simmered between them.

Their direction shifted, and he angled toward the narrow stream just to their left. He turned their canoe and got them further into the canal before setting the paddle inside and grasping an overhanging branch to hold them in place. They remained bobbing in the gentle water, and he could tell that she waited to see what he'd do next.

One of his arms snaked around her stomach and held her tight. Tears rolled down her face, and she shook. He'd do what he had to do to keep her safe.

He wanted to fix things for her. At least, he could try to ease her conscience for the only thing that made sense as an explanation for her tears so far. "Mari, I'll protect you." He hoped his whispered words would find their way inside her, and that she would know he spoke the truth. "We did what we had to do."

"Maybe."

"Things will work out. We'll camp out for a few hours then continue to the border. We'll be free of this place soon."

"Okay." She leaned into him, her head shifting ever so slightly as she searched the vegetation along the sides of the river for people. "What's the first thing you think you'll want once you get home?" He stiffened behind her, and she sighed. "I didn't forget about your memory loss. Just, what do you think, or what comes to mind? Like air conditioning."

"That'd be nice, but it's probably not at the top of my list. You naked and both of us in a real bed would be the first thing I'd want, and definitely more than once. When we're ready to let the world back in? Grilling a steak, potatoes, a cold beer, and good company. That sounds right."

Her face heated at his words. "Nice."

"What about you?"

"Safety. You." She glanced back at him. "A life where you're a permanent fixture by my side. Those would be top contenders. Also, I'd like a place to stay where I'd be protected. I could do without a lot, so long as I had that." A shiver coursed through her as she pressed against him. The thickness to her voice told him she was overwhelmed, even though her words rang with truth. Her tone hinted that what they discussed had a high probability of being unattainable, because the guerillas had found them.

His arm tightened around her stomach. "While you're by my side, you don't need to worry, Mari. I'll take care of you."

The sky had already begun to darken, and for a moment, her nails dug into his legs. "I know you'll try, Chris. I just hope we have that chance, that we make it out of the jungle alive."

CHAPTER 11

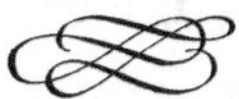

MARI

Secure between Chris's legs in the canoe, Mari let her mind wander. She'd started her journey through the treacherous Darien Gap with the intent to cross the border and eventually make her way to the States—alone. Now that Chris was by her side, she couldn't imagine doing it any other way than with him. He offered her stability, safety, and a tether to sanity in the dangerous swampland that was rife with killers.

If the need arose, she was one, too. It had been necessary—it was Chris's life or that man's. That's what she understood.

She wasn't a stranger to death or to killing—she'd grown up in a tough environment and mingled with dangerous people in her youth. This was her first time pulling the trigger and ending a life, but it wasn't a foreign experience. Death came in all forms, and who wielded the death blow depended on the situation. It could be from a disease, such as her aunt's, or a senseless slaughter, which was what happened to her parents, or what she and Chris had done to ensure their own survival.

Mere inches from the narrow bank on either side of their canoe, Mari kept a vigilant lookout for both people and dangerous wildlife. Risking a quick glance behind her, she caught Chris's intent predator-like expression in the glow of the moon, and her breath hitched. Fierce, single-minded focus radiated from him. With his jaw clenched, he scanned the surrounding area and the trees, all while keeping them on course. If there was a threat, she had no doubt he'd neutralize it.

Still, she wanted an additional reassurance. Keeping her voice low so it didn't travel and put them in further danger, she asked him, again, the question that was most on her mind. "Are we heading in the right direction to the border?"

"Yes, in a roundabout way. We'll follow the stream several miles until we find a good place to rest, preferably closer to morning."

Leaning back into Chris once more, Mari pulled her gun out, getting ready in case they were ambushed. They weren't terribly far from the guerrilla camp, and she had no idea if they would come across more insurgents or others with dark intent. They could very well be outnumbered. Chris moved silently through the jungle and navigated the canoe in the same manner. In the time she'd known him, he never ceased to amaze her. She craved him. He'd hacked away at the barrier she'd tried to keep intact between them, and more often than not, she found herself brushing her hand along his hard body or leaning in for a breathless kiss.

She nibbled on her lip as she contemplated the differences between him and the other men she knew. There was no comparison. He trumped them all.

"How is it that you move like a ghost?"

He didn't answer, and she felt his body tense behind her. A slight tremor ran through him.

"Chris? Are you alright?"

Silence met her question.

Cautiously, she turned around and caught the haunted look that seized his features. "What is it?"

He winced. "Just a flash of moving through the jungle with some others. Nothing clear." With a shake of his head, he resumed the same sure motions with the paddle, moving them swiftly downstream. "About another hour, and we'll break."

They'd traveled a good distance, and from the look of the sky, morning would lighten the horizon in a few hours. She wanted to get their camp set up and put up their hammocks to catch a little sleep. She hoped they'd find something as camouflaged as their former campsite.

A few chunga palm trees were on their right. Several drops of sap glistened from the bright moonbeams and made her glad they weren't stopping there. The palms were covered in long, sharp spines, laden with bacteria, and deadly in the jungle. One scrape was all it would take for an infection to set in, which was definitely not wanted in the hot and humid environment. Bacteria thrived there.

Monkeys and birds called to each other from the canopy of trees as the sky continued to lighten. Soft rays peeked through the break in the leaves overhead. Her grip stayed tight on the gun while she let the serenity of the wild sink into her. If the jungle hadn't been infested with drug trafficking, guerrillas, kidnapping, and deadly wildlife, its appeal would have been greater. *Well, without the intense heat and insects, too.*

They quietly glided through the water, with the jungle's symphony their only company. Silence generally meant danger of the human variety. Aside from their mishap with the men who'd attacked them, things looked good.

In time, she would confess her secret about their relationship, but it wasn't the right moment. They'd found a rhythm together, a chemistry that burned bright, and a mutual goal—to escape the rough terrain.

"The area right before the bend looks good, with lots of vegetation." Chris pointed. "If we can make our way through the plants and bushes without having to use the machete, we can camp here for a few hours."

Her spirits lifted. They could rest, eat, and hydrate before beginning their travels again in the morning. She knew he'd push on, forgoing sleep. He was probably stopping for her, but she was grateful.

With a shove on the bed of the shallow stream, Chris brought them against the bank. "Hold the paddle here, Mari. I'll get out then help you."

Her fingers curled around the wooden handle, the end of which was still shoved into the riverbed. The current pulled, and she strained to keep them in place.

Once off the canoe, Chris bent down and gripped the side of it. "You can lift the paddle up now. Just put it inside, then grab my shoulder to steady yourself as you get out."

Before she stepped out, she slipped her pack on, dragged the other two closer, then tossed each of them onto the ground near where he stood. She did as he'd instructed, pleased at how much easier it was to get out of the canoe this time than it had been when she was with Hannah.

"Move back a little," he said. When she complied, he pulled the canoe out of the water and dragged it over to a thicket of plants. He picked up a branch he'd found by the canoe's hideout then arranged it to cover their tracks. "That'll hopefully keep us hidden." He slung the remaining two packs over his back then moved around her, deeper into the jungle. "We'll find somewhere close, but out of range of a flood if it rains tonight."

If heavy rains came, there would be risk of the waterways flooding, and waking to that would suck. Mari tried to place her feet where he did. The forest floor was wet, and it sucked at her boots, making it hard to walk. Falling behind Chris, she found it difficult to match his much larger stride. Forcing a burst of energy, she took a large step forward, but her back foot caught on a root, and the slick ground slid out from under her. She went down hard. Her palms smashed into a plant before sinking into mud. Something moved, and she felt a burning sensation crawl up her arm in a succession of fiery bites. Whipping her hand up, she scurried back from the spot. A line of red ants—fire ants—moved up her arm, attacking her. She cried out before clamping her lips together.

Chris lunged at her and brushed her off with his hand. When he got them off, he lifted her to her feet, and she moaned. The back of her right hand and arm throbbed and burned.

"Are you being bitten anywhere else?" He tightened his hold on her and pressed her against his chest.

She shook her head then raised her arm so he could see the trail of bites, along with the instant redness and swelling. "I can't believe this."

"At least it was isolated to your hand and arm. Could have been a lot worse." He slipped an arm around her waist and led her to sit at the base of a tree.

She whimpered as her injury burned in painful pinpricks. Her fingers went numb. Chris unzipped his backpack and rummaged through it before pulling out some pills and a canteen. She took the medicine from his hand and swallowed them with a gulp of water.

"I know it hurts like a bitch. Is anything swelling? Your tongue? Any difficulty breathing?"

A few tears leaked from her eyes, and she shook her head. "No, it just burns and itches like crazy." She worried that the welts would open and become infected. Stabbing pain rode her nerves like a rollercoaster. "I'm not allergic. I can breathe okay at least."

"Let's get you down by the water, and you can put your hand in there for a while. It's the best we can do without ice."

He picked her up—why, she wasn't sure, but she didn't complain—and carried her to the edge of the stream, helping her to rest comfortably with her arm dangling in the water. It was dark enough that she didn't worry much about enemies sneaking up on them. They still could, but she was well hidden by the tall grass around her. They'd have to come right up on her to see where she sat.

He crouched next to her, playing with the long strands of her ponytail. Time ticked by, and his presence eased some of the fears running rampant through her mind. This wasn't the first time she'd been bitten by the horrid insects. They gave her the creeps, but there was no way to avoid them in the jungle.

She was thankful that she hadn't fallen into the bacteria-ridden spines of the palm when she tripped. There'd been one close by. The ants' bites were awful enough, and she knew she couldn't scratch them. Her misery would last longer. As more time passed, she relaxed further. The water helped.

Chris stirred beside her. "Will you be okay if I go set up our camp? I'll only be gone for a few minutes."

She swiped at her tears. "I'll be fine. I'm just upset."

He bent again and brushed a kiss over her lips. "You'll be all right. Get some rest, and you'll be good as new."

She nodded, then Chris moved swiftly behind her to set up their camp a short distance away. No longer did she worry that he'd abandon her. He exuded competence and strength. That wasn't what bothered her—the stress of their predicament did. Since he wasn't by her side, she allowed herself to give in to her self-pity and open up the floodgates for a good cry for a few minutes. Tears rolled down her cheeks, and her shoulders shook in silent sobs. Dropping her forehead to her uninjured arm, she took several steadying breaths, willing the pity party to go away. She'd wipe away all evidence of it before he returned.

Fate must have intervened to send me to him—someone so innately good, capable, and powerful. It wasn't something she was accustomed to. The only constant in her life, after her father had been killed in the street in her youth, had been the one who'd caused her the greatest distress, and from whom she ran even now.

Not too long after she'd rubbed the tears from her face, Chris came to sit next to her, their makeshift fishing line in hand. "I thought I'd catch us some fish for dinner rather than leave you too long to hunt." He dropped the line, complete with a wiggling bug on the end, into the water. It floated downstream, squirming on the surface. It didn't take long.

Keeping her face averted, she gritted her teeth against the feel of his weighted stare. "I told you, I'm fine."

He grunted in response right before he jerked the line, setting it. He must have felt a nibble. Following the line of transparent thread, she smiled as he pulled a small fish from the stream. "At least they're biting."

"Yeah, but we need a hell of a lot more than that." He cast the line in again and settled in to wait for the next one. By the time he was finished, ten fish lay next to them. "I'll clean these and start a fire. Are you feeling well enough to come to camp with me, or do you want to keep your arm submerged a while longer?"

"I'm ready." She pulled her hand out, and he inspected it.

"The swelling looks like it stopped."

Soon, the welts would form small blisters, and they'd have to cover them with bandages. *God, I'll have to deal with this for a week.*

Chris looped a piece of twine through the fishes' gills,

stringing them up so he could carry them. Taking her good hand in his, he helped her to stand and walk to where he'd set up their things. "Have a seat over there, and I'll get all this cleaned and cooking. Should be ready in no time."

It seemed that their roles had reversed, and she wasn't sure how she felt about it. The only thing that looped through her mind was that they wouldn't be moving out just after dawn like he'd planned. They were delayed again, and it was her fault. If only she'd been more careful.

CHAPTER 12

MARI

"Are you comfortable?" Chris positioned the mosquito netting around Mari's hammock in their new camp.

"I'm better now." The sky was dark with threatening clouds, and they were about to turn in. It was late in the day, and they'd planned to spend a few of the hotter hours resting. Chris busied himself with his hammock, climbed in, and drew the gauzy curtain around him. They had eaten their meal and put out the fire. With full bellies, they were ready to sleep. Almost.

A light rain fell, slipping through the gaps in the leaves overhead. Their spot wasn't as protected as the one they'd been in before, and it made her feel vulnerable. It was farther from the guerrillas' camp, though—at least she hoped it was.

The ground sloped uphill. Chris had positioned himself closer to the river, saying if an enemy came, there was a high probability they'd come that way. He wanted to be the first line of defense.

~

CHRIS

Chris woke to the usual melody of the jungle. After making a quick catalog of the noises, his muscles eased. The usual pre-dawn sounds buzzed all around them. Careful not to wake Mari, he slipped from his hammock. For a moment, he stood over her, just taking in everything about her.

Through the mosquito netting, he followed the rise and fall of her chest. A thin T-shirt outlined her breasts. Some time ago, she'd stopped wearing a bra. It only added heat and caused chafing in the jungle. The fewer clothes, the better, so long as they were slathered in DEET to prevent as many bites as they could. Malaria wasn't something either of them wanted to experience.

Her hand rested flat against her abdomen, and he checked the swelling of her arm, as they'd decided to wait to bandage it until she woke. At least she hadn't scratched the welts open in her sleep.

She faced him, rocking in her hammock, and he wanted to smooth away her worry lines. Things would get better, or so he hoped. For the hundredth time, he wondered at how he was married. Something deep in his psyche, unwilling to surface yet, spoke of heartache. Something had happened in his past, and he worried about what would happen when the memory came to light. *Did it have to do with a problem between them?*

For the life of him, he couldn't fathom leaving his wife alone, where she would be forced to flee for her safety, which was what she was doing.

Am I the reason for her running, or why she's in the jungle? He flinched. Shoving the thought away, he had an idea of something she could take joy in, which would be another step in bringing them closer. All he could do at that point was try to heal whatever rift had occurred between them.

Trying not to wake her before he was ready, he carefully unzipped his backpack and withdrew the map. There were a lot of things in his pack he couldn't account for, though being a soldier helped him understand most of them. Mari's fear about him joining the guerrillas didn't sit right with him. There was something else, some kind of connection or bad blood between Mari and the guerrillas. He would figure it out in time.

Cupping his hand around a small penlight, he scanned the rivers on the map and made note of their locations. There it was—the spot he wanted to take her. It wasn't too far. A grin spread across his face, and he put the map away before he went in search of food for them.

Simple berries and bananas seemed to make her happy, but coconut milk was preferable, and they ate the meat inside, too. It kept dehydration at bay and contained nutrients they needed. He scaled a palm tree then knocked down two green coconuts. Mari preferred them—she said they were sweeter. He repeated the process to reach some ripe bananas and found a bush that held berries that were safe to eat. Gathering everything, he went back to where she rested and set about opening the coconuts.

He heard a dull thud and whirled around, raising his gun against the threat. Nothing moved. He scanned the area and saw the culprit. A ripe coconut had fallen on its own. *This is why we never sleep under the coconut trees.* Falling coconuts could seriously injure them.

Chris's machete striking against the outer shell of one of the green coconuts caused Mari to jerk awake, and Chris shot her a sheepish smile. *Shit, I should have done this farther from her.*

"Hi," she croaked.

He ate up her curves as she shifted into a sitting position

while stifling a yawn that caused her shirt to stretch tight across her chest. "Sleep okay?"

"For the most part. At least the worst of the cramping in my arm is gone."

"Good." After opening the second coconut, he rose to kiss her. "We got lucky with the ants. If you hadn't jumped up when you did, you would've been covered in them."

She shuddered. "I should be good to go today, maybe after we eat." She stood up, and dizziness caused her legs to give out beneath her.

Chris lunged and caught her, steadying her on her feet. "Maybe later in the morning. You may be having a slight allergic reaction to them."

Mari's lip trembled. "Yeah, you're probably right."

With a gentle squeeze, he lifted her fully and carried her to a spot he'd covered with banana leaves. He helped her onto the makeshift mat before he handed her the opened coconut that was brimming with milk. "I'm sure you'll feel better in a few hours."

They ate together in companionable silence, even though he was fully aware of what occupied her thoughts. She wanted to leave the place, and really, he didn't blame her. He knew there was something she wasn't telling him. He felt it in his bones. "Mari, is there anything else you want to tell me about the guer-rillas finding us?"

"About those two?" She frowned. "No."

"Are you sure you didn't meet Hannah before you left your aunt's home?"

Mari lowered the coconut. "No. I told you, I literally ran into her here. I'd never seen her before." He could see her temper prick in the color that infused her cheeks. "I can't say the same about you, though. She knew you, and when you first woke, you definitely reacted to her."

His anger simmered, but he pushed it aside. It was true. Hannah infuriated him. Why, he wasn't quite sure. Something about her presence brought out his instinct to fight. "I can't remember how I know her." *The damn amnesia still plagues me.*

Her face fell. "I'm sorry, Chris. It bothers me that you two know each other. That's all. Especially since…"

Since I supposedly abandoned her. "There was no way I would have left you for good, or intentionally. Or for her. There had to have been a reason I was pulled away."

She avoided his eyes, which narrowed in suspicion. He hoped sooner or later she'd trust him enough to share whatever secret she withheld from him, and he hoped it would happen before it was too late. An internal clock ticked inside him, urging him to reacquaint himself with Mari and to unravel the mystery of their meeting here. The guerrillas were only one piece of the puzzle.

"I can't explain it. Just that we come from two different worlds. Here, we're on equal footing, but the fact remains… You're military. Nothing good comes from those in authority here. Power corrupts, and drugs and the money they bring are the ultimate motivation for everything they do."

He ground his teeth. "Mari, I was military before, wasn't I? Why are we together in the first place, if that's how you feel?"

She launched the coconut at him, but he deflected it. "Do you want me to leave?"

Circling her much smaller wrists with his hands, he dragged her into his lap. "Stop. You're blowing this all out of proportion."

She bared her teeth, her words forced out between them. "You stop bringing up Hannah. I already told you what I know."

He reared back. *That was still bothering her?* "Okay, fair enough." Taking in the rapid rise and fall of her chest, he gave in. "Look, I was wrong to say that. There is no way I'd leave you. I'm sorry. It's this thing between us. You need to confide in me, to trust me. I won't leave, no matter what terrible secret you think you have."

A moment passed before she gave him a small nod. He wrapped his arms around her body, and she leaned into him. The electricity that sizzled when they touched was one of his favorite things.

The secrets he sensed between them made him wary, but he gave her the space to tell him when she was ready, even though it felt as if he'd run that gauntlet before—and lost. "I've got a surprise for you after you eat." He set her down and rose to pack up their stuff, transferring the extra supplies from the third pack to his. He buried the bag under a bush with a mound of leaves covering it. They didn't leave anything useful behind. Anything could happen in the jungle, and he would be prepared.

"What kind of surprise?" Mari asked around a bite of one of the berries.

"You'll see soon enough. Eat up. And we can head out."

It didn't take long to pack up the hammocks and mosquito netting. Everything else, they would wear. He dropped her boots next to her and discarded their broken coconuts away from where they'd camped. They wouldn't be returning, but it didn't pay to leave a trail, either.

Mari tugged on her footwear, careful of her sore hand and forearm. On shaky legs, she stood up. Chris had both packs on his back.

He threaded his fingers with hers as they walked to where the canoe was stashed. He dropped her hand then pulled the boat from its hiding spot and set it into the water. Holding the side, he reached out to help her in. Once they were both seated, he paddled them in the direction they'd been headed in the night before.

Mari twitched in her seat. "Is the surprise that we're heading out early? That we're staying on track for the border?"

"Yes and no," he responded, unable to hide the smile in his voice. "You'll see soon."

The jungle stirred with the first rays of light through the previously dense clouds. The humidity began to rise, and the scent of rain hung in the air. They would have another downpour that day, for sure. At night, the rain would pound down on them, cooling the temperature for a short while. To some degree, it was welcome, especially because they would need to refill their canteens. They had a few hours of light remaining in the day, and they would take advantage of it.

Chris stayed vigilant for any ambushes in the surrounding bush or ahead in the water. He didn't anticipate any trouble, as the guerrilla camp in this area was a good distance behind them, but one never knew. Soon, cascading water mixed in with the usual jungle sounds.

Mari glanced over her shoulder, a brilliant smile on her face. "A waterfall?"

He laughed along with her excitement. *God, she's beautiful, and when she smiles, stunningly gorgeous.* His heart flipped over in his chest.

It didn't take long for their little stream to meet up with the sparkling blue lake fed by the waterfall. The sight was magnificent.

"Are you sure we can do this, that it's safe?" She nibbled her lip as she scanned the area around them.

"I'll keep watch. Besides, the cool water will be a nice relief for your bites."

Chris maneuvered their canoe over to the edge of the lake and helped her out before tying it to a nearby branch. The vessel bobbed in the rippling current. He left their packs to rest along the bottom of the canoe, which would make it easier for them to jump in and go if the need arose, or they could easily grab them if they decided to make a run for it. Either way, they'd be close.

Mari immediately pulled off her shirt and tossed it on the seat, followed by her boots and pants. As he stood and shed his clothes, she'd already unbraided her hair and shaken it out. With an impish grin, she swung her legs over the side of the canoe and stepped into the water.

Mere inches behind, he slipped his arm around her waist and tumbled them fully into the refreshing water. Twisting in his embrace, she laughed, releasing bubbles to the surface. He immediately let her go, and she broke for the top. Following, he closed the distance between them and again circled her waist, pulling her soft, slippery body against his.

Her arms wound around him, and she sealed her mouth over his. That was all it took. Sparks flew, and his skin felt like a current passed over him from her touch. As he lifted her, she automatically wrapped her legs around him, and he took them waist deep, closer to the waterfall. The roar of the water couldn't compete with their igniting passion.

Arching against him, she dropped her head back, and he rained kisses on the curve of her neck. Her breaths came in little puffs, and he cupped a hand between her legs, reveling in her heat. Gliding his finger along her opening, he teased her, drawing whimpers as she pushed against the flat of his hand. He rubbed her clit, and she cried out.

Wrapping his hand firmly in the back of her hair, he tilted her beautiful face back to his and slanted his mouth across hers, their tongues tangling as he positioned himself at her entrance. She moaned and wiggled, trying to impale herself on his thick, throbbing shaft. *God I want her. All the damn time.*

Teasing her clit with his finger, he moved her lower and thrust deeply, seating himself all the way in. She broke their kiss, arched, and cried out. He latched onto her nipple and teased the taut bud. He pulled almost all the way out, only to slide all the way back in, over and over again. Her frantic little sounds drove him over the edge, and as he took her mouth with his, his hunger grew ravenous.

Another swirl of her clit, and her body squeezed his like a glove. Her back bowed as the orgasm seized her entire body. A scream burst from her lips, and he swallowed it with his mouth, increasing his pace until he followed with his own climax, just seconds after hers.

With her thighs tight around his waist, he held her in his arms. He was still inside her, and he never wanted to leave. She was heaven. With a quick but thorough glance around the lake, he checked for any unwanted visitors. Nothing had changed. The area looked secure. Satisfied, he walked them deeper into the plunge pool until the water reached his shoulders. He kept Mari in his arms, content with the closeness of their joined bodies.

She tilted her head and angled into the crook of his neck. One arm supported her above the water while he rubbed her back with his other hand, shifting the wet strands of her hair to the side.

"I like your surprises." Her husky voice slid around his heart.

He chuckled, pleased with her reaction. "How are you feeling?"

"Amazing, although I think I may need a nap." She snuggled closer. Her hand toyed with the short hairs brushing the back of his neck. "If the jungle was always like this, I'd want to stay here with you."

He tilted his head and snuck a peek at her face. "We'll figure out a way to visit tropical paradises in the coming years. There are so many places we can go. So long as there aren't any active missions, we'll spend time doing what we love."

Her body stiffened. "Missions?"

"Hmm?"

Pulling back, her hands on his shoulders, she stared at him, her mouth open in surprise. "You said 'missions.' What did you remember?"

He frowned, unsure of why his saying that would cause her such worry. Then he realized exactly what he'd said, and with it came a flash of whirling helicopter blades, gunfire, and the burning on his head after the bullet grazed him. There were loud noises, then something propelling his parachute off course, too far from the intended target. He vaguely remembered something like a drone flying by. Whatever it was, he chose to keep it close until it revealed itself entirely. "I don't know exactly. I can see a helicopter above me and hear a lot of noise. There are gun shots and…not much else afterwards."

Her arms wrapped around him in a fierce hug. "I'm scared, Chris. I feel like we just found each other." He felt her shudder as she pressed against him. "Things are so different. I don't want to lose you."

The desperation in her embrace sent tendrils of wariness through his mind. He ignored them. She was in his arms, and nothing would tear them apart.

CHAPTER 13

MARI

Water dripped off of Mari as she lifted herself out of the small lake. The slight breeze felt pleasant on her bare, wet skin. Tired and still itching from the ant attack, she walked over to the base of a palm tree, intent on picking up a coconut she had watched fall to the ground.

Focused solely on the round orb, she stumbled a little over a stick. "Ow."

"You okay?" Chris shouted from the water.

Turning in a circle, she checked to make sure she hadn't unearthed anything she needed to be careful of. Sharp, piercing pain stabbed her ankle, and she cried out. Her leg spasmed in horrific agony, contracting over and over again. Water splashed her, and she looked up, working to focus on how fast Chris appeared before her.

"What the fuck just happened?" He gripped her shoulders tight, panic swirling in the depths of his green eyes.

"My leg." Her body locked up with the next wave of misery. As it subsided to a dull burn, she pointed to the pile of rotted wood off to the left. "Snake."

Chris picked her up and ran to their canoe. Setting her inside to lie on an incline, her heart above her leg, he carefully inspected the bite without touching it. "Did you see the color? Do you know the type?"

"Yes." She groaned. It was bad, very bad—the worst possible snake that could've attacked her. "Fer-de-lance." It'd had dark-brown triangular markings along its body. Mottled green and black made up the rest of the discerning pattern. It was deadly. She was screwed.

"Shit." He riffled through his pack, pulled out a vial, inserted a syringe, and filled it with antivenin. He swabbed her skin and quickly injected the medicine. "Okay, babe, let's hope the first dose works." Vial and syringe set aside, he tore through his bag again and withdrew a canteen. "Drink. You need to stay hydrated."

He laced his fingers with hers, and she held on tight. *Holy hell, the pain is unbearable.* Pulling her naked body into his lap, he cradled her, allowing her to dig her nails into his arm without complaint when the pain came. Her nerves fired as if they were locked into the on position. She saw the snake—it was a baby, but still able to cause intense agony.

She'd need more than one dose, and she knew it. "Why not more?" Panting from the venomous poison that attacked her body, she had to know. *How many vials will I need? Ten? We don't have that many.* Tears ran down her face.

If she survived, this would surely delay their progress. More than anything, she wanted to get out of the jungle. *Have to leave.* They would come for her. It wouldn't be long until they figured out where she was. No one would save her then, if the snakebite didn't kill her first.

God, the pain. "Morphine?" Begging wasn't beneath her. In fact, she'd swallow all their pills to escape this awful agony.

"I'm sorry, Mari. It won't help. The only thing that will is the antivenin."

"Give me more." *Seriously, I'm fine with begging.* They were moving. Chris's arm brushed her as he paddled them along the water, retracing their prior path to the waterfall.

Why back? She must have looked at him with her question written all over her face because he answered.

"We have one vial. That probably won't be enough. I'm going to have to raid the guerrilla camp to get more."

No. There's no way. He'll be killed. "It's not safe." In between the worst of the gut-wrenching agony, she tried to talk to him. The world phased in and out around her as she suffered. She could only manage brief moments of clarity.

Chris shifted her, and she cried out. She couldn't move her leg—a temporary paralysis had set in. *If only it would stop the pain.* Moaning, she fought to stay awake as she watched Chris drop the paddle in their canoe and inject her with another shot. At least she knew the vial was less than a month old from the date scrawled across the label. It would be safe for a few more weeks without needing to be refrigerated. With that, she was lucky.

Black dots swirled through her unfocused sight, competing with her churning stomach. Sweat dripped down her face, and chills racked her body. Another bout of intense pain seized her, climbing up her lower leg to her thigh. It was spreading. Panting, she clawed for consciousness, but she didn't win. Blackness eclipsed her vision.

~

CHRIS

"Fuck, Mari! Wake up." Chris felt the talons of fear sink into him the moment he laid Mari down in their canoe, shoving their packs beneath her back and head. He had to raise her heart above the wound. The bruising began at the snakebite, and he feared it would cause tissue damage, or worse, necrosis. *Fucking hell, this is bad.*

The canoe drifted as he worked on her. The wound had been bleeding cleanly for about thirty seconds, so he set about cleaning it with the utmost care, careful not to push on the injury itself, focusing on removing any excess poison on her skin. If it was safe to do so, he'd have sucked out the blood from the wound with a vacuum pump, but that wasn't the recommended procedure. They could only wait it out and pray that the injections would do their job and neutralize the dangerous venom. Still, it bled, and he would need to watch it closely for signs of blistering and discoloration. In time, when they were out of immediate danger, he'd bandage it to keep bacteria out.

He filled another syringe with antibiotic, which he'd taken from the two guerrillas they'd disposed of at their first camp. They only had one more vial left. Injecting her with it, he prayed that it would leave her free of infection and that the antivenin would take effect. She could lose her leg. He'd seen it happen, and the process wasn't a pretty sight.

The swelling continued, and he adjusted her body in an attempt to isolate the venom. There was a little inflammation around her ankle caused by the bite. Bruising mottled her leg, spreading upward. *I already suctioned the fuck out of the antivenin vial with the syringe, so I'll just pray that I got everything I could into her.*

He lined up the bottles of antibiotics, and he gave her all of what was left. They had six hours until things would get really bad. They'd know after about two hours just how bad, given the visible effects. He didn't plan on letting the worst happen, but that meant that he'd need more vials. According to the hand-written notes on his map, the guerrilla camp was close to three hours away. He'd make it there in less time. He hoped she'd sleep—and not freak out—while he was gone. He'd leave his pack with her. That way, she'd know he was returning.

Short-term memory loss could occur from a fer-de-lance bite. It wouldn't be good if she woke and couldn't remember that he'd planned to get more meds from the camp.

Gritting his teeth, he paddled as fast as he could. Blistering sunlight shone down on them. There was nothing he could do for protection from the rays. He needed to be able to glance down at Mari, to make sure her chest moved in an even pattern, verifying that a constricted airway wasn't a cause for concern.

Every now and then, she'd twitch, and he could see the pain, as it caused her features to go taut. It was bad even while she was unconscious. No wonder she'd passed out. Chris saw a mental flash of a man in fatigues sprawled on the ground, surrounded by a handful of others, all dressed alike, who stomped a snake to death. A realization struck him: he'd known grown men in a similar situation.

Those damn snakes were unpredictable, aggressive, and easily excitable. Fucking hell. Chris clenched his jaw. They needed a break. It was as if the jungle had suddenly turned against them, first with the guerrilla attack, then the fire ants, then the snake bite. *Bad things happen in threes, and that was three. Please be done with us now, Karma.* He hoped good luck was due to come their way.

He paddled the canoe as if possessed, and they arrived sooner than he expected. The guerrillas must've already swept the area—that's what he'd do. With that in mind, he figured the safest place could quite possibly be in their tree hut. He maneu-vered the canoe into a more secure spot than where Mari had stashed it before. He slipped one of his shirts over her head then threaded her arms through and tugged it down. The end of his shirt fell to the middle of her thighs. Thankfully, it was loose and not constricting. At least she'd have a little bit of coverage. He lifted her and their packs then carefully stepped out of the boat and walked to settle her beneath a canopy of leaves.

There were footprints all over the place. The guerrillas had obviously been there already and hadn't bothered to disguise their presence. They wouldn't expect to find anyone else back there, which was one good thing that worked in their favor. Chris set Mari down for a moment so he could hook up one of the hammocks and pulled the netting from the pack. Then, he picked her back up and placed her in the hammock with her injured leg dangling from the side.

Before he left, he went out and plucked a coconut from the ground. After opening it, he filled one of the empty canteens with the milk. Wanting to make sure she stayed hydrated, he coaxed as much as he could down her throat. He left it capped and next to her for easy reach in case she woke. She needed to flush the toxin out. When he returned, he'd make her drink a veritable lake.

In a matter of seconds, he dressed then strapped on every weapon on his body except one handgun and a knife. At the sight of one of his knives, he remembered when he'd caught her throwing knives when she was angry or bored. He placed the weapons beside Mari before dropping the netting around her.

He'd given her two doses of antibiotic and a full vial of antivenin. To up their odds, she would need more, and fast. From the recesses of his panic-stricken mind, he seemed to remember reading a story about a woman getting bit and pulling through with no damage after a quick injection of ten shots. Most didn't fare so well.

It was late afternoon, the hottest time of the day. He downed the other coconut he'd split before setting off for the guerrilla camp. With his map, he had a general idea where it was.

The pace he kept was grueling in the heat, and he sweated by the bucket load. It didn't matter—all he cared about was getting what Mari needed and returning to her. Rather than focusing on his exhaustion, the humidity, and the fear that he could lose her, he thought about what he'd gained with her in his life as his feet pounded the distance to the camp.

He sensed movement not too far ahead, so he slowed and took care with each step. Through the leaves and branches, he could see a large group of men in camouflage milling about. He dropped to his elbows and army-crawled closer. Three men were deep in conversation, their expressions deadly serious. He listened as their voices carried to him, wanting to hear any intel that could up his and Mari's odds of getting out prior to an ambush.

A group of three men were situated closer to him than the rest. All wore the tan-camouflage pants and shirts. One of the men seemed to command the respect of the other two, and Chris zeroed in on what he was saying.

"The captains are looking for her—this is serious. All we have to go on is mostly from the guide who dropped her off. She paid a good sum of money to ensure her safe passage. From there, she traveled on foot. If we return her to the captains unharmed, we'll be rewarded and given a full supply of guns and ammo for our regiment. We're going to split the men off in groups of two and send them to flush her out."

"Assuming she's alive," the shorter man said.

"She better be." The leader slapped the men on the shoulder. "Now go. You two travel north of here. And if you find her, I'm told she goes by the name Mari."

Rage slammed into Chris. None of this made sense to him. *Captains?* That told him it was either mafia or cartel—which would make more sense—that was after her, but the manner of search he just heard the man describe seemed off. Someone else was fueling the hunt. *If they come anywhere near her, they'll pay with their lives. She's mine.*

The leader signaled for his followers to get into formation. He began to address them. It was Chris's chance. He saw tables stacked with guns, but farther down, he spotted medicine and spare clothing. While the group was distracted, he crawled in slow increments over to the last table, which was near a dusting of brush. Threading himself through the bushes, he took care to check for dangerous wildlife. *All Mari needs is for me to be bitten and then killed before I can get back and protect her.*

Carefully, he reached around the side of the table and slipped as many of the little packs from it as he could. He looked down at the assortment. He'd grabbed vials of antibiotics and syringes that were wrapped in baggies. Needing the antivenin, he tried again. There would be less of that, and he hoped it was the right kind. With an eye on the soldiers, he moved with caution. If one of them shifted their focus from their leader, they'd catch him in the act.

The guerillas didn't stray from giving the man in charge their full attention. It was probably considered treason to look away. *Fanatics.* As he checked the small bag he'd just swiped, his heart soared. *This is it.* He took everything he'd grabbed. Out there, it paid to be prepared.

As he started to slither back, two of the vials clinked together, and a few of the men turned their heads in his direction and noticed him. *Shit.* He twisted and dashed to the tree line just as an uproar from the troop sounded. He crashed through the brush, purposely weaving away from the direction where Mari was. He circled the camp as they closed in.

The pop of gunshots made him sprint faster, and branches whipped him in the face, arms, chest, and legs. He thundered through the brush, slipping here and there, but not going down. He could see the river—he was close. Sparing a quick glance over his shoulder, he counted four men leading the pack, their guns in their hands. One raised his weapon as Chris burst through the trees and dove, head first, into the river.

With the vials secured in his pocket, he took a big lungful of air and swam beneath the surface as a trail of bullets surrounded him. He ignored the stinging in his shoulder and continued with powerful strokes, never breaking the surface of the water that carried him further downstream.

The bullets that peppered the water let up. Only one or two came too close for comfort. His lungs burned, but he kept going. He needed for them to give up and the distance to increase. He deliberately continued with the wrong direction, taking a few more strokes before risking a breath then dunking his head back under. Switching directions, he moved farther from the edge and powered on, this time going the right way—toward Mari.

When he absolutely had to, he surfaced for another breath before plunging back under and swimming. He focused on how long he swam, gauging how far he'd gone and how much longer it would be until he reached the general area where Mari slept.

On his next breath, he looked back to see if any followed. No one was there. He'd gotten lucky. Taking inventory of where he was, he guessed he had another ten minutes of swimming until he reached the bank where Mari was. He needed to hurry. Blood was in the water from the bullet grazing his shoulder, and crocs were a problem.

When he pulled himself out of the water, he began jogging to where Mari was. In no time, he'd be by her side, and they'd be on their way again.

If the medicine worked.

CHAPTER 14

CHRIS

Ten shots had been administered. Chris ran his fingers through his hair and paced. He could only wait now. The bandage she wore was freshly changed, and the puncture marks looked good. They were lucky. He'd heard of—and even seen—some cases where the wound would pus, the toxin virtually eating the tissue.

As often as he was comfortable, he woke her long enough to ply her with liquids, hoping to aid her body's fight. Evening had passed, and night ushered in on its heels. He still needed to slip out of their camp to survey the perimeter. In the light of the moon, he'd tied tripwires all around them. They were not easy to spot. Even if someone got past them, he'd taken other measures and set traps to alert him.

Needing something to do, he went outside their hideaway and did another sweep of the area. Through the trees, a patch of brown and green shifted, and he crouched down. Careful of the root buttresses spreading over the ground from the tree, he maneuvered behind the thick trunk.

There were two of them.

Staying low and peering around the edge, Chris tracked the guerrillas as they headed in the opposite direction. That didn't mean he and Mari were in the clear. The men could easily swing back around. In a little while, he would have to look for them again.

Each moment that ticked by eased the tension in his body. He waited a good thirty minutes. With no one in sight, Chris ducked back beneath the fallen branch to check on Mari. Relief washed over him when he saw her lashes flutter open. "Good to see you're back." He lifted the netting and brushed her hair away from her cheek. It hung loose in long waves.

Mouth curving into a grin, she gave him a wink. "As if there was any doubt."

He handed her the canteen so the water could ease her scratchy throat. "Not a one. You pulled through like a champ." He talked in whispers, and she mimicked him. "How are you feeling?"

She took another gulp before answering him. "The intense pain is gone. For that I'm grateful." Her large brown eyes filled with tears. "I swear the jungle hates me. The longer we stay here, the lower I think my chances are of making it out."

With his fingertip, he brushed aside a tear that escaped. "I'll keep you alive. Stop worrying about that. Tell me what you're feeling so I can figure out what else you need." He pulled out the vial with antibiotic and prepared another syringe. "I want to make sure you don't get an infection, so bear with me for a sec." He wiped her skin with an alcohol pad and quickly gave her a shot.

"How does my ankle look? Will I lose my leg?" Her voice cracked, and he ached for her.

"No, babe." The pads of his fingers gently caressed her cheek. "You're going to be good as new in a few days." He peeled back the loose bandage, cleaned the wound again, and replaced it with a new one. The bruising was still there, a sign of internal bleeding, and the swelling remained, but it hadn't gotten any worse. In fact, it appeared to have decreased some.

"How much antivenin did you have to give me?"

"Ten shots. I debated over another one, but you improved after an hour from the last injection. I think we're in the clear."

She frowned. "I didn't think we had that much."

"We didn't. I was able to give you several injections before our vial was dry."

"So what'd you do?"

There was no avoiding telling her. "I took more from the guerrilla camp."

Her pupils dilated and covered her rich brown irises. She reached for the gun at her side and curled her fingers tightly around it. "Are we safe?"

"Somewhat." He grunted. "I rigged the area around us, so if they cross the perimeter, we'll know. That'll buy us some time."

"Why?"

"Just a safety precaution." He chose not to add to her stress with the near-capture experience he'd had—it'd been too close for comfort. "We're going to try to camp here for a few more hours. We'll stay in the canoe as much as possible, or I'll carry you. If we had a week for you to recover, that would be ideal, but we don't. A few days off your leg and traveling by water is all we can risk." He clenched his jaw, worried they'd ambush them even with the few hours he wanted to give her.

She grabbed his wrist. "What happened?" Alarm pulled her features tight. "I can tell you're holding something back."

He hooked his finger in his hammock and secured it, stopping it from swinging before he took a seat. All the while, Mari scanned what he wore, obviously noticing the weapons strapped all over him, before her focus caught on the dark spot and tear on his shoulder. "Were you shot?"

Palms up, he tried to stop her rising concern. "It's nothing, I swear. Just a graze."

It hadn't worked. He could tell she was panicked. "They saw you, didn't they? Are they coming? How much time do we really have?"

"Yes, they saw me." His jaw pulsed. "I led them away. We should be good for a while. That's not all, though. I overheard the leader of their group talking. They're looking for you, specifically. You were referred to by name." He waited a beat, hoping she'd interject, but gave up after she said nothing. She pressed her lips into a tight line. "There was no mention of Hannah. You're to be captured, unharmed. Why is that?"

She shifted, confusion and fear vying for dominance over her features. "I don't know why the guerrillas are after me. Maybe because Hannah killed the one chasing me? Like you said before, there could have been another—his partner—who saw him go after me. Then, when he didn't return—when he was found—the other one probably told the leader. I guess."

The events she described churned in Chris's brain. *Doubtful, although I guess there's a slight chance that could be it. What about the cartel captains?* He'd hoped she would confide in him. He would give her some time. He'd do everything he could to keep her safe. "You need to stay as calm as possible. Try to get some rest, and let your body heal some more. I'll keep watch."

Mari flashed a small smile, did as he said, and shut her eyes. He stayed, watching her as she fell into an inconsistent, uncomfortable sleep. She awoke every so often, a grimace of discomfort marring her beautiful face. More time would have been ideal. He pulled the medical supplies out, quickly cleaned his shoulder wound, and placed a bandage over it.

He'd heal. His focus was Mari. He continued with the antibiotics and debated over another injection of antivenin, but so far he thought she was going to recover. Any damage sustained would reveal itself soon.

Tired of wrestling with the dilemma, he readied another antivenin shot and gave it to her. She barely stirred, exhaustion riding her hard. He replaced the netting over her then bent down and grabbed another can of DEET, which he reapplied to try to deter bug bites. He slipped back outside, checked the area, and did what felt right—he took up position to watch for the enemy.

~

CHRIS

The jungle settled into its nocturnal harmony. Each tree's leaves played a different tune in the gentle breeze. Nighttime animals scurried around, some calling to each other. A light drizzle made the leaves glisten in the moonlight and the dirt beneath Chris's boots slippery. Dawn was due to arrive shortly.

Mari had slept seven fitful hours. In that time, he'd given her another dose of antibiotics. It was time to do so again. He prepped the needle then swabbed her skin. The tiny prick of the shot caused her eyelids to open, and she cleared her throat. "Hi."

"Feeling any better?" He caught the sleepy expression that softened her features and made him want to kiss her even more than he already did.

"Yeah. I think so. My ankle itches though."

He closed the distance between them and shifted her ankle

into a shaft of moonlight. Peeling back the dressing, he inspected her injury. There weren't any angry red lines or pus coming from it. "It looks pretty good. Could be a sign it's healing." He cleaned it again and taped a fresh bandage over it to ward away bacteria and infection. In an ideal environment, he would have left the loose covering off. But in the jungle, there was no way he would take that chance.

"Our roles are reversed, huh?" She grinned, her natural spirit overriding the last traces of fear he saw. "Have to say I sort of prefer taking care of you. Sitting here sucks." Crinkling her nose, she grimaced. "Ah, I have to go to the bathroom."

"Being immobile is hell." He helped her from the hammock, carried her outside their camp, and placed her on the elongated web of tree roots that grew several inches above ground. Where he set her was a perfect little v shape that acted like a seat. He tugged up his T-shirt that covered her to her thighs and helped her to bunch it around her waist.

With reluctance at leaving her side, he went halfway around the huge trunk to give her some privacy. "Try not to put too much pressure on your leg."

"Could you maybe not listen?"

He chuckled. "What would you like me to do? Hum a song?"

"That would be nice. Or maybe just talk to me?"

"Okay. Here's the thing. I'm starving, and we need to eat to keep up our strength. I've been toying with the idea of hunting, but I'm worried about leaving you alone for too long."

"I'm done."

"That was fast." He went around and picked her back up. Red colored her cheeks, and she refused to look at him. "There's nothing to be embarrassed about. Shit, I can't even tell you how many times I've been in awkward situations with my brother."

Her hand jerked against his shirt. "What?"

"I…" They stood there together, him holding her tight to his chest, the sounds of the jungle loud in his ears. An image filled his mind of a man who had his head thrown back in laughter, with an ever-present scruff over his square jaw. "Fuck. I have a brother."

"What's his name?"

What is it? He frowned. She should know this.

"Don't give me that look." Her eyes sparked with aggression. "I told you we were barely together, barely married. Besides, your memories should come back to you naturally." A flash of uncertainty drew her brows together at his silence. "We had a sort of shotgun wedding. You were on vacation. I was infatuated. It was sudden." She sucked in a breath then clamped her lips together.

Hmm… Still doesn't sound right, but I'll get the full story from her eventually. Stepping over another root that threatened to take them both to the ground, he covered the distance to their camp and ducked inside. After settling her in her hammock and making sure she was comfortable, he paced the small circular area and let the small window to his past open. "I can see his face. Sort of. His name is Trevor, but he went by Trev. Something happened. I can't remember what."

"What do you mean? Like he was in an accident or—"

"No." He absently brushed her concerned question aside. "I just know there's a problem, but I have no clue what it's about."

She snagged him with a hand as he made another circle around the confining space, and he immediately stopped, not wanting to topple her from the hammock.

Her face begged him to listen, so he did. "Chris"—her hand cupped the side of his face—"since you're recalling little parts of your past, it has to fully come back. You're stressing over it, though, which is understandable but maybe not productive. So let it go, and know they should slip right back in on their own schedule."

Her gentle touch fell away, and as he ran a hand over his scratchy face, he growled. "It's so damn unnerving."

"Of course it is. Hey, when's the last time you slept?"

"Huh? Oh, I have no idea."

"Well, I'm completely awake. I've got the gun you gave me, and I'm a dead ringer at shooting. I'll cover us from here while you grab a couple of hours."

He hated that she was right. He'd seen her shoot, so he didn't worry much about her accuracy. *What good will I be if I'm not alert?* "Yeah, maybe just a little while. But wake me up as soon as you're getting tired." He locked his gaze with hers. "Promise me."

She waved away his concern. "Yep. No problem."

Part of him worried that, once he closed his eyes, things would go to hell.

CHAPTER 15

hris's breath had sawed in and out. "What the fuck did you do?" He faced off with his brother, his heart a bloody mess. With barely restrained violence, he slammed his fist into Trevor's jaw. "She was going to be my wife." *Someday.* "She chose me."

Trevor took the hit, and out of frustration, Chris punched him again. Jessie swore there was no one else. Anger and pain sizzled along his taut skin as the image of his fiancée, naked and in bed with his brother, tore at his gut.

With his surfer looks and easygoing personality, Trevor had no trouble getting women. Chris didn't either, but that was beside the point. Normally, none of that superficial shit would have bothered him. A small part of his brain realized that he'd dodged a bullet, and that his brother would never stab him in the back.

Chris was the levelheaded one, analytical to the core. From a young age, he'd watched out for his younger brother against an abusive father and a neglectful, alcoholic mother. He'd been a technological genius. The sliver of himself that could see logic knew that Jessie had been banking on funding her future when she'd said yes to his proposal. What she got instead was a view into a life with his SEAL brothers after she had met a few of them. Several of them came from a life lived on the streets and they were thick as thieves. For the most part, this group of guys were better than whom Jessie probably envisioned herself with. They were blue collar, which wasn't what Jessie was after.

Their dad liked to use him and Trev as punching bags. When he wasn't hitting them, he'd go after their mother, who was an easy target. He and Trev spent their time watching each other's backs, and their mom's as well, until one fatal night when she'd had too much to drink, lost in the misery of a failed marriage and abusive husband. She took a fall down the stairs and never woke up. He and Trev made a pact to always be there for one other.

Then Jessie came along and played a number on them. Both of them had fallen for her, Chris more so than his brother. She'd been fun-loving and carefree with Trev, and went to every sporting event he took interest in. With Chris, she'd listened for hours as he talked about the latest and greatest technology. She was able to be what each of them wanted most at any particular moment. Some part of Chris's brain had withheld his other life for a while when they were together, the one with his brothers, their time in the SEALs, and what they did now. That should have been a red flag, but she was so damn beautiful. She'd played him.

She swore she loved him and said yes to moving in with him. She was the first girl he'd been seriously interested in.

Trevor had been a one-night stand, or a week's worth of them.

"I didn't know, man." Trev had held his hands up, palms facing out. "She said she was single. I never would have touched her, I swear."

"Where is she?" Chris's fists clenched against his sides, and he needed an outlet but fought the urge to slam them into his brother's face.

"That's the thing, bro. I don't know. It was casual between us. It didn't mean anything. Then, the next thing I knew, she hooked up with Bradley Stanton. You know that prick."

As if his brother had slapped him, the name drained his anger. He was still pissed, but not seeing red. "What'd she want with him?"

"Come on, man, you know the answer to that." Trev ran his hands through his hair then hooked them behind his neck.

"Money." *Fuck.* That bitch had been using them. Bradley's bank account trumped theirs tenfold. The realization she'd played all of them had slammed home.

Chris's body shook, and he jerked awake. Light streamed through the canopy of leaves. Out of reflex at being startled awake, he automatically grabbed the gun and pointed it at Mari. "Shit!" He lowered the pistol. "Sorry." Dropping his head to his hands, he groaned at the memories that had plagued him during the couple of hours of sleep he'd managed to grab.

"You okay?" Her sweet voice made him feel ten times guiltier.

"Yeah, I'm so sorry. Waking me isn't always the safest thing to do."

She laughed. "I'm not afraid of you, Chris. I know you'd never hurt me."

He straightened up and turned to fully face her, drinking her in. Everything about her was beautiful. Jessie had been, too, but her beauty only ran skin deep. If Jessie were in Mari's position, she would be long gone. Taking care of anyone other than herself didn't fit into her agenda. He just hadn't realized it soon enough. Mari, on the other hand, genuinely cared for his well-being. Jessie was fake, all blinding smiles or dainty tears to obtain her end objective. If Mari was irritated, mad, or scared, she showed her emotions and reacted with passion. Not one part of her tried to be something she wasn't, or so he hoped. The only thing that concerned him was if her secrets would impact their relationship.

He scrubbed his face, trying to shake the images of Jessie. "I'm okay." Surfacing from his dark thoughts, he realized she was hovering over him. He wrapped an arm around her waist and pulled her on top of him in his hammock.

She giggled and tucked herself against his side, her head resting on his chest. "Tell me what you dreamed about. You shouted in your sleep, so it had to be something major."

Chris frowned. "Since I shouted, I should check and make sure no one was around to hear me."

Her hand flattened against his chest. "Stay. We'll hear them approach. You set all those traps, right?"

"Yeah, still."

"Please, Chris." Her fingers toyed with the neckline of his T-shirt. "Tell me."

Dammit. I don't want to share this with her. But secrets always have a way of biting me in the ass. She's my wife, and I should trust her. He relaxed back, enjoying her touch as he came to a decision. "I dreamed about my brother, Trev. We were our only surviving family, at least until we joined"—*shit, I wanted to keep this separate for just a little longer*—"the military, but that's not what the dream, or the memory, was about. Growing up, it was just us against our abusive prick of a father." *And then a bitch who came between us.*

"I can't believe you never told me any of this." With a shake of her head, she dropped her hand to rest on his abdomen. "I'm sorry, Chris. I didn't know. What about your mother?"

"Dead." His voice sounded flat even to him. He wasn't sure why it bothered him. She'd given up. She'd chosen the bottle over protecting her sons. Maybe she'd tried when they were little, but as they grew bigger, stronger, and more able to protect themselves, the fight left her. "Anyway, my brother and I both fell for this one girl. We always swore we'd have each other's backs, no matter what. But Jessie. Fuck, she played us. I had no idea Trev was seeing her. And he didn't know I was either, or that we'd planned to live together. It was insane. How she managed to keep us from knowing all that was a brilliant mind-fuck in itself."

"What happened with you and your brother?"

"We eventually found out. But I had a huge problem with it. Trev is—"

"He's what?" Mari tilted her head back, and he looked down at her, catching her inquisitive expression.

His fingers played with her hair, and he felt content to open up to her. "We're kind of opposites in relation to how people perceive us. Trev's super laid-back and easygoing, while I'm more introspective. He jokes around, and I've got my nose buried in work."

"Hey." Mari pushed against him, lifting herself up so their gazes locked. "It's her loss and my gain. I get to have you in my life and to love you. Not her."

His body tensed beneath her, and he studied her face. When she'd admitted she loved him her eyes had gone wide, and that's when he knew she meant it. Sincerity and something else softened her features.

He'd slept the day away, and the moonlight cast a silver glow across her face, accentuating the planes of her cheeks, her spiky lashes, and her plump lips. Her hair fanned around them in that look he adored. But it was her pulse keeping a steady beat against his chest, and her pupils, that confirmed what he'd hoped. She wasn't lying. She did love him.

After slipping his hand around the back of her neck, he tugged her closer and crashed his lips against hers. She opened hers for him in a willing surrender. Their tongues tangled with equal passion.

He broke the kiss, both of them breathing heavily. "Babe, I want nothing more than to make love to you, but I'm worried about your injury."

"It's on my leg and ankle. I think I'll be fine." She pushed against his hands, which cradled either side of her head.

"I'm not sure you will. Blood flow will increase. Your heart will pump faster and harder, and if there are any lingering toxins, I want your body to fight them off rather than spread them through because I couldn't control myself for a few hours."

Sagging against him, she pouted, which had to be the most adorable thing he'd seen her do yet.

"Fine," she half-heartedly growled. Settling against him once more, she drew lazy circles on his chest. "Then let's talk about something else. I need to keep my mind off taking advantage of you."

He chuckled. "Tell me about your aunt. Did I ever meet her?"

"Oh." Sadness coated her voice, and her fingers froze for half a beat in their hypnotic pattern on his body. "No, you never met. I went back to Colombia because she was dying. There was no one else to care for her. No family."

"What was she like?"

"Loud." She laughed. "God, she was loud and demanding. But she had this incredible artistic eye and could sew anything she set her mind to. All the clothing in her store was hand sewn.

And her customers loved it. The quality was amazing." Her voice quieted, and her body relaxed further.

God, he'd give anything to remember their life together, no matter how short she'd said their time was. Even thinking that, his instincts pricked. They'd been doing that a ton since he woke and found Mari looking over him that first night in the jungle. While he wanted to pay attention to his gut, he didn't know where the alarm stemmed from.

The only thing he could do was protect her.

Time passed swiftly as they shared aspects of their lives with one another. The hammock swayed with their weight, and the wind that'd picked up gusted through the leaves. It was the middle of the night, and he hoped the storm would abate in the morning. Thunder rumbled in the distance, and he followed the gentle rise and fall of Mari's even breathing. She'd fallen back asleep.

In a matter of minutes, heavy rain fell, forcing its way through the protection of the trees and pelting them. Even though the wetness was frustrating in the jungle, making travel more difficult, it was a great way to get clean—even more so than bathing in the streams.

Turning his head, he let the patter of the raindrops lull him back to sleep, with Mari wrapped securely in his arms.

CHAPTER 16

MARI

Sleep came swiftly, and Mari welcomed it, knowing she needed additional time to heal. Snuggled against Chris, she felt safe until her dream swirled into focus.

Her aunt's store was closed. At eleven in the morning, that was unusual. Going around to the back, she climbed the stairs to the second-floor apartment. Doorknob in hand, she turned and pushed the door open. Her frown deepened because it had been left unlocked. Her nose crinkled as she crossed the threshold. It smelled rancid.

"Aunt Linda?"

A horrific round of wet coughing was her answer. Mari rushed inside, following the sounds. "Oh, Aunt Linda." Tears welled and tumbled down her face. Her aunt was curled up in bed, bloody tissues strewn around her. Another bout of hacking seized her frail body, and she wiped more blood from her mouth.

Stretching a hand out, her aunt tried for a feeble smile. "Mari," she rasped. "God knows I love seeing you, but I told you not to come."

Mari knelt beside her. "You told me you were sick. There was no way I was going to leave you to fend for yourself."

With her hand clasped tight in her aunt's, she leaned closer to hear her thready voice, which was so different than what she'd been like while Mari grew up. Her loud, boisterous aunt was dying—a husk of the larger-than-life person she was.

"It's too dangerous for you here. Go back to Venezuela. Things have changed over the last several years. Not for the better."

Mari gave her aunt's hand a gentle squeeze. "I'm here now. You just need to rest and not worry about a thing. I'll take care of you and the store."

"No." She curled into herself, paying for forcing words out with another fit of coughing.

Mari rushed to get her a fresh glass of water. After she helped her aunt into a more comfortable position, she gave her the water. "What's important is your health. I don't want you worrying."

Panic-filled eyes met Mari's gaze, and Aunt Linda whispered, "Oh, darling, you've a knack for arriving in the eye of the storm. The store is the least of our problems. If *he* notices you, and he will, there'll be trouble."

"Whatever it is will work itself out. I'm here now so you can get well. Please, just rest."

"Don't open the shop." Linda clutched her hands, squeezing as tightly as she could, and pleaded with unmasked terror. "Go back home. I'm grateful to see you before I leave this world. I love you, Mari. But I want you safe. Please, for me, *go*."

Mari jackknifed into a sitting position, causing the hammock to swing precariously. With her heart pounding against her rib cage, her gaze darted all around. She was afraid something or someone hid nearby.

~

CHRIS

"Chris."

A sexy voice wove into his dream, and he lifted his hands to grip her hips, pressing into her soft, pliant body. Heat was all around them, consuming him from inside. Their bodies were slick where they touched. She shifted. An elbow pressed into his chest, and something clicked that he wasn't dreaming.

In a fast blink, he worked to focus his eyes as he woke from their late-afternoon nap. A form hovered over him, and his mind played tricks, changing Mari's long, dark braid to Hannah's platinum-blond one.

"Hey, Chris." Her husky voice filtered in, and he let himself follow the strings of memory from the image, which he superimposed over Mari's. The past materialized as he walked into an office he'd been in many times before—because it was his. His gut reacted as he noticed small details. The papers on his desk didn't look right. Someone had been in there. The faint smell of perfume in the air told him who.

Hannah.

Something pricked at his intuition when it came to her. He didn't trust her.

"Chris."

Mari's insistent voice snapped him back to the present, and her features came into focus. He scowled at the loss of her slight weight pressing against him. "Why are you on your feet?" Still in the hammock, he was met by her frown.

"I had to go to the bathroom, and you were totally out of

it." She plopped her hand onto her jutted-out hip. "What's going on?"

Chris grunted. "Did Hannah tell you anything about why she was in the jungle?" He pushed himself up and snapped, "And sit down."

With a roll of her eyes, she eased back into her hammock. "No, she didn't tell me anything. Oh, wait. She said she was going in the opposite direction we would be headed."

"Deeper into Colombia?"

"Yes, but I don't know exactly where. The entire thing was weird. She was there one minute, making me promise to help you, then gone as soon as you and I were sort of settled. There was one more thing. She said there were people, or a person, who would be looking for you. The message I got was that it would be bad if they found you."

He frowned. "I know her." He unhooked his hammock, his brain churning, trying to analyze everything he remembered and put the few puzzle pieces he had into place. Stuffing their things into the packs, he lifted Mari and set her by the base of the tree so she could lean against it before he took her bed down, too.

"You remember?"

At her quiet tone, he zeroed in on her unsettled features. "Not everything, just a snapshot of a memory with Hannah."

She gave a curt nod, her lips pressed into a stubborn line.

"Something bothering you?"

She shook her head quickly, and when she failed to meet his gaze, he eliminated the space between them and tilted her chin up with his hand. When they were facing each other once more, he studied her features, looking for clues for why her mood shifted. Her almost-frightened look shook him. "What is it?"

She shrugged. "I don't understand what Hannah is to you,

and at times, the thought of your memory coming back scares me." Tears gathered in her eyes. "I'm afraid I'll lose you."

"Baby, there's no way." His thumb caressed her lower lip, and he bent, brushing his lips over her. A spark leapt between them. Before they gave into their desire, he pulled away just enough. "There's nothing to worry about."

He shouldered their packs before he lifted her, cradling her to his chest then slipping from their tree fort. "Pull your gun out since my hands are full."

"I can walk."

His answer was another grunt while his gaze swept the jungle around them. In no time at all, they reached their canoe. He set her on her feet then removed the vines and brush he'd used to camouflage it from travelers or guerrillas in the area. After he freed the canoe, he helped her climb in then followed.

"Mari, get down so you're not visible."

"If I'm lying down in the canoe, I can't help to spot potential threats," she argued.

"They're after you and not me at this point. While they'll think about stopping me, they'll for sure come after us if they see you. This is easier and gives us more of a shot to get out of here safely."

There was no arguing that logic, so she flattened herself along the bottom of the canoe, her gun still in hand and resting on her stomach.

Every nerve ending buzzed as he dipped the paddle in one side then switched it to the other, his gaze constantly searching. They were out there, so it was only a matter of time. If they could get out of this area, using the cover of night, they stood a good chance of reaching the border without incident.

After traveling for several hours, the heat of the day became unbearable for both of them. They needed to stop and rest until it was cooler. Mari was doing remarkably better, and his worry for her eased. No blistering had occurred around her snakebite, and her skin looked to have suffered no permanent damage. Chris suspected the young snake's bite only contained a fraction of the venom an adult fer-de-lance would have injected.

Thick trees enclosed the spot he'd decided to stop to rest in, and after they'd secured and hidden the canoe, they ate. Mari stepped away to wash her hands and face by the river, and he waited for her to come back.

Chris leaned back against the tree as Mari sauntered over to him, the natural sway of her hips teasing and tempting him to pull her onto his lap. Her long, thick mahogany hair was pulled away from her face again. He wanted to slip his fingers through it and see it fanned out around her exquisite face. *My wife.*

Every minute, hour, and day they spent together, they grew closer, moving in sync with one another. Still, there was a part of him that found her claim difficult to believe, but he wanted her, because with one touch his desire for her struck like lightning, like a match to a flame.

Mari bent down, her full breasts pushing against the thin material of her T-shirt, and snagged the canteen. She straightened and moved before him. He grabbed her hand and tugged her down. Her throaty laughter filled his ears as he brushed a few stray strands of hair from her neck. Her body cradled into his, and she trailed a finger down his chest.

He took in the knives strapped to her outer thigh. "Why did you marry me? Was it just to gain a ticket out of Colombia?"

She jerked her head and held his gaze. Her expressive eyes burned with passion, but not the kind he'd come to enjoy. She was angry. "At first, yes. I would do anything to leave this place. Aside from a few good things, such as my family—who are all dead now—there is nothing this place can offer me. It takes and takes and takes. I wanted out."

He moved his hand to cup the side of her face, skimming

along her cheek before resting it on her neck, where her pulse jumped against his palm.

"You were different. The thought of where you came from was exciting. You were a way out, sure, but you became more." Her features softened. "So much more. I… You're protective and cunning. Nothing will stop you once you want something. Not only that, you're kind and loving. I'll admit this all didn't come together until our time in the jungle—but I saw a glimpse of those traits and wanted them for myself."

The jungle was harsh—beautiful, but unforgiving if a wrong step was taken, hydration ignored, or tiredness allowed to cloud judgments. Through the constant nausea the jungle provoked, he and Mari came together, celebrating the beauty of life.

"Beauty is one thing, but not everything. You're so very handsome, but that's not what makes me want to fight for you, to stay with you, to share my life with you." She placed her hand against his chest, her palm pressing against his heart. "You're mine, and I love you."

The last, she said in a throaty whisper. His lips crashed down on hers, devouring her. She opened hers immediately, and he swirled his tongue inside. Needing her, he tugged at her shirt, exposing her sun-kissed olive skin to his gaze. She helped him, whipping the offensive material from her body. Her body was trim, toned, and soft in all the right places.

It didn't take long before she freed him from his pants and straddled him. As he thrust into her, her head arced back. Over and over, he sank into her warmth. He slipped his hand between them and teased her with his fingers. In no time at all, she convulsed all around him, and he followed her climax, gripping her hips.

She fell against his chest, her movements still graceful and her pupils fully dilated. "I love you, Chris," she whispered under her breath.

His hand rubbed up and down her back. *This fiery woman is mine.* But something held him back, and he didn't return her words. "We need to keep moving. It's going to get harder on us the longer we stay here."

Lifting her, he got to his feet, her legs still wrapped around his waist, before she released them and slid down his partially-clothed body. For a brief moment, her head rested against his chest. "How long do you think we have until we're out of here, across the border?"

"We backtracked. We've got a long trek ahead of us, but with the canoe we can make our way through the network of streams as long as possible. That'll save us a lot of time."

They fixed their clothing, slung their packs over their shoulders, and moved toward the stream, not far from where they'd rested.

Deep inside, the reason he was there tugged at him, urging him to figure it out before more trouble found them.

CHAPTER 17

CHRIS

They made their way down the stream. Mari fingered a knife. As she slipped one from the sheath around her thigh, he grinned. They were his knives, but in her hands he found them sexy as hell.

"What happened to all your knives?" She had sheaths sewn into her pants to slip them in, where they'd be safe and secure, but they'd been empty until she'd found his. And he knew they were his because one of them had a chip on the handle. She'd taken them before he'd woken to find himself in the jungle.

"Caught that, did you?" That throaty laugh of hers caused him to smile. "When I paid the guy to take me to the entrance of the Darien Gap, he changed the rules while we were on the water." She shrugged. "Money was no longer enough. He wanted all my weapons, and a few side benefits, so I threatened him."

Anger surged in him, but she only grinned and shook her head at the wicked scowl on his face.

"We came to a swift agreement. He'd continue with what he promised, and I agreed to surrender my knives without burying them in his flesh." She shrugged. "It was a fair trade. One of the knives he took from me may be recognized. It'll only bring him trouble—quite possibly, death."

He grunted, already imagining his hands around the guy's neck, crushing his windpipe.

"So, I took yours. I figured you wouldn't mind, especially since you know how crazy good I am with them."

Dark thoughts swirled in his head, not about Mari handling weapons, but about himself. They were nothing new to him. In fact, his pack held a plethora of them, including C4 and the detonators for it. *What had I been planning to do?* He couldn't keep ignoring it and sweeping it under the rug—nor the captains who were searching for her. "Why are cartel captains after you?" His words carried the dark promise he was capable of delivering if his back was in a corner. In a sense, he was already there.

She stiffened in front of him, then her head whipped around, sending her braid against her opposite shoulder with a thwack. "How should I know?"

Interesting. The paddle slipped in the water, continuing to propel them forward, even though his body stilled in preparation for pushing her to gain the answers he sought. "Not working, Mari. You know exactly why, don't you?"

A stricken look flashed across her features, so fast he would have missed it if he hadn't been studying her reaction. "Pretty sure we've talked about this. We already know the guerrillas are on to us, so why not the captains? They could've been in the camp and gotten identical information as the rest of the guerrillas," she snapped at him, anger coloring her cheeks.

"That may be so, but that's not what I heard when I snuck into camp."

She visibly paled before him. "Cartel members were there?"

"No. They were talking about you, specifically. So, Mari, what secrets are you keeping?"

She spit a slew of Spanish, and anger deepened the color staining her cheeks.

His instincts told him that whatever she was withholding was a threat. "You can hide behind anger all you want. There's something you're keeping from me, and with the commotion you're raising, we'll have company very soon."

She blanched, falling immediately silent. Narrowing her gaze, she swept the tree line on either side of them, and behind. He did the same.

They saw them at the same time. Two men cleared the bush, one trailing slightly behind, making a path toward Mari. They were too focused. *Shit!*

The men fired shots, all aimed at *him*. Dropping back, he fell into the canoe as the bullets flew by. One tore into the fibers of his shirt. *Damn, that was close.*

Mari stood, her body tense and her arm back. She let her knife fly at the exact moment Chris extended his hand and pointed his gun at them. He sat up then put a bullet through the forehead of the other guerrilla, whose gun was partially raised. It slipped from his grasp and dropped to the ground as he fell forward and face-planted into the narrow stream. The other man gurgled, the blade protruding from his throat. Mari leapt from the boat, jerked the knife from his neck, and whipped it along his tan camouflage pants as he crumbled before her. His fate mirrored his partner's. She raced back to the water and hopped in the canoe, the blade gripped tightly in her hand.

Damn, she's hot. In silence, they continued up the stream. She wasn't off the hook yet, but he'd let it go for now. They had been arguing too loudly. They had to learn from their mistake and be more careful.

"We've got about an hour until we near the mountains. Then, we've got to ditch the canoe and walk the rest of the way." He peered at her leg, but it looked good. She would be okay.

Shoulders drooping, she gave a quick nod, her gaze never leaving the dense foliage that flanked their path. They traveled in silence, his muscles flexing as he propelled them further along their watery path.

Movement caught their attention in the thicket of bushes just before the bend in the steam. "Mari, wait here please," Chris commanded as he cautiously set the paddle down and sprang from his perch. He covered the ground in a low dash then lunged at three men who'd neared their path. They wore black and resembled one another in look, in carriage, in association. Each had a machine gun strapped to his body and a pistol in hand. They were drug traffickers. No doubt about it.

As the closest one lifted his gun, Chris slammed the butt of his weapon into his forehead. The man crumpled at his feet. A knife stuck out of the second man's throat, and he grinned at the cause. Mari. The third's trigger finger was already depressed, and bullets sprayed. Chris leapt to the side, and a bullet narrowly missed his bicep as he returned fire. *Head, heart, and gut.* His target dropped while the gun continued to discharge. Kicking it away, Chris then looked behind him. Mari popped up from the side of the canoe, her arm back, ready to launch another knife. When she saw him standing there, whole, she visibly relaxed.

He shook his head as he bent to lift the man he knocked unconscious over his shoulder. They needed this guy alive—for now. Mari had jammed their transportation at an angle, lodging it diagonally between both banks. It wouldn't go anywhere until he shoved it free. He dropped his load into their canoe then settled on his seat and picked up the paddle. They needed to hurry. Reinforcements would've heard the gunshots.

He braced his feet widely in the canoe and heaved them forward with the paddle. "Tie him up. Make sure it's tight."

She scurried to do as he said. She removed the unconscious man's weapons and made sure they were well out of his reach before she tore one of the shirts that'd been in her pack and set about securing his ankles and wrists. She covered his mouth with a strip, too, so he didn't shout to draw attention when he regained consciousness.

Without sparing him another glance, Chris increased his rowing efforts, and they sped along the waterway. Mari leaned close. Canteen in hand, she pressed it to his lips.

He'd caught sight of a tattoo on all three of the men's hands —a sharp-angled blue butterfly. It'd immediately registered in his brain. Flashes from his past flipped like a series of pictures in his mind. There was a conference room with a group of men, including his brother and him, around the table. The memories were fragmented and over in seconds, but told him enough. They'd had dealings with this cartel before. He knew it had affected someone close to him. He'd remember—he was confident in that. The thing that struck him was the sense that this cartel had unfinished business with those he cared for.

"It's been too long since either of us has had anything to drink. I added some of the powdered electrolytes to the water." Her words pulled him from his thoughts, and he complied by accepting the canteen from her.

She was right, they had to stay hydrated, alert. He sucked it down, leaving half for her. It tasted like Kool-Aid. She pressed the canteen's opening against her lips, and he followed the movement of her throat as she swallowed.

As Mari started to sit back down, she kicked at the man at

her feet. "What are we doing with him?" Anger swirled in her eyes, along with something else—*fear?* Her features were pulled tight as she glared at Chris.

"Is this the secret you're keeping?" Tension formed between Chris's shoulders. "Do you know them personally?"

Dread and fear rolled across Mari's face, and the play of emotions didn't go unnoticed by Chris. "Why do you say that?" she snapped. "We should just dump him overboard. He's an unnecessary risk."

When uncomfortable or hiding something, she reacted with anger. It wouldn't work this time. He could play this game. Silence stretched between them, and his gaze never left hers. As the seconds ticked by, he watched as her mind turned, discarding each excuse before it reached her lips. It had to be what she'd been keeping from him—this group of men knew something he didn't.

First, the guerrillas were after her. That he could understand, as she'd killed one of their own, and they most likely knew about it. Then he learned the cartel was involved, and some of them showed up. He repressed the flash of rage at the thought of either of those factions after her. Something wasn't adding up. Sure, there were drug traffickers who ran through the jungle on a regular basis, but there was a deliberate method to their formation, their search, and their lack of immediate fire at her—also confirmed by what he'd overheard. It all stood out to him, plain as day.

"Look." She dropped her head into her hands and groaned. "The Ramirez cartel is here because of me. They're here to take me back. It threw me when I saw that." She pointed to the man's hand. "He's one of the captains."

Shit, that's what the tattoos mean. "Why do they specifically want to bring you back?"

"I don't really understand *why* I'm so important. One of

their members has a thing for me. It's stupid." She scrubbed her face then lifted tormented eyes to his.

"Do you care for him as well?" His voice dripped icicles, even though he knew he had no ground to stand on. If she'd indeed felt abandoned by him, she could have gone to another. She'd been a woman stranded and in a difficult situation, and he didn't really have any right to judge her, especially when he only had bits and pieces of his past. More would come, he hoped.

"Oh, God. No way. I knew I'd have to leave as soon as my aunt was placed into the ground. He'd come for me. He's very powerful. You don't tell him no, not ever. The only reason he hadn't followed through with his promise—threat—was because he knew Aunt Linda was dying. I had a stay of execution."

Her haunted face tilted up toward him, and he pressed his lips together. He longed to take her in his arms. Getting them to safety came first. And where there were some cartel members, there would be more. He pushed them faster down the stream, hoping they weren't headed for a trap.

"We'll travel a few more miles. Then, we're going to stop and question him." Chris held her attention for a moment longer. Fear for her made him lash out. "And by 'we,' I mean me. You'll stay back, out of his reach. Let me do this."

Annoyance flashed over her face, and her eyes narrowed dangerously. But she nodded once then turned around to look out for a trap. *I'll pay for that. No doubt.*

They kept going for four more miles before they found a secluded spot to pull over. The vegetation was relatively thick, and there was a natural place to stash their canoe.

Chris slung their prisoner over his shoulder and trudged behind Mari as she settled a ways from the stream, between clusters of trees and bushes. With a thud, Chris dropped the man to the ground, and Mari backed up enough that he could do his thing.

Chris slapped the man repeatedly on each cheek until he lifted his lids to expose his groggy, unfocused gaze. When the fog slipped further, the cartel member jerked back as much as he could.

Chris pressed a knife to the man's throat then slid his other hand behind the gag and tugged. He allowed the ruthlessness he kept in check to show on his face as he leaned forward, sneering as he spoke his next words. "I have a few questions that you're going to answer. Do you plan to cooperate, or should I make my point clear first?"

The man struggled beneath him, muffled Spanish curses leaving his mouth as his eyes hardened with cold determination.

So, he's not going to cooperate. Chris chuckled, and the sound was dark and disturbing even to his own ears.

Mari turned and did a sweep of the area before moving back to the canoe. She would keep watch, and Chris would extract the information they needed. She jammed the paddle into the riverbed to hold their position.

Not far from her, Chris brought the tip of the knife against the man's throat, and his eyes went wide. "Who, specifically, is after her?" Blood trickled down the man's neck, and his mouth opened partially.

Their hostage smirked and mumbled in heavily accented English. "She knows who."

In a quick move, Chris withdrew the knife, stabbed him in the leg, and twisted the blade, his hand automatically covering the hostage's mouth as he jerked the blade out. The muffled scream lasted several seconds. Beads of perspiration dotted the man's forehead, and panic swirled in his dark eyes.

Chris removed the knife and pressed it to the man's side. Applying pressure, he leaned further over the man. "Not what I asked." The blade slipped through the man's clothes to inch into his side, in slow and agonizing increments.

Gasping, the captain clamped his lips together.

"I see this is going to take a while longer." He pushed the blade in another inch or two. "I'm aiming for your kidney, if you hadn't already guessed. Time's ticking. Better talk." He worked the captain over, alternating where he slid the sharp blade in. Cut after cut, the captain held his tongue. It wasn't until Chris began relieving him of his fingers that his weak, raspy voice gave up something worthwhile. "Juan Carlos."

Chris's hand stilled, and rage filled him. Why, he couldn't really say, but the reaction was there—bitterness coated his mind at the familiar name. The memory would come. Either way, he knew it meant something very bad. "And why is it so important that Mari is returned to him?"

The captain laughed. Blood bubbled and leaked from the corner of his mouth. Chris smiled at him with a dark, sinister grin that instantly caused the captain's laughter to die a quick death. "Wants…" Raspy, labored words whispered from his bloodstained lips. "His legacy—baby she's carrying."

Chris whipped the knife out and shoved it back at his throat, increasing the trickle of blood. "What are you talking about?"

A weak finger lifted and pointed to Mari, and the sneer that flitted across the captain's face was eerie in its intent. "Engaged." The captain laughed, choking on his blood to the point where he couldn't take another breath. Fury filled Chris's veins, and in one swipe, he severed the dying man's carotid artery. Lifting the captain, Chris tossed him into the stream. The crocs would finish him off, drawn to him by his blood trailing in the water.

Turning back, he caught Mari's stunned gaze with a furious one of his own. "What the fuck was he talking about?" He took the paddle from her hands and pushed them forward in a savage motion. *We're married. That means…* "Why would our marriage have been a secret, Mari? Who's the father—Juan Carlos?"

"What? Ew… No way." She scrunched up her nose. Seconds passed until her mouth formed an O. "*Dios mio*, that crazy asshole. Mateo must have lied to his father. I swear. But… as far as us being married, we were never seen together in Colombia, Chris." She shifted, breaking eye contact. "Venezuela was where we met, and where we were going to build our life. Things changed. You left. I didn't think you'd ever come back."

Her eyelids closed, shielding him from seeing inside her, but he still noticed the pallor on her tan skin. A sick sense of déjà vu swirled in his gut. He'd had enough of being played to last him a lifetime from just one relationship gone bad.

"I'm *not* pregnant." Her voice was strong and sure. "I last saw Mateo six months ago. I'd be showing if I was."

He growled, incapable of anything more.

"I'm not positive why his father would think that. As for the engagement, I never agreed to it, never said yes, and took off as soon as I could after my aunt passed away. That was all on Mateo." She scowled. "Saying no to him isn't something people do. He is a powerful man, and I'm his obsession. I always have been. Still, it was his lie, to himself and apparently to his father."

He peered into the depths of her eyes, weighing the statement for truth. It wasn't the pregnancy part that bothered him, but the idea that she'd strayed from their marriage. She hadn't said no. She'd traded him for someone with more power and more money.

The sound of the paddle dipping into the water and the natural cadence of the jungle around them filled the silence that stretched between them. He'd been with another who'd used him, and he'd let her. He'd kept blinders on even though there had been signs. He didn't allow himself the luxury of ignorance again as he drank in every detail about Mari, every reaction. Her fingers played with the hilt of her throwing knife. *Nervous.*

She does that when she's angry, defensive, and agitated. Her lips were pinched together, and her color was high. He knew she'd start yelling at any moment with her quick temper.

Narrowing his eyes, he kept her in his sights while watching for movement out of his peripheral vision. The paddle continued to glide through the water until he switched to the other side, propelling them forward. "Keep your voice down." He shoved aside his feelings of betrayal and the urge to hunt Mateo and Juan Carlos down and kill them. "Why would Juan Carlos or Mateo think you were pregnant?"

Her chin notched up, and her eyes flashed in response. "I'm *not*, especially because I'd have to sleep with Mateo to get that way. That never happened."

"Are you telling me that the engagement wasn't real?"

Shoulders sagging, she groaned. "I've known him since we were children. Back then, we were friends. Somewhat, anyway. He ran wild, and because of who his father was, no one dared to stop him. The first time we met, I was playing outside my aunt's store. I don't know. He seemed drawn to me, and I liked the excitement that surrounded him. It was different than all the other kids, the poverty, the fear."

Chris grunted.

With a wave of her hand, her focus snapped back to his face. "When we first met, Mateo had just met his half-brother, and he was angry. It was a recurring theme for him."

"How close were the two of you?"

"I wasn't his girlfriend, if that's what you're getting at. But he'd staked some sort of claim, and you'd have thought I was, given how boys maintained a safe distance from me. Mateo wasn't around very much. His father kept him busy, and when he wasn't with him, he was with his friends and whatever girls hung with them while they club-hopped. The business side, the side where he terrorized people... I didn't really see that first-hand for some time. Even then, he sort of shielded me from that side of his life." Mari scrubbed a hand over her face. "When my aunt found out about our weird friendship, she lost her shit. My parents were killed in the street when I was very young. Guess whose family was responsible? More than anything, I wanted to leave Colombia, to make a life somewhere else." A sad smile curved along her lips. "I almost did, at least for a while, when I lived in Venezuela, until my aunt got cancer."

"Mari, you're avoiding my question. Were you and Mateo engaged? Why would he think you were pregnant?"

"He told me when we were young that he'd marry me someday. It became clear to me that, because of that confession, he kept his distance for the most part. He wasn't ready until his brother came back not too long ago with a pregnant wife." She shook her head. "Mateo was furious. Alejandro was a step ahead of him, and their father was pleased. That enraged Mateo."

"Did you want to marry him?" Chris's temper notched up even more, simmering beneath his controlled demeanor.

"No," she snapped in a firm voice. "I'd just come back to take care of my aunt and run her store for her, hoping she'd go into remission. None of that worked out. Mateo stormed in one day and told me I was his fiancée and we'd be married as soon as he settled a problem." For a moment, she pressed her lips into a firm line as she regained control of her shaky voice. "I buried my aunt and knew I didn't have long before I had to make a run for it. Before my aunt passed away, a woman came into the store. I recognized the necklace she had—it was impossible not to. I just didn't know which brother she belonged to. It didn't matter. I helped her. Eventually I learned she was Alejandro's wife. Aside from what I did for her, I had my own problems with the family. I knew there would be no going back. So I left."

Chris maneuvered to a particularly dense area along a curve

in the stream and pushed them to the side, indicating that she should get out. He lifted the canoe and hid it in a crop of bushes and tall grasses. Obscuring their footprints as they went, they moved aside the brush carefully rather than using a machete. It was slow going. When a small clearing opened up, he pulled her to a stop.

"I need to figure out what we're going to do." Focusing on her face, he noticed the fear lurking beneath the stubborn set to her chin. He pulled out a canteen and passed it to her before taking some for himself. He raked his fingers through his short hair. "How long have you been running from him?"

She shrugged. "About six months. I never stayed in the same place for very long. I holed up in rooms people would rent me, hoping Mateo wouldn't find me. I had some money. That was all I allowed myself to grab before I left. If I hadn't gone then, someone would have come to drag me to Juan Carlos's house. It was only a matter of time. Mateo was almost possessed when we—or, I should say, *he*—talked about us marrying."

"So no real engagement, no baby, no sex?"

Her lips peeled back, and she bared her teeth. "I *told* you, no. When we were children, I liked him. He was charming. As a teenager and adult, I did not. My family didn't want me to get too close to him, and my aunt feared he'd hurt me."

He plucked a blade of grass, then he twirled it between his fingers, never taking his focus off her. "He didn't leave anyone to watch over you?"

Her skin seemed to leach of color. "I don't know. I left at night and out the back. I promise you, I didn't want anything to do with him as a teenager. My aunt told me Mateo's father's men killed my parents. They were gunned down in the street— their lives casualties of a drug-related territory dispute in town. Their blood mixed with the dirt not far from where my aunt's shop was. Juan Carlos is ruthless, and Mateo is so much more so."

"And he still wanted to marry you, knowing you hated his father?"

A bitter laugh filled the air, and Mari's anger flashed across her taut features. "I never spoke to him about it. My aunt made sure I knew to be careful. I'm no fool. I'm from Colombia, Chris. Survival is in my blood."

He nodded. That was true. His wife was tough, something he admired about her very much. Still, the news sat ill with him about Mateo, and something pricked at his consciousness.

"You still doubt me?" Her voice continued to rise. "After all I've told you?"

"No, I believe you." With that revelation, his rage came. It simmered below his skin, ready to erupt. He knew that name, *Mateo*. He hadn't shared that with Mari. Nor had he shared that he recognized the Ramirez cartel name. Bits and pieces of his past filtered in to create a bigger picture. Death, torture, and senseless killing was their motto, and drugs were their livelihood. They would not threaten Mari—he'd put an end to their reign of terror.

Their gazes clashed, and he knew she saw the steel in him. "We aren't leaving. This ends here."

CHAPTER 18

MARI

"No!" Mari lurched to her feet. Glaring down at Chris, who had his back to a tree, she clenched her shaking hands into fists. "Going back is death. There is only going forward. No one survives this jungle twice."

His hazel-green eyes met her wide-eyed stare. His face was a sea of calm determination.

Why is he insisting on doing this? While his reasoning behind what he said was admirable, she was no fool. She'd been lucky to get out when she had. *What would happen when they returned, when I'm spotted?* Their best option was to stay on their current path.

Fear ruled her emotions and reactions. *I can't go back.* She had to make him believe her. Her hand brushed against her pants in frustration. The shape of his dog tags in her pocket sent her reeling. *What are my options? Should I hand them over, giving him that piece of his past, his identity? It could distract him and make him want to go home to the States, rather than pursue this death mission.* Their very presence symbolized he had another life—even though it was one that didn't include her. *Would everything fall into place once he laid eyes on them?* It could be an even worse fate for her. If she did return them, she'd lose him for sure. *But he'd be alive.*

There was her other concern, the one that'd ruled her decision to keep them from him. *What if he just leaves me?* Her time was running out—the cartel would surely find her at that point. He couldn't save her—not even those in power in her country could. There wasn't any authority in her world that she could count on, at least none she was familiar with. Corruption ran rampant in South America.

Staying firm with her decision, she pushed forward with her strong sense of self-preservation. Getting away and making a fresh start for herself in America was her goal. Going back would compromise that.

They would die.

Her mind spun. She could leave him and push on herself. They weren't terribly far from the border—she'd been following on his map. Fighting wasn't something she was afraid to do. As a Colombian woman in a drug-ravaged world, she knew her way around a blade and gun. Around death.

Her pack slung over her shoulder, she clipped him as she moved to maintain their direction out. "No. We're leaving." Over her shoulder, she glared. "Or at least I am."

His hand grasped her elbow, jerking her to a halt, and she sneered at him rather than allowing her tears to fall. "Let go." Yanking on his grip, she dug her heels in. Nothing terrified her more than facing off with Mateo or his family. She would not win.

"Stop being stubborn. You know I'm right," Chris said.

"I know you're dictating, and that's not going to happen. I'm telling you, I won't return there." *I'll lose more than my freedom. I'll lose you.*

"We stick together, Mari." Chris's voice left no room for arguments. "You're my wife. I won't let anything happen to you. That includes taking care of any threat that means you harm. Juan Carlos and Mateo do. If we leave, they'll only follow—trust me. It ends here. It ends now."

Oh, God. He's right. They'll never stop. Mateo had wanted her for his wife since they were young—even more so since she'd returned to Colombia. She had no clue why he'd chosen her. With Mateo's brother's success, she would pay the price. There was no doubt about it in her mind. Mateo's jealousy ran deep.

She took in the determined set to Chris's broad shoulders. The emotions shining in his eyes were what stopped any further protest. *Would I ever find a man that even came close to what he's come to mean to me? Who has such integrity, quiet determination, power—and, best of all, his protective and loving heart?* The fight left her. She would take the chance and risk her secret coming to light. Maybe, just maybe, he'd love her anyway.

She frowned, and her shoulders slumped forward. It wouldn't be easy going against such a powerful man. But Chris was right that it wouldn't end if she left. Mateo would hunt her down. With Chris by her side, she stood a chance of being free —for good.

He pulled her to him, wrapping his arms around her. "It has to be this way. Men like Juan Carlos… You know they won't stop. Especially if Mateo told his father you're carrying his child. In their eyes, that makes you their property." Pressing a kiss on top of her head, he brushed several loose strands of hair from her cheek. "I'll keep you safe, Mari. We'll figure out a plan."

"The two of us aren't enough to take them on." She curled her fingers around his shoulder and leaned back so that she could look at him. "What are we going to do?"

"No, we'll get help. But first we eat, get enough to drink, then travel through the streams to save our strength. When we make it out of the jungle, we'll put our plan into action." He stroked the side of her face with his palm. "We're going to take their legs out from under them first."

With furrowed brows, she shook her head. "Take me out?"

"No. That's sort of defeating my vow to protect you, isn't it? We're attacking their livelihood first." A shit-eating grin curved along his mouth, and she laughed.

Game on.

CHAPTER 19

MARI

Chris and Mari took the time for a short nap. They'd need it with the distance Chris wanted to cover. They were going to try to double their pace, which would mean very little rest and grueling hours in the heat. For the time being, he wanted her to take it easy, and for her to regain her strength. She brushed at a mosquito that landed on her arm. The little buggers only momentarily distracted her.

As he played with her hair, watching over her, she let sleep claim her, chasing on the coattails of her anxiety. Soon, she'd be ready to fight by his side. That part didn't scare her. Getting captured, or Chris being injured or killed, did.

With each gentle tug on her braid, she let herself relax further. Even so, the problems they faced were never far from her mind, and the last time she'd seen Mateo danced through her memory.

Her fingers had smoothed the shirt she'd just folded in her

aunt's store. In the small apartment above the shop, her aunt fitfully slept. With a few hours to spare, Mari had decided to work in the boutique. The bell above the door jingled, Mateo came in, and her stomach clenched with tension.

"I know your aunt told you that I've been looking for you. I would have expected better from you." Mateo gripped her upper arm and pulled her close. "Next time I request your presence, you'll respond immediately." His free hand gripped her chin and forced her to meet his gaze. "You were always to be mine. From the first time we spoke all those years ago, I knew it. I told you then you'd be my wife someday—that day has come."

That was what Aunt Linda was trying to warn me about. "We were children, Mateo." Her skin crawled from his touch. "Let me go."

A slow smile spread across his face, sending chills racing along her spine. "No, Mari. That's one thing I will never do." His mouth crashed over hers in a too-rough kiss.

It wasn't her first from him, but it damn well would be the last. Her gut churned with anger, and she shoved his chest with the flat of her palm. Bile clawed its way up her throat. The smell of him and his touch made her ill. When he pulled away, she fought against touching her bruised lips. "I won't marry you."

"It's funny that you think you have a choice." He dropped his hold on her arm and strolled around her aunt's shop. "Since I've always been generous where you're concerned, I'm going to give you an early engagement gift. I'll postpone our wedding so that you can bury your aunt. From what I've seen of her, it won't be long. After, you'll come to me freely."

"No."

In what seemed like slow motion, he turned to face her once again. His brows arched high on his forehead, and his eyes flashed with menace. "You'd rather we're married now? That can be arranged."

She clamped her lips together, not trusting herself. There were so many things she wanted to scream at him, but what she needed most was time.

"Mari." Her body shook, and she jolted back to the present, momentarily fighting the arms that embraced her. "Babe, I've got you. Take it easy." Chris held her cradled against his solid chest as he walked them over to where they'd stashed the canoe.

The foreboding in her mind dissipated some, and she dropped her head against him, savoring that small moment. Too soon, he would release her, and they'd be on their way again. Her fingers grazed across his chest to rest against the strap of her pack, which he'd slung over his shoulder along with his. While the jungle fought against them, sapping her strength and tossing dangerous wildlife in her path, he seemed relatively unfazed.

She was native to this harsh land, and thought it should be the other way around. *He* should be exhausted and worried about going back through the jungle.

Chris deposited her in the canoe, dropped their packs in, and shoved them off and into the small channel. She bent and rummaged in her pack for her canteen. Her fingers closed around it, and she pulled it out. As she unscrewed the cap, she kept her face turned away from him, unwilling to let him see the mental exhaustion and deep fear that had taken root inside her. They were so close. Even though she understood with every fiber of her being that Mateo wouldn't give her up, even if she escaped to the States, she fought the urge to scream and throw her canteen, or drop her head in her hands and sob. But that wasn't everything at stake. She was going to lose everything. *I'll lose Chris's trust. Him.* Soon, he'd find out about her lie.

Giving in to dramatics wouldn't do her any good. She

needed to shove her worry aside and be present, especially with all they were up against. The sound of the paddle breaking the water, the canoe slicing through it, and the reassuring calls of animals helped her gain a modicum of control. Then, she made the mistake of looking at Chris.

"You're unusually quiet. Is there something else that's bothering you, Mari?"

"Aside from the trek back through the jungle and facing the Ramirez cartel?" In a deft move, she twisted her long hair into a bun and secured it. The air left her lungs in a rush, and she faced him, her fears bare to his view. Her shoulder lifted in a shrug before she let it drop. "Obviously capture, torture, and death are a terrible possibility. But, that's not everything."

He frowned.

Shifting, she gazed at the spidery vegetation as it grasped for their canoe. "There is more. We were so close to making it out of here. This place keeps sucking me back in. I'm afraid I'll never escape and that you'll leave me. Or you'll realize you don't love me and I was a mistake. One you can easily brush aside before you go back to the States." With a gulp, she faced him again and rushed out another truth. "I'm afraid something will tear us apart."

CHAPTER 20

MARI

Mari stretched in her hammock and blinked the sleep from her eyes. The sky, still dark, had begun to lighten a fraction. Brilliant rays of orange and yellow glowed against indigo blue. She shifted in her bed. The pressure in her bladder had woken her before Chris. Soon he'd be up and they'd be on their way. Again.

She and Chris had tried to sleep together in one hammock, but as usual, it was too damn hot and they were bathed in sweat. It was nice, though, and she wished she could curl up against him all the time. He was addictive.

With care, she shifted and let her legs dangle over the edge of the bed. Chris stirred as she stepped out—an eyelid popped open, and he grunted. She whispered, "Bathroom," and he dropped back into sleep.

A step to the left, and she ducked behind a tree. It was still too close. Staying in line with where they camped so she didn't get turned around in the twilight, she went a little further before she stopped by a clump of plants. She took care of business as fast as she could, stood back up, and then fastened the button on her pants.

Stretching, she started to make her way back until she heard a twig snap. Alert, she palmed one of her knives in one hand. She thanked God that she'd slipped them into the slots in her pants when she woke.

Rather than risk a confrontation on her own, she took a step forward. A hand clamped on her shoulder, squeezing and holding her in place. A growl escaped her throat, and her vision tunneled. Flipping the hold on the knife, she swung her arm back and sank it into the person restraining her.

The blade sliced deep into his thigh, and she pulled it out just as quickly. Twisting, she faced the person head on. She moved her hand fast, in and out, delivering quick stabs at vital points. The man howled.

Another man stepped forward, yelling, "Control her!" *Fuck no. That won't happen.* She gripped the blade tighter and thrust it up, making contact with the first aggressor's stomach.

Blood flowed from all the wounds she'd inflicted. He was no longer a threat. His partner, quickly covering the distance between them, was.

"Chris!" She shouted a warning, just in case there were more. He could be caught unaware.

The injured man raised his arm to strike her, and she fought a laugh. *Good luck.* Goon Two jerked her over to him, his hand clamping on her raised one, the one that gripped the knife tightly in her palm. The bones in her wrist twisted in agony, and she cried out as he wrenched her to him.

A gunshot sounded, and the pressure on her wrist released. A small hole bloomed in her captor's forehead. Free from his grip, she stepped back. Goon One received the same treatment, and he crumpled fast, already part of the way there from having lost a ton of blood.

Chris wrapped his arm around her, and she sank back into his body. She'd know him anywhere. The solid feel of him, the aura of competence, confidence, and danger that emanated from him, was ingrained in her psyche. His chin dipped to her shoulder, and he nuzzled her neck.

"Are you okay?" His voice, hoarse from sleep, sent a shiver dancing on her skin.

"Another day, another attack." She turned to meet his gaze in the early rays of dawn. Determination in the hard glint of his green eyes shot an additional jolt of awareness through her tense muscles.

"Trouble seems to follow you around." He dropped a few more kisses along her neck, his voice creating a delicious vibration on her skin. "I don't want anything to happen to you."

"I'm fine. It wasn't anything I couldn't handle." She shrugged in his hold. "It's not like they were going to seriously hurt me if they think I'm pregnant—which is stupid, since I'd be showing by now. It'd be their death if they harmed me."

Kicking the foot of one of the dead guys to release a little pent-up frustration, Mari's focus snagged on the additional outline around his jagged butterfly tattoo. "Oh." *Shit!*

"What is it?"

"More of them. The extra outline on their tattoos means these two are part of Juan Carlos's 'inner circle'—his captains."

"He's serious about getting you back." Chris's voice had turned predatory. "He won't."

She twisted to look at him, scrutinized his serious expression, and pressed her mouth into a stubborn line. Needing him to take it down a notch, she tried to deter him about the captains, and from the possibility of them harming her. "Chris, we're in the jungle. The odds of something happening are extremely high, but probably not from the cartel guys. There's a small possibility they're here for some other reason, and we happened to be in their path. Win-win for them. Well"—she chuckled—"not really. The win went to us."

He tugged her away from the dead men and back to their gear.

She held the side of his face, and her body softened at the emotion blazing in his eyes. The dog tags burned a hole in her pocket, and she fervently hoped he'd mean that when she returned them to him.

"It's not just them, it's what could've happened." The intense weight of his gaze caused her to hold her breath. "I care about you. Whether I remember my past or not, you're it for me."

Her heart expanded until she thought it would burst, and she confessed what she'd come to know as truth. "You're it for me, too. I love you." No matter how long they'd known each other, he was the only man for her. She wanted a life with him. His sheer strength fed her and gave her the courage to fight for a better existence—with him. She wanted to go to bed every night in his arms and wake up to his kisses.

"I mean it. Whether I remember my past or not, I know my future." His hand settled on her hip, and he drew her close. "I love you too, Mari." In a brief caress, he brushed his lips across hers before resting his forehead against hers. "We need to move faster, be smarter, and finish this before they have any chance to strike at us."

Her fingers shook, and she swallowed a whimper. "I still think we can leave all this behind us. In the States, they have no power. We'll be free."

A sad smile lifted the corners of his lips. "No, Mari. We won't. Their reach extends into the States. I remember having dealings with them before—just not why. Nothing will stop them. Especially if they think you're carrying Mateo's baby, Juan Carlos's next legacy. We'll finish this here."

Going back meant even more risks than she was willing to share. Part of her wanted to give him his dog tags—a link to his past—and to plead with him as she did so to stay with her. But the rational side, the one who grew up in a country that chewed up its inhabitants and spit them out more often than not, didn't want to take the chance. "I'm worried," she whispered as she pressed against him, "that you'll remember something in your past and no longer want me."

"The past is just that, the past. I don't care who or what I was. I know what I want." With a finger under her chin, he tilted her face so she looked at him. "I want you."

Now. But soon you won't.

CHAPTER 21

MARI

The heat. Will it ever let up? Mari cursed her cramping, aching muscles. The jungle was not to be taken lightly. Nausea took root and refused to go away. It hadn't rained that day. The rainy season was still in full effect, so it eventually would. She wished with everything in her that the downpour would happen soon.

She trudged behind Chris, not wanting him to see how close she was to dropping. Smirking, she fought the hysteria that badly wanted to bust free in a maniacal cackle. She walked to her doom. Nothing good would come of confronting the Ramirez cartel.

She should know. When she was young, she hadn't understood and had continued to open her heart up to the angry and hurting boy, Mateo. But their friendship changed as the years went by and she developed a healthy awareness of what type of people he and his family really were. Still, she was careful. Her aunt coached her to be. "Keep the enemy close," she'd said. So Mari had. *Look what it got me.*

Her gaze trained on Chris's back, and she watched the muscles shift beneath his thin olive-green T-shirt. If she had an abundance of saliva, her mouth would have watered, but instead she was sweating all of the fluid in her body out. The only reason she'd agreed to go back, to confront the demons of her past and present, was because of Chris. He was hell bent on saving her. She saw that now.

If she survived the last leg of the jungle, maybe they could be together.

She stumbled over something on the ground then dropped to her knees, her hands breaking her fall. A tremor shook her, and her body gave out. Strong arms wrapped around her, stopping her from face-planting into the dirt.

He pulled her against his solid body. "We can stop here for a little while."

Mari laid her head onto his chest, willing her body to rest. Over and over, he was there for her. She'd started to look at him in a new light not too long after he'd regained consciousness. Without knowing it then, she'd opened her heart to him. That, she didn't regret—she even cherished the experience. What concerned her was that she'd deceived him about their relationship. *If only what I said was real.*

They'd be out soon, just not in the direction she desperately wanted to go. Her body shifted as he pulled one of the packs off and rummaged through it. "Here, drink this," he said, thrusting the canteen in her direction.

That she could do. With greedy gulps, she downed as much of the sweet water as she could hold. Feeling mildly better, she passed the canteen back and snuggled back against him. Her eyelids fluttered down until his deep voice rumbled against her ear.

"We need to eat again." He pressed some berries into her palm.

She shuddered. "I can't eat. I'm too nauseous." Sparing a glance up at him, she noted the hard set to his mouth. Her temper snapped, and she yelled, "I'm not pregnant."

He frowned. "I wasn't thinking that. The nausea is from being malnourished and constantly fighting dehydration. Not to mention the pace we travel." Gently, he took her hand, urging her to eat.

Shit, I'm taking my frustration out on him. I'm so tired. "I'm sorry, it's just been a long trek, and it's getting to me." She took one of the berries and popped it into her mouth, forcing it down. Even though her stomach cramped viciously, she made herself eat them all, refusing to throw them up. Chris pulled some dried meat out, and they ate some in silence. She could only get a little down, but the protein would help, and she understood that. A couple sips of water, and she prayed her strength would be enough for the next several hours. Sleep sounded like heaven.

"We'll rest here for an hour or two to regain our strength."

Dusting off her hands, she sucked in a breath at the speculative look on his face as he stared a hole through her.

"But you could be pregnant. We haven't used protection."

Her mouth formed an O, and she pushed on his chest, standing. Pacing, she wrung her hands. With all her other worries, she let herself get caught up in their passion. They'd been reckless.

"Mari, don't worry. I shouldn't have said anything. It's highly unlikely with the malnutrition and dehydration we've experienced, but the thought has crossed my mind." He ran his hands through his short hair. "I don't know if we ever discussed it or not, but do you want kids?"

With you. She gave him a small nod. *As long as you stay by my side.*

CHAPTER 22

Fog hung heavy, casting an eerie stillness over the jungle. While it was beautiful, it hid the dangers lurking within the vegetation, including snakes, scorpions, bacteria-infested palms, and even humans who used the thick soup to shield themselves before attacking. Soon, the sun would climb the sky and burn away the last remnants of the morning haze.

Mari and Chris slowly picked their way through the forest, placing each step only after scanning the ground, their gazes doing a constant sweep. The swoosh of the machete as Chris cleared a trail for them vied for Mari's attention with the sounds of rushing water. The mouth of the river neared. They'd come upon it in a matter of minutes. Through the awakening forest, they heard more than the motion of water. The distant hum of a motor buzzed.

Their path suddenly opened up, and Chris put the blade away while she stepped around him, curious to see if she could see the water through the trees ahead. A small glimpse of the murky water was all she saw. A mixture of relief and despair washed over her.

Chris's hand settled on the small of her back for a brief moment, and she longed to press into his touch. With her nerves stretched taut, she took measured breaths, as they would soon cross the river and exit the Darien Gap.

They'd already had to ditch their canoe and had no choice but to wait for the next boat—the same route she'd used to cross to the jungle—carrying brave souls who wished to challenge the Darien Gap for their freedom. She'd hoped to do the same, but instead they'd turned back, and she would have to face the grueling passage yet again if they were lucky enough to make a go for the border a second time, unless Chris had another way out.

The tug on her belt loop had her looking over her shoulder. Chris tilted his head to the side, and she shifted, going where he directed. He pressed close to her ear, and his whispered words sent a shiver down her spine for more than one reason.

"We'll wait out of sight. No telling if the next boat that comes will carry cartel members or people trying to escape to the border."

He lowered to the ground, and she followed, scooting close to him. The heat was hell, but even that didn't stop her from wanting to be near him. They'd face a nightmare soon. Every moment she had with him would count, especially since she didn't know if it would be their last.

He handed the canteen to her, and she took a long drink before giving it back. His focus stayed fixed on the riverway, so when he spoke she jumped a little, not expecting it.

"Tell me again, how long were you in hiding, and are those places still available if we need them?"

She battled exhaustion from the mountain they were

climbing with this plan. Each step felt as if she took it backwards. For a good six months, she'd fought tooth and nail to escape. After they crossed the Gulf of Uraba, their success or demise would be determined.

"The one closest to here is an abandoned hut on the outskirts of Turbo. It provided the perfect shelter for some time. The town doesn't have much to offer other than a beach, a nice park, and a few restaurants and bars. We can go there to start."

They lay next to each other on the ground, and she was thankful for the shade that shielded them from the intense sun.

"What about the man who took you across the river? Is there more than one?"

His voice stayed level, his questions quiet, and she knew he was gathering intel and filing it away in that analytical mind of his.

"I'm sure there is more than one guide. But I only saw the one guy. Oh wait, there was someone else, but he was leaving, so I didn't deal with him." She rubbed her forehead, briefly closing her eyes. "Maybe they do work in shifts."

"Is there anywhere you want to go?" He spared her a glace before returning to surveying the water and the shoreline.

Longing lanced her heart. "Yes. I want to stop by my aunt's home one last time. I know it's not entirely safe. Mateo should have people watching it." It'd been so long, and for it to be left undisturbed... It was probably foolish to hope no one had broken into the place.

"We'll figure it out."

The distant hum of the engine increased, and Mari perked up some. If they could make it to that hut, they'd have shelter and be able to eat and sleep, she hoped for at least a week. Chris was a machine. They'd be heading out after he thought she'd gotten an adequate amount of rest. One way or another, it would all be over soon, even if it didn't end in her favor.

CHAPTER 23

MARI

Chris and Mari waited patiently as the last passenger got off the boat that had motored to the muddy shore. Determined, desperate faces disappeared into the thick vegetation as their group stuck together in a clump of eager bodies. She huffed. They had no idea what was in store for them. The jungle housed more dangers than they'd experienced in the corrupt streets of her homeland. It was a beast all of its own.

Seeing their intended transportation getting ready to shove off, Chris and Mari moved as one. Just as the boat inched away from the shoreline, Chris grabbed onto the ridge, and the boatman jumped a mile. It was the same man who'd brought her over, and she stifled a laugh at his reaction. No love was lost between the two.

The gaunt face of the guide met hers. A grin, riddled with missing teeth, leered at her. With her back ramrod straight, she took a step forward. She had knives again. He'd pay this time, not her. Fingers curling around the hilt of one of the blades she'd taken from Chris, she allowed him to see the dark smile and the eager promise on her face.

Chris's hand clamped over hers, stopping her from freeing her blade. "You'll give us a ride across." The statement was directed at the boatman, dripping with authority and leaving no room to argue. The man actually shivered as he stared at Chris in confusion.

They were lucky, and she knew it, because their wait for the boat had only been three hours long. It could have been days, with no way to summon the boat and no way to tell when the next one would cross over to the jungle.

A familiar gleam entered the boatman's eyes as his mouth curved back up into a sneer. He thought he held the power. *Fool.* Not even the breeze dared to stir. Her vision tunneled, and she waited to see who made the next move. She was ready to throw her knife if needed.

"We'll be taking that knife back, too." Chris yanked the boat back and took Mari's hand to help her climb aboard.

Anger colored the man's face a deep red, and he sputtered. "Why would I?" His hand covered the knife's gold handle as he attempted to hide it from them.

"It belongs to her." He waited a beat as he settled himself in the boat, edging between the boatman and Mari, effectively cutting off her access to him, and vice versa.

The man shook his head, his body tense. He gripped the throttle, his knuckles leaching of color.

"Bartering is one thing. Swindling a lone woman while she's in the middle of crocodile-infested waters? Nope. That's not happening." Chris leaned forward, his face inches from the boatman's perspiring one. "Your choice is simple. Take us across and return the knife to her, hilt first, or I throw you from the boat and take us back myself. You can take your chances with the crocs."

The guide's hand quivered before he slowly grasped the hilt of the blade that stuck out of his shoe. With narrowed eyes, Mari went on alert. Rather than risk a physical confrontation on the water, she spewed the truth that would make him want to get rid of it.

"It belonged to Mateo Ramirez. What do you think he'll do if he or one of his associates notices you have that, hmm?"

A small cry escaped the man's lips, and he thrust the end of the knife at her. Snorting, she took it from him.

The boat reversed, and the man avoided eye contact as he steered them across in silence.

Chris's soft, commanding voice cut through the noise of the motor and the slap of the water as they traveled, leaving no room for argument. "You won't say anything about us. If you do, we'll find out, and you won't like the consequences."

"I'm no fool. Between you and the Ramirez cartel, I'd be crazy to say anything. Just get off my boat and go far away when we reach the other side."

Her body stiffened as she took note of how Chris tensed while his gaze surveyed the approaching port. Where their thighs touched, his muscles hardened to stone. He was in warrior mode, and she knew nothing would get past him.

Pressing her hand to his arm, she looked around, needing a physical connection to him to ground her. They were back. In a matter of seconds, they'd step off the boat. It would be two against hundreds when Mateo and his father learned they were here. She had no doubt the boatman would tell someone if he thought he could make a profit.

The boat touched the opposite shoreline, and Chris jumped out, turning to reach a hand to help Mari exit. Clasping his hand, she stepped off, her gaze staying on the boatman. Chris tugged her, and she went with him, their pace picking up. The heat was still brutal, but she was used to it by then, and it wasn't as bad as it had been in the jungle. In the arms of the jungle, it was suffocating, the humidity oppressive, and a constant nausea plagued her, one of the side effects of the wilds that refused to be tamed.

They passed rows of boats, curved around a bend, and she found her hand grasped in his sure one again. They crossed another dirt road, and she knew it wouldn't be long before they came upon a small section bordering the village where she'd taken refuge. Each place had been temporary, and she dared not risk overstaying her welcome. She was lucky when she stayed there before, and she knew it. Now, with the stakes even higher, she wondered whether someone would out her once they learned that Mateo or Juan Carlos had demanded her return.

Since she'd agreed to come back, she risked more than just her life—she gambled with Chris's, and it ate at her very soul. The dirt road led exactly where she knew it would, and they weaved through small huts with precarious walls. Windows were cut into the structure, allowing air to flow through. No doors barred any from seeing inside. Some had cloths tied to one side that allowed for privacy, but the heat worked against the homes that would never have electricity. The village reeked of poverty, which Mari was uncomfortably familiar with, despite the money she'd been able to use for escaping. It'd come from her aunt's lifelong stash.

"This way." Tucking a loose strand of hair behind her ear, Mari tugged on Chris's hand as she urged him to follow her lead. "There's an abandoned hut on the edge of the village. We can stay there for the night."

Few people were out, as the hour had turned late. Danger existed as a way of life there... everywhere, really. She'd grown up walking hand-in-hand with it. With all the upheaval, the people were on high alert. There was no telling when the cartel or the supposed authorities would come in and wreak havoc on those who lived here, especially with Juan Carlos and his son hunting her. Mari repressed a shiver.

They ducked inside, finding a corner away from any intrusive eyes. They dropped their packs, and she found Chris's gaze in the small amount of moonlight that stretched through a window. She sat on the floor and leaned forward onto her hands, her nerves suddenly getting the best of her.

"Come here." Chis lifted his arm, and she moved to curl up against him.

She noticed the gun at his side. They might need it, and she was glad he was a fierce fighter. They'd both need to be if they were going up against the head of the Ramirez organization. Her body tensed. This could be the last time he held her, the last time that she felt safe and no longer alone. There was every chance that he would be taken from her, and her life would spiral downward in a nasty way.

"Hey. We won't be alone in this. I'll find a way to contact my brother so we have reinforcements." Chris nudged her chin up with a finger, locking his gaze on hers. "Don't worry. They waged this war first. We showed up, and we're gonna finish it. Everything will be okay. Do you trust me?"

Warmth spread through her. *Yes.* There was no doubt in her mind. He'd become her world, and after everything they'd been through with his injuries and then hers, she trusted him to keep her safe. With a nod, she leaned against him and let her eyelids close. They would need rest for whatever Chris had in store for tomorrow.

~

CHRIS

Voices filtered into Chris's awareness, and he blinked the last remnants of sleep away. Mari was still pressed against his side. They'd shifted to lie flat at some point during the night, but she remained curled into his body. He brushed a lock of hair from her face then dropped his hand to her hip, giving her a gentle squeeze.

The noises beyond their tiny shelter were unhurried and natural. People were going about their day. He detected no panic or tension. They were safe for the time being.

Mari stirred, and he tucked his chin to watch her awaken. She took his breath away. *So fierce. With a blade, gun, or verbal barrage, she grabs life by the balls.* He loved that about her, as well as the vulnerable side, which she buried deep, but which he glimpsed every now and then when she thought she was alone, with no one at her side. And when they were finally safely out of there, he promised himself that they would have all the time in the world to explore each other fully.

"Morning." She flashed him a smile as they stood and stretched. Mari bent to rummage through her pack then produced a small bag she'd filled with berries. After they had a miniscule breakfast—he was so hungry—they drank their fill of water.

"Are we going to just go and confront them?"

The worry on her face made him feel like shit. "Not yet. We're going to do some recon." After another sip of water, he took her hand, ready to strategize. "Tell me everything you know about their day-to-day operations, what they hold dear, where they ship their cocaine from, their coca fields, and their routines at home."

Mari tensed and sucked in a breath. "We're only two people.

I don't know what you expect us to do against an army of Ramirezes."

"You'd be surprised what we can do. But we'll save the heavy lifting for when we have a team to help us."

She studied him and looked as though she was weighing the risks. When he fell silent, the unnatural stillness that surrounded him would intimidate her, and she would run for the hills—if she didn't know he'd protect her with his very life. He had to make her believe they stood a chance. He gave her a pleading look.

"Okay then. Let's get to it." She launched into a recounting of what she knew, which he followed by mapping strategy. She gazed at him with a wondrous expression in her dark eyes, in awe of his strategic prowess.

CHAPTER 24

CHRIS

Shouts of children echoed in the distance as they played close to their homes or darted through the tiny community with each other. Chris reached for Mari, wanting the physical connection to her. As they made their way to town, they walked hand in hand down a dangerous dirt road known to shelter thieves. The small village had been a haven, but they needed supplies in order to put their plan into effect.

Chris shifted closer to the willowy trees that lined the road, pulling Mari with him. They drew attention with their packs, his sheer presence, and her natural beauty. He understood why Mateo wanted her and had put her on a pedestal for when he was ready to settle down. It wasn't going to happen, though. Chris would punch those false expectations right out of Mateo, along with his father's organization and the drug-trafficking legacy that he expected to fully inherit.

He would demolish them. Steel lined his veins.

He pulled her deeper into the cover the vegetation offered. Giving the Ramirez cartel any warning so early in the game upped the cartel's chance of winning, and he would see to it that they did not win. His mouth twitched, and he firmed his jaw. This was war, something he was well versed in.

He only wished his brothers were with him.

Faltering a step, he focused on that last thought, working to push past the headache that always gripped him when he tried to force a memory. Six blurry images swam in his mind's eye. No matter how hard he attempted to tease them into focus, the sudden pain in his head worsened.

A soft touch on his forearm had him looking down into Mari's upturned face, and he grinned in resignation. He knew what she'd say: stop forcing it. The memories will come when they're ready.

"We'll be there soon. It's only about half a mile," she whispered. "Are you sure about all this?"

"Hell yeah." They would stock up on food and ammo, and he wanted to see if they could get any more intel from the people Mari knew. They traveled together with greater ease, walking through the forest adjacent to the dirt road. As in the jungle, birds called to one another, and an occasional monkey swung by, traveling through the branches up ahead. But there was a big difference between the jungle and the copse of trees they were in, in terms of the heat. It was cooler, and he was thankful for that.

The sounds of people—of living—filtered through the trees, and they stepped farther away from the road. Surprise was still on their side, and he wanted to keep it that way for as long as possible.

"Do you know many people here?" Chris kept his voice low as he questioned Mari.

"No. Not here. But it's a larger town, with restaurants and shopping. It's not like the one we just came from."

"Then we run an even greater chance of running into cartel or military people."

She tensed beside him. "Yes. I avoided this area—skirted around it—on my way to the tiny village we just came from."

"Well, maybe we can grab a shower somewhere and a change of clothes."

Mari groaned. "That would be beyond amazing."

A few more feet, and they would be there. Chris's awareness notched up, listening to and discarding noises, testing the conversations they could hear against anything they knew to be wary of.

Screams filled the air. Several consecutive pops of a gun jolted them both into movement. *Shit!* They sprinted to the edge of the forest, to a place just before the trees gave way to a back street. Shops lined the view in front of them, and a few people raced by.

The chaos seemed to be coming from what he assumed to be the center of the town. He spared a glance at Mari as he released her hand. She quickly grabbed her gun, and her other hand gripped a knife, ready to let it loose should she need to. Determination pulled her features tight. Switching his attention from her to the area around them, he cataloged every roof, every hiding place, and the people moving away from where they planned to go.

In times like these, their connection expanded then contracted to a laser-like focus. He read her energy, and his training kicked in. Their coordination wasn't unfamiliar—he knew he'd had that same unity with others, at some point in time.

After dashing from the cover of the trees to the back of one of the buildings, they edged close to the corner. Shouts and crashes filled the air, and he took advantage of it, moving closer, with Mari at his back. Weaving in and out of people going in the opposite direction, they covered ground to take them to another cluster of buildings.

"Town square," Mari said under her breath.

Inching between two buildings, they kept watch for movement past the narrow path they edged along. Chris was first. The pop of bullets volleyed back and forth between two groups. He couldn't see them yet. There were only a few more steps until he got to where he needed to be, and he chose those with care.

On a roof almost directly across from the narrow passage they were inching away from, three men took cover. Their heads popped up, and deep scowls etched their craggy features. It was obvious from their clothes and coloring that they weren't from the town. The three of them shouted a few words back and forth before they yelled down to the five cartel members a few feet from them, who returned fire. *Russian.* The knowledge of who crouched on the rooftop surprised him. There had to be a connection.

"Shit," Mari said as she peeked around him.

People fled in a mad dash through the square, taking cover where they could. One dark-haired woman, who wore a flowing skirt and sleeveless top, strolled through the open street amidst the chaos, her face tilted to the roof. Something about her carriage sent alarm bells clanging through Chris. *Do I know her?* He stole another look at the men. *Does she know them?*

Squinting, he took in the details of the woman. He stepped forward, recognition causing his mind to spin and dark edges to eclipse his vision. *Hannah.* She'd passed about three feet from where he and Mari were.

The sight of a brunette Hannah jolted him with such force that the world around him faded away, to be replaced by images from the past. Memories rushed through his mind, and the sights and sounds of the present ceased to exist around him.

He staggered against the side of the building as images erupted of Trev, his blood brother, and his street-turned-military-brothers, Hayden, Tank, Keegan, Jack and Hawk. Their family had extended to include Trev's military team: Liam, Matt, and Connor. The love he had for all of them came flowing back, along with the intensity and danger of the wars they'd waged, the hostages saved, the wounds, the betrayal. They'd come. They never left a man behind, especially not one of their team, their family. They were probably somewhere in this country right now, searching for him.

His vision flashed back, and he focused on the very person he suspected was responsible for the mishap during their last mission, which had resulted in his amnesia, in his being stranded upside down in a tree, and in his gunshot wound.

Hannah wasn't from Colombia. Nor was he. He remembered that they'd worked in the same building at the CIA until the day he and some of his SEAL brothers were sent to rescue hostages when an aircraft went down. She'd been on that plane. The very reason for him being there was to rescue her and several others, so why she remained—lived—shed a dark light on what she probably was: a spy, possibly Russian.

He shook his head to clear it as the voices escalated in their volume and speed. The Russians hurled words from the roof to the men below, who may or may not have understood them, but he did: "We had a deal."

"Chris," Mari hissed at his side, her fingers digging into his bicep.

He blinked. The world flooded back in full force, and he watched Hannah's long legs carry her in graceful strides farther away from where they were. He could go after her and maybe find out what the hell had happened and why.

If he did, there would be a choice. He could capture Hannah or remain by Mari's side. The tug on his arm brought his attention back to Mari.

She's not my wife. In fact, he'd never met her before he came to Colombia. Betrayal welled up in him, warring against visceral images of the two of them together and how she'd taken care of him and remained by his side when he was most vulnerable. They'd built their trust, and she'd told him she loved him. The part of him damaged by Jessie wanted to grab her, shake her, and demand to know what game she played. Pressing his mouth into a frustrated line and clenching his hands into fists, he willed himself to cool down and to confront her only when the time was right.

The urge to go after Hannah subsided further when he remembered the very real threat that Mari faced. There was no other option for him. If he didn't help her, she would most likely die.

He turned part of himself off, focusing on where they were and what needed to be done, something he could definitely do. "At least they cleared the people out."

"Right." Mari nodded. "Fewer people to recognize us."

"We still need a few things."

Chris grabbed her hand and pulled her along as they left the little walkway between the buildings.

He clenched his jaw. Why she lied about being married to him didn't matter at that moment. It wasn't the right time to have that discussion.

CHAPTER 25

CHRIS

They bought food with the cash Chris had hidden in a pocket of his backpack. Even in the small village, they'd stuck to English rather than Spanish when they spoke to one another. He and Mari ate then stored what was left over in his pack. He wiped a bead of sweat from his forehead. It was damn hot, but still better than when they were in the jungle. They left the little community and pushed on to their next location. This time, they hotwired a closed-top Jeep, as the distance was approximately fourteen hours to Buenaventura, the port he wanted to target. From there, they would visit the surrounding coca fields.

Dusk settled around them, and shadows elongated. Soon, it would be nightfall, and he hoped to reach their destination prior to that, but it looked like it wouldn't be possible. When the Jeep ran out of gas, they left it and continued on foot.

In silence, they pushed on, and he set a fast pace, one she

met without complaint. They were close to one of the main ports, which the cartel used as a drug-trafficking route. He'd checked the map before they'd stopped. "It should take about an hour." At Mari's nod, he increased his pace, which she matched. He wanted to get there before it was fully dark. Time passed swiftly as they picked their way along their intended path.

It was a good time to confront her. Out of the corner of his eye, he skimmed over the curve of her cheek to the stubborn set of her mouth. The internal fight he waged allowed him to understand why she would have said what she did—to ensure his protection. She lied to him and pretended that he meant something when, at least at first, he didn't. But she wasn't Jessie. Her actions over their time together spoke louder than his missteps and blinders with his past-relationship fiasco.

For some time, they risked walking on the road, listening for the sound of cars. None came, at least not while they were in sight of any approaching traffic. That could change at a moment's notice, so they remained alert.

It wasn't long before they veered off the path that led to the busy harbor for the perceived safety of the trees. She had her fingers hooked in the pack's straps, and he had to force his attention to her face rather than the T-shirt molded tightly across her breasts. Whether she was his wife or not, he wanted her in every sense.

Mari leaned against a tree and shoved wispy strands of hair back from her face. She dropped the pack at her feet and stretched her arms overhead. "Why did you want to stop?"

Chris hesitated to say anything and instead stepped in front of her, closing the inches that separated their bodies. Bending down, he slid his hand behind her neck, beneath her braid. His other hand dropped to her hip and drew her against him while he brushed his lips over hers. She instantly softened against his body, and something eased in him. There was no hesitation, only desire.

When he leaned back and she opened her eyes, he looked within, wanting to see inside her, all the way to her soul. The wall he saw on occasion wasn't there—there was only passion, need, and warmth. She cared. No matter what her reasons had been for the deception and the lies about them being married, he believed she had feelings for him. The rest would work itself out in time, because he had no doubt she'd initially sought his protection under the guise of being his wife.

Putting some space between them, Chris tugged on her braid. "When did we fall in love?"

"What?"

He didn't miss how her body stiffened. It was miniscule, but there regardless. They weren't married. He needed to reassure himself about exactly where her loyalties were. His instincts told him they were with him, but he'd traveled down that path once before, and he would not do that again, especially when it could literally mean their death—or his, depending on the outcome of her goals.

A small smile spread across her face, and she eased back against the tree. "You caught me off guard. I thought we were going to talk about hitting the coca fields." As she tilted her head, her features softened into a wistful expression. "I can tell you about when I lost myself completely, knowing you were the one I wanted, always. When I saw you for the first time in the jungle, when we cut you down and I realized who you were, I didn't know what to think."

He rested his hand on her hip, unable to stop touching her. For good or bad, she'd already become a part of him. "So you didn't fall for me again right away?" Her small gasp drew him closer. *Screw the heat.* No matter where they were, he wanted her.

"You went to attack Hannah. I worried. Then when you

woke and focused on me and my gun was gone in a flash." She shook her head, and a small smile teased the corners of her mouth. "You move so quickly. I'll admit, those moments made me cautious. Then there was every time you showed me concern and compassion, when you looked at me and your eyes darkened with desire, when you put me before you every single time, and when you touched me with such care." She blinked back the fine mist that coated her eyes and softly laughed. "My feelings for you deepen with every moment we spend together. I don't know what I've done to deserve you, but whatever it is, I'm very lucky."

Fuck. No matter the reason their paths had crossed, he was damn grateful. Even though she skirted around whether they'd met before their time in the jungle, he didn't really care in that moment. He pulled her forward by increasing the pressure on her hip. For a few minutes, he would indulge in the softness of her lips. Then, they'd get down to business and hit the cartel where it hurt them the most—their inventory.

CHAPTER 26

CHRIS

*M*ap in hand, Chris studied the few places Mari had identified as Ramirez coca fields. Their plan was to go there after they hit up the marina. If they struck the surrounding farmland first, there would potentially be tighter security on the outgoing shipments. The farms would be relatively easy, even though she seemed nervous.

"Stop biting your lip. You're going to make it bleed." He brushed his thumb over her swollen bottom lip. "This is a piece of cake. Trust me."

"I do. I'm just worried. There are no rules for them. They don't care who they hurt." She pressed her hand against his chest. "And no one has been able to stop them before."

He covered her hand with his own and gave it a gentle squeeze. His unease at her lie melted away with one look and one touch from her.

He wanted to weaken the organization and send as many of

the cartel members as he could scattering as they attempted to salvage what he and Mari would destroy with C4. That way, there would be fewer of them around their intended target, Juan Carlos. "It'll be fine. We're observing first, and you're telling me everything you know while we watch them." After the explosions went off, his brothers would know he was close by. That's when they'd team up together and do the real damage.

She bobbed her head in acceptance and stuck close to him as they slipped through the banana-shipping yard, keeping out of sight of the workers and security. Crouched down, they dashed for the cover of crates until they made it to the building where they housed the equipment. A rusted ladder was screwed against the side of the steel wall, and they climbed the rickety steps to the roof. From there, they would have a great view of the harbor and all the workers. Lying flat, they peered over the edge, and Chris was thankful for the cover of dusk.

"Tell me what you've heard about how they ship the raw cocaine out. I already know about the barrels. When it's darker, I'll go down and check them. But what else?"

A shiver coursed through her, and she pressed tighter against his side. He could tell that she was terrified of what the cartel would do to them if they were caught. They wouldn't be.

"The crates. Sometimes they'll pack the stuff flattened and in tinfoil. They'll line the inner flaps of the boxes. With the bananas on top. The barrels"—Mari pointed a quivering finger at rows of blue canisters on a large barge—"are filled. I don't know, it may be something like two to five hundred thousand dollars' worth. I'm not sure how much is really in the crates with the bananas."

"All right." Workers were packing up to go home for the day, leaving the wooden pallets where they were, probably to be loaded tomorrow. From what it looked like, this shipment was set to go sometime tomorrow. Security guards—well, men with machine guns—patrolled the grounds. Once he was closer, he'd be able to tell if they were private sector, paramilitary, or cartel. It didn't matter, so long as they hit the intended targets hard and got out before they were identified.

The sky darkened, and so did the marina below them. The occasional flare of a cigarette or cigar as one of the men took a drag was the only artificial light. A thrill at being back in action raced through Chris. It brought back the times he and his family —the ones he'd run with when he was younger—would cause trouble. *Too bad they aren't here. They'd fucking love this, too.*

With his hand on Mari's shoulder, he nudged her, then moved to caress the curve of her neck. Leaning in, he whispered his intentions. "I'm heading down. I'll check the boxes—"

"They'll be in the bottom flaps."

The pulse in her neck fluttered, and he chuckled. "Right. I kind of figured that'd be what they'd do. The top would be too easy to find. Stay here, and no matter what, be quiet. Unless"— a wave of dark intent swept through him—"someone comes up here and tries to start any shit with you."

She nodded with wide eyes. He brushed a kiss on her forehead before he carefully made his way to the rusty ladder.

Steering clear of the armed men, Chris sprinted over to a group of boxes on top of a pallet. As quietly as he could, he turned one upside down and opened the bottom with his knife. Nothing was there. He was about to check more, but the boat drew his attention. A guard strolled along several feet away, right in Chris's path to the ship. Crouching, he waited until the man moved on, saying something to his buddy as he caught up to him. They didn't follow a standard patrol pattern. *Untrained amateurs.* When it was relatively safe to dart toward the vessel, Chris took off.

He was a ghost. They had no clue he was there. It made sense, since he was part of a Special Forces group—Gray

Ghosts. They'd been doing this type of stealth shit since they were young and mostly homeless. It wasn't until much later that they decided to make it legal. The gauntlet thrown down by the authorities was too sweet to pass up. Their entire group took the tests for the Navy, and he regarded it as the best decision they'd ever made.

It was either that or jail. It had been a no-brainer.

He reached the ship and boarded, keeping to the darkest areas, and almost tripping on a crowbar. He grabbed the crowbar and quietly pried open one of the tops. *Bingo.* He dipped his finger inside the barrel and tasted it to be sure—sure enough, it was full of uncut cocaine, just waiting to be shipped out.

Not happening.

He swung his backpack off his shoulders, pulled out some of the C4, and attached the plastic explosives to a cluster of barrels. After setting the detonators, he grabbed his pack and moved down the line, checking random containers as he went. They were all full of the powdery stuff. In what felt like no time at all, he finished securing the charges then made his way off the boat. There were still more boxes he wanted to check, but with the quantity onboard, he doubted he'd find any more. Plus, he wanted to make sure he had enough explosives for the operations at the coca fields.

Taking the same route he'd used to reach the boat, he returned to Mari, and they made their way to the outskirts of the marina. The detonators he had used weren't remote. Instead, he'd set timers on them, programming them to go off in sync. They needed to get further away, closer to the first field he wanted to strike. They wouldn't know what—or who— hit them.

Their distance wasn't great, so they would be at the first field in no time at all. They raced full force along the road, jumping into the shelter of the trees if they heard the slightest whisper of voices or vehicles. They encountered one Jeep and stopped to wait in case any more came along. He figured it was most likely the second shift relieving the armed men at the docks.

Five minutes later, the explosions began. Mari's hand jerked in his, and the look of terror that flashed over her features in the pale moonlight only fueled his determination to put an end to her worries.

There was no need to worry just yet. They'd secure a place to sleep for a few hours and put the next phase of their plan into effect when they awoke. The fun was just beginning.

CHAPTER 27

CHRIS

High above the ground, Chris detached the ropes that had secured Mari and him in high, thick branches the night before. The sun would crest the horizon in about an hour, and he wanted them to be on their way before it was fully light out. Mari stood one limb over with her hand on the trunk of the large and sturdy tree they'd chosen as their sleeping quarters.

"See? It wasn't so bad." With a wink, he slung his pack over his shoulder and began the climb down.

"It was terrifying." A grin curved along her lips. He dropped to the ground and stood nearby so he could help her down. There were a lot of people combing through the woods next to the road that led to the harbor. From their vantage point, and obscured by the thick branches and leaves below them, they'd listened while remaining unseen. Mari had shivered every once in a while.

Dammit. I want her out of here. Safe. The next step will be anything but that.

With his hands on her hips, he turned her to face him, needing to see her expression. "There's no going back at this point. I can get you out and on your way to the States safely, while I finish this." He forced one of his hands to fall from her. "What do you want to do? Last chance, Mari."

Her fingers curled around his forearms, and a determined gleam flashed in her eyes. "This is my problem—my fight—and there's no way I'd leave you to handle it alone. I'm with you all the way."

He dropped his hand from her hip. "Let's go, then."

"Wait." She tugged on his hand. "This isn't fair. You don't need to fix things for me. We've done enough damage. Let's just leave before it's too late."

The concern and truth in her words firmed his decision to stick by her side. "Not happening."

She huffed as she pointed diagonally to the south from the road they were on. "The closest field is that way."

As they set off in that direction, Chris swept the area for signs of people. The farm was close. He'd already noted all the places Mari knew, memorized where to go, and figured out the best combinations to strike. They would hit them in random order instead of destroying only one place at a time, which would make the cartel think there were more groups attacking their livelihood. It was very possible the cartel would figure out the numbers they were up against. Knowing it was a small group—two, to be exact—would give them a tremendous amount of confidence and only increase their aggression. Chris and Mari needed every advantage they could get. And soon, they'd need his team's support.

A small part of him felt guilty for destroying the farmers'

livelihood, and he knew Mari felt the same way. But the cartel had to be stopped.

He'd started to remember so much more of this life—everything, in fact—and there was another reason he wanted to wipe out this particular threat. Before he had set out on the mission that led him to Mari, he'd been at Liam's. Trev and Liam had a hand in helping Mateo's brother's wife, Liv, escape her husband and his family. After a shootout at Liam's farm, which was his team's new base of operations, things were better. They were progressing. All was relatively quiet there, but they all knew Juan Carlos would be back again.

What Mari didn't seem to know was that Mateo was dead. *She runs from a ghost. Well, not entirely. Juan Carlos is after her, and he's very real and very deadly.*

More and more, he found himself staring at her. She tugged on her hair until she realized what she was doing and flicked the thick braid behind her. Concern flashed across her face with a quick flare of panic every now and then. While her story behind their relationship wasn't true, he sensed her feelings were. He'd even given her an out, and she hadn't taken it. Part of him wanted to send her home. He could contact his team and have them swoop in, pick her up, and deliver her to safety. But then she'd be gone, and it was her fight, too. He couldn't quite deny her that.

It didn't take long for them to reach the outskirts of the coca field. He drew her closer to him. Workers would be arriving shortly, but he still didn't believe there weren't guards on the premises unless they relied solely on the landmines, which he knew would be placed strategically around the grounds.

Chris guided Mari to sit by the base of a tree, where he took the time to rifle through his bag. He found the small, lightweight tools and the device he was looking for. He palmed the device then slung his pack over his shoulder.

With the tools, he set about altering the mechanics of the detonators, which were his inventions. The screws were undone quickly, and he made the necessary adjustments. A simple alteration could change them from timed to remote detonators—whatever he needed on the fly. He closed the box and put the screws back in place then motioned for Mari to help.

"Put your hand under this."

"What? Why?" Her nose scrunched up.

"It's a metal detector. I altered the setting so that it can detect any type of metal—or at least enough that we can locate where the mines are and not step on them."

"Oh." She held her hand out, and he floated the box over her ring, far enough away to simulate how deep the mines could be buried.

A low hum erupted from the equipment as he passed it over her band. He pressed his lips together at the sight of it. *Who gave her the ring?* "Thanks. It works." Grasping her hand, he toyed with her small piece of jewelry. "Did I pick this out for you?"

Her face lost some of its color, and she shook her head. "It's my aunt's," she whispered. "I—um, she gave it to me so we could use it. My uncle died some time ago, and she wanted me to find the same happiness she had with him."

"And I was okay with that?"

"Yes. You understood the sentiment behind the ring."

He dropped her hand, still feeling the need to question her and wondering how long it would be until she told him—if she would. He would rather she told him than the other way around. No matter what, they'd eventually have that discussion, but Mari could be unpredictable, letting her emotions rule her responses. "Even though I'd have wanted to buy you something bigger?"

Her expression turned wistful. "That's sweet, Chris. But the history behind the ring makes it mean more to me than something brand new." She closed the distance between them and wrapped her arms around his waist. "You've shown me what a relationship should be, and that matters more to me than anything."

With his hand on her hip, he tugged her closer. "How is that, exactly? We've been in a jungle, and you said I deserted you so that you had to flee the country… or at least try to."

She shook her head. "None of that matters. You've been here for me from the moment you opened your eyes in our tree canopy. You've cared for me, kept me safe, and shown me love."

He pulled her in close and enfolded her in his arms. After a few minutes, he grasped her shoulders and shifted her back a little. "We have to get a move on. The workers will be here soon, and I want to set the charges." He bent to pick up the box once more then slid a tiny panel open to reveal a thin, long collapsible piece of metal, which he extended to drop the box closer to his feet. The scanner would be their very best friend as they searched for exactly where the mines were.

"Climb up this tree and wait for me."

Crossing her arms over her chest, she glared. "No. I already told you I'm a part of this. That includes whatever crazy idea you've got going."

Fighting laughter, which he knew she'd take offense to, he grinned. "You want to go through the fields with me to figure out where they've buried mines?"

"Yes." She extended her hand, palm up. "I'll use that, and you can do whatever it is you're planning on doing."

"Do a wide and slow sweep so we can walk side by side, like this." He took the device from her and showed her how to do it before giving it back and linking their hands together so they didn't stray apart. His right hand was free, and he gripped his gun in it, ready for any surprise they might encounter.

They started through the field, staying between the planted

lines, and he hoped their journey would be a safe one. Leafy plants surrounded them in all directions, rising up along the hills. It was a drug addict's paradise. For Chris and Mari, the place was the source of their enemy's income, the base. He planned to destroy it and handicap the cartel's revenue.

Many farms were hidden, with the coca plants growing between others for camouflage. The labs were also protected by trees, with the mixing and processing done under a tarp to hide from the prying eyes of the military, should they fly overhead and find them, which would lead them to burn the crop.

For the time being, Chris and Mari would leave the fields alone. The manufacturing part at the heart of the farm was where he planned to strike first. It wouldn't stop them. But it would sure slow them down and piss them off. Keeping the cartel off balance would work in their favor.

"We need to get to the lean-to." It was where the coca leaves were processed into paste.

Mari's brows furrowed. "The workers will be here soon."

"We should have enough time. If they get here while we're making our way back, we should be able to crawl out between the crops. Sort of." They weren't that high or dense.

Scanning the ground in front of them before they stepped was a slow process. When they arrived at the lean-to, their time was severely limited. One section of the area was a square, marked off by logs that kept the leaves in. When the loose leaves were within the square, the workers would stomp them down until they turned brown. When the desired color was achieved, the plant was mixed in a vat of gasoline and sulfuric acid then left to process for several hours. The next step would be to strain it into a paste, or "pasta," before processing it further into a powdery substance.

Chris bent around the edges of the lean-to and attached a small amount of C4. At the base of the barrels that contained the chemicals, he added more. "Brush the dirt over the plastic so that it's camouflaged. Be careful not to disrupt the detonators, though."

They worked quickly and hid the explosives as best as they could. The sound of vehicles urged them to hurry, and he camouflaged the last of the C4 before he motioned for Mari to run through the crop, following the same path they took to get there.

The mines would most likely line the perimeter of the fields in order to keep military out. Not only was it the source of the cartel's money, it also sustained the farmers that worked the land. Even so, he had no qualms about destroying what they would turn into a drug and infiltrate society with. There was no good that would come of leaving the operation intact.

With a hand on her back, he crouched next to Mari, urging her to hurry. They hunched down and stayed below the top lines of the coca plants as much as possible as they rushed to reach the outer edges before the workers saw them.

His heart pounded as they cleared the field and surged into the jungle beyond. Banana trees lined the crops, mixed in with a few additional trees and shrubs.

Mari whirled to face him, her face flushed and panic pulling at her features. "What now? You're not blowing it up with the farmers in there, are you?"

He shook his head. "We'll travel to the next one and set up the explosives there at night. But during the day, I want to understand their work schedule." He'd already noted the time of day the workers arrived. Padding that time with an hour just in case they began early, he knew when they'd strike. Or they'd hit them at night. That would be safer and easier.

No matter what, with Juan Carlos's inner-circle captains closing in on them, the detonations needed to happen soon.

CHAPTER 28

CHRIS

In the thick of the forest, Chris and Mari froze as the motor of a vehicle rose above the chirping birds. They weren't far from the dirt road, and had even been on it for a portion of their journey. Ten minutes later, they arrived at the next coca farm, and they'd taken to the woods rather than risking being seen. The sound of a twig snapping had Chris whirling around.

Four men with machine guns in hand, converged on them. In typical black garb, complete with black bandanas or ski masks, it was obvious who they were associated with. He shoved Mari behind him and opened fire. Air whooshed beside his ear. A knife struck the man farthest to the left—Mari had thrown it.

Cold enemy eyes widened in shock. *Be afraid.* He knew what he looked like when he did that. It used to freak his brother out. A cruel grin stretched across Chris's mouth with the knowledge of what these men would soon find. Shoving that thought from his mind, he tunneled his focus.

Bullets peppered the space around them, displacing the air and kicking up dirt by their feet. A few of those should have landed. They missed on purpose. Noting the butterfly tattoo on one of the men, he knew Mari would be unharmed, but that didn't mean she was safe. They had orders to retrieve her alive, but wounded might be acceptable. He was expendable.

"I want the last one alive," Chris growled, loudly enough that Mari could hear. He aimed for the man's legs and fired. The scream that sliced through the air would only bring more men. Their time contracted even more. Mari sank a knife into the man's gun hand. He fell to his knees and dropped his gun. He reached to pull out his blade, but not before Chris put a bullet through his good hand.

They rushed him together. Mari went to the others and kicked their weapons away, just in case. As she bent to retrieve her knives, wiping them on the dead men's clothing, Chris pulled the one from the living man's wrist and moved it to press against his neck. "What do you know about us?"

The cartel guy spit at him, and Chris laughed. While he applied enough pressure to break the skin, a few trickles of blood ran down the man's neck. "That didn't answer my question. You can start with telling me what you know about us." He motioned from himself to Mari. "And finish up with what Juan Carlos plans to do."

"And Mateo." Mari growled.

The cartel guy paused, his anger giving way to confusion. "Mateo's dead."

Mari stumbled behind him. *She truly didn't know.* A cold smile of intent spread across Chris's face. The guy he was interrogating looked as if he was about to piss his pants. He was definitely of a different caliber than the captains.

During the shootout in town he'd remembered Mateo had died. His relief at her reaction—and her ignorance about Mateo's death—doubled. There was also no way she was pregnant, given that Mateo had died about six months before. Her stomach was more than flat, and their time in the jungle had made it start to go concave, her hip bones and ribs too prominent for his liking.

A soft plop told him she'd dropped to the ground. Small puffs of air fell from her mouth behind him, and his tense muscles eased slightly. She would be okay—it had to be relief. He couldn't spare her a glance while he held the guy at knifepoint.

Boots scuffled, shifting in the dirt, and Mari's hand fisted his shirt by his hip. Chris flinched as she dug into his skin. As the pressure increased, he pushed back on her, not letting her shove him aside. He didn't want her to do something she might regret later.

Fuck.

"Move, Chris! I'm free now. We can leave, there's no reason for them to come after me." Her voice was shrill, emotion carrying each syllable. "But *he's* in my way."

"No. We need more information. Juan Carlos is still hunting you."

"I'm not pregnant," she almost shouted. "It's clear just looking at me."

The knife in Mari's hand flashed, and Chris grabbed her wrist, stopping the downward arc as she tried to end the man's life. He jerked his gaze to hers and saw wildness swirling in her amber orbs. "Not yet." With care, he moved her arm to her side and shifted in front of her, effectively blocking the man on the ground. *Juan Carlos will kill her if he learns she isn't pregnant.*

"Hurry up," she growled.

Behind him, she paced. Chris clamped his hand around

their hostage's bicep then dragged him to sit against the base of a tree. In fast succession, he stabbed the man in the legs and kicked him when he cried out. "Shut up." Chris got in his face again. "Stop wasting my time. What're Juan Carlos's orders?"

Pained defiance carved into his hostage's features, and Chris increased his efforts. "You'll be useless to them," he whispered close to the man's face. He cut off two of the man's fingers, and his screams filled the air.

Stillness settled around them, except for their captive's whimpers. He positioned his knife across the guy's other hand, a move that he knew would get through to the man. Without his fingers, he couldn't hold weapons. He cut halfway through, pausing when the man cried, "Wait, I'll tell you!" in a frantic tone. "Get her. Bring her back."

"That's it?" Chris's brows rose, and he positioned the knife to plunge into the guy's stomach next.

"Yeah, man. He wants the baby unharmed. It's all that's left of his son. Now let me go!"

Chris yanked his gun free then shot him once in the head and twice in the heart. He dragged the guy deeper into the brush, knowing it wasn't perfect, but they needed to get going.

He wiped his knife off and motioned for Mari to move with him. They set off at a slow jog—he didn't want her to overtax herself. They had a good distance to travel until the next farm. In a few miles, they would stop and rest.

He pushed her, but not once did she complain. Her features were shuttered, masking the emotions he knew would come out sooner or later.

When it looked like she was about to fall down, he slowed and waved her farther from the road so they could rest for a little while. She dropped down to the ground, lying on her back. Her chest rose and fell as she gasped for breath. He took a canteen from one of their packs and handed it to her. He'd long since shouldered their gear, not wanting her to have to carry the extra weight. He was used to it.

Several minutes passed as he waited for Mari to talk to him. It didn't take much longer. She shoved the loose strands of hair from her face and sat up, hugging her knees with her arms.

"I don't even know how to process this. I've been running from what Mateo would do to me, the prison he'd force me to live in, and now I find out he's dead. It's freeing, really, but I know I'm not entirely safe."

Chris met her troubled gaze with a determined one of his own. "No. Not until Juan Carlos has been stopped. We have a few more farms to hit, and then we'll go after him at his home."

Her body shivered when he said that last part, and he understood. Juan Carlos's home would be heavily guarded. But he was up for the challenge. And while he'd like to stash Mari somewhere safe, he knew she wouldn't let him.

"We're close." He reached for her and squeezed her arm. This woman was amazing—she hadn't even blinked at what he'd unleashed on the cartel guy, and he knew she would have done the same or worse herself. "Let's take care of this next field, set the explosives, and detonate both of them. We'll camp up high again." They needed the rest before the shit-storm they were about to face.

CHAPTER 29

MARI

After they grabbed a couple of hours of sleep—but it wasn't enough because it never was—Mari kept pace with Chris as they descended yet another tree. Nightfall had come a few hours before, and the sound of workers in the coca field they were watching were long gone. It was the third farm they'd targeted. The number of miles they'd covered was crazy, and her body was furious with her.

At the base of the tree, a few feet from the farm, she waited for Chris to determine their next moves. Her world had shifted again. Shock sank its teeth into her and refused to let go.

Mateo is dead.

In a sense, she was free. Her gaze sought out Chris once more, taking in the strong lines of his back, legs, and broad shoulders. He didn't know her biggest lie to him—that she wasn't his wife. It would be for the best if she cut ties and left him. She'd fulfilled her part of the bargain with Hannah.

The ache that squeezed her heart at the thought of walking away from him stole her breath and kept her rooted to the ground. *No. There is no way I can just walk away. Not since I fell for this man. And I have. I love him.* For the first time in her life, she'd found someone who made her crazy, melting her with one look, one touch, one kiss.

It wasn't fair. She had to tell him and really give him the choice to leave and not to engage further with the Ramirez cartel. Her hand slipped into her pocket, and she touched the dog tags she'd hidden in the tiny zippered hiding spot. He deserved to know.

"Chris—"

"Wait a sec, Mari." He reached behind him, his pack already on his back, and squeezed her hand. "We need to leave now. We've got about thirty minutes. It'd be much easier if we can find a Jeep or something." With a shake of his head, he gave her a lopsided grin, and his sexy dimple on the left side almost made her sigh.

Well, hell. She'd have to hold her secret a little longer. Relief made her go weak in the knees, and she struggled to keep up with him at first as he led her deeper into the trees. "Where are we going now?"

"We need to program the detonation at the fourth field then get ourselves moving so we're in town, closest to accessing the cartel."

"My aunt's place is there."

"Perfect. We'll go there before attacking Juan Carlos's home. I can contact my team from there, too, if they're not already close by."

"Your team?"

"My brother and the other guys I work with." He flashed her a smile. "The timers are set to go off fifteen minutes apart, so that the Ramirezes are scrambling all over. Which means we don't have a lot of time. We need a vehicle."

This was war. Chris wasn't one to mess around. What really worried her was how they would make it out alive after they laid waste to the Ramirez organization.

Absently, she twisted her long braid around into a bun at the top of her head. With her hair out of the way, she adjusted the pack that she'd pulled out of his grasp once more. *How much C4 does that man have?* "Are we setting explosives for every farm around here?"

"As many as we can." They continued to go farther from the field they'd set to detonate in about the time it would take them to get to the other one. Her heart thudded against her sternum, and she pushed herself to keep up with his crazy pace. He wanted to strike so many. Fear and excitement battled each other as they neared the first field. Continuing on the same path they'd taken to plant the explosives the first time, she followed and watched him set the timers.

The barrels of cocaine at the harbor had long since exploded, and she knew they wouldn't have too many chances to get to Juan Carlos once the fields were destroyed. Part of her knew from the very beginning that her opportunity for escape was slim. Her nerves were strung tightly, but if she was going to die, she wanted to do it by Chris's side, carving as much of a chunk out of the Ramirez organization as they could.

He motioned for her to leave, and they raced through the field, taking care to stay in the same line they'd first used, with no deviation and no chance to step on a landmine.

"Come on, I think I know where we can get a Jeep." This last farm placed them to the east and closer to the harbor. He backtracked to the port, since this farm was closer. It didn't take long before the sound of an explosion crashed through the night. The hairs on the back of her neck rose in anticipation of the cartel's pursuit.

When they got to the harbor, they squatted down by a forklift and surveyed who patrolled the perimeter. As they counted off the guards, they noted the semi-routines of the men. Chris indicated that she should follow his lead.

Soft light illuminated the area, and Mari saw the devastation from the bombs Chris had set. Black painted the ground in several areas, and the boat that had held some of the barrels was in shambles. It would be impossible to navigate the water.

They ran low to the ground, straight for the metal structure they'd climbed the other day. The rickety building was still intact. Pressed against the wall, Chris tried the door and found it unlocked. After he carefully opened it and surveyed the interior for people, they slipped inside. The smell of rotten fruit, dirt and dust, and the tiny scent of iron was the first thing to hit her. *Blood.*

Something happened in there, and not too long ago if the smell was any indication. It was just shy of repulsive, but not to the point of decomposition, which would make her gag and want to keep the door propped open.

A small amount of light pooling on the cement floor from a few well-placed windows near the ceiling gave them a general layout of the building. Garage doors lined one side, along with several larger shapes. Machinery, most likely. At least that's what they looked like in the small shafts of moonlight.

She curled her fingers around Chris's shirt and stayed close. When he stopped, she plowed into his hard body nose-first. She rubbed it and stifled a curse.

He tucked her to his side, and she almost laughed with relief at what they'd found. An open-top Jeep. Her tired body sagged against him, but then she clambered up, slid over to the passenger seat, and sighed. A quiet chuckle left Chris.

"Stay here. I'm going to set up a distraction."

Mari watched his retreating form, but fatigue won, and she remained in the seat. Fifteen minutes later, he whispered off to her right that he was back. She waited for him to join her, but he went over to the garage door that took up one side of the building and did something with the lock. He pushed the door up, ran back, climbed into the Jeep, and turned over the ignition. Alarmed voices filtered inside, and Chris lurched the vehicle forward and past several men, who opened fire on them. As they increased their speed, Mari held onto the oh-shit bar with white knuckles.

The popping sound of bullets pinged against the Jeep, and Mari pulled her gun out, twisted in her seat, and returned fire. At least she tried, by following the shadows and sounds of the weapons. It was still dark out, and Chris hadn't turned on the headlights, which gave them a slight advantage. If the lights were on, they would be an even easier target.

As they passed through the entrance to the harbor, Chris yanked something from his pack, which rested between them. When he got it free and pressed the button, a succession of explosions rocked the air from where they'd just traveled, dulling her hearing.

They drove until they came to a fork in the road. Chris turned left, which would lead them away from the town they needed to visit, and agitation spiked her blood. "What are you doing? This isn't the way we need to go."

Part of her tried to calm down, but her out-of-control temper eclipsed that attempt. She gripped his forearm, willing him to look at her again.

The Jeep swerved off the road, and she cried out when they crashed through a clump of branches before skidding to a stop. Chris shut the vehicle off, hopped down, and went around to her side. She glared at him.

"Are you okay?" He grinned. "We're ditching the Jeep to point them in a different direction. We'll walk back to the town. We aren't far off, but I wanted to throw a tiny misdirection at them."

She rolled her eyes and climbed down before yanking her pack from the floor of the vehicle. She fell into step beside him, and her temper cooled, allowing the unease of her secrets to take its place. They would face an insurmountable hurdle next, and she couldn't go into it without sharing what she knew— what she'd lied about.

She mulled it over as they passed the next mile in silence. The village they'd take shelter in—the same one that housed her aunt's shop and upstairs apartment—loomed up ahead.

"We need to find somewhere we can sleep the next few hours."

"My aunt's home. If no one sees us go in, it should be okay, at least for a little while."

Chris nodded. "Tomorrow, we'll wait and see what they do. I'll find a way to contact my team. Then, we'll go after Juan Carlos at his home."

CHAPTER 30

CHRIS

Safe in Mari's aunt's apartment above the store, she and Chris listened to the sounds in the street below. Chaos had ensued shortly after the first farm detonation, but he suspected the one that caused the most upheaval was the hit at the harbor. Chris grinned as Mari sank down beside him, their backs resting against a single bed.

"Did you find what you wanted?" He tugged her braid before dropping his arm around her shoulders.

She rested her head against him. "Yes." In her hand, she clutched a few pictures. "These were really the only things I'd hoped to keep." She swept her hand around the small, one-room living space. "Everything else is just stuff."

With a squeeze to her shoulders, he brushed a kiss on top of her head before peering out the small crack between the cloths, draped over the window and shielding them from sight. They had a second-floor view of the street if he angled his line of sight just right. And he did, getting up to look down on the activity happening below. "We can't stay here too long."

"Why? They don't know we're in here. I'm sure the guerrillas and possibly a cartel member or two reported that I was in the Darien Gap. Especially since they were Juan Carlos's chosen ones. They wouldn't expect me to return."

The cartel swarmed the streets and searched the shops around them, no doubt for evidence of who participated in the raids. He and Mari wouldn't have much time until they were discovered. Narrowing his eyes, he looked at who else was down there. The military walked between the cartel members, turning a blind eye to the injustice that occurred. "I would."

"You would what?"

"I would check here. Overlooking any avenue isn't smart." They could spare five more minutes. Then, they needed to move out. He scanned the rooftops, checking for anyone lying in wait.

"Chis, I need to tell you something." She cleared her throat. "I'm not your—"

"Well, shit." He chuckled. His team was here.

"What?" Agitation and fear lined her rising voice, and he turned with a grin.

Flat on the rooftop across from them, Hawk lay with his sniper rifle. He moved the curtain a tad, waiting until he felt the full weight of Hawk's focus looking back at him. The moment was enough that he knew things would go their way. In a flurry of hand gestures, they signaled to meet in twenty minutes.

The noise in the street slowly died down, and he pulled his pack close. "Put your pictures and anything else you know you'll want inside." He frowned as she wrung her hands together. "I'm sorry, babe. What'd you want to tell me?"

She shook her head. "Can't we rest here a little longer?"

Chris turned and really looked at her. There was a slight tremor in her hands as she unwound her hair and picked up the brush at her side. In slow, even strokes, she worked through the long strands.

Taking the brush from her hand, he separated a section of her hair as he settled her between his legs. With Hawk—and probably a few others on their team—watching over them, his worry eased, at least for the time being. He took his time and combed through her hair until it felt like silk between his fingers. When he finished, she leaned fully against him, tilting her face up to his.

"Thank you."

"What's bothering you?" He brushed a few strands from her cheek, his gaze crawling over her somber features as he cupped the side of her face.

"I need to give you something." She shifted and put space between them so they now faced one another. Her hand dipped into the pocket of her pants. "I've had these since Hannah and I pulled you from the tree. Instead of showing them to you while you were struggling to remember, I kept them."

Her hand uncurled, and in her palm were his dog tags. *So that's where those went.* She dropped them into his hand then curled hers around his, so that the military tags were between them. It was an unusual thing for her to be afraid to keep from him.

"Why?"

"I was scared you'd remember everything, especially since your division is on them. I worried that if I gave them to you, you'd become someone else. You'd turn against me, too. I know it was wrong, but I needed your protection to escape."

"I'm still the same person, and I would have helped you." He pulled her against him, wrapping his arms around her. "This doesn't change anything for me." He slipped his dog tags around his neck and tucked them beneath this T-shirt. They could have helped to jog his memory from the onset, but then he wouldn't have played along with her little lie. Maybe it was a good thing she'd held them. "I understand why you'd be concerned, but it's different in the States. There is way more good than bad in the armed forces. We're there to protect the people in our country. It's our job." Chris tweaked her nose. "The corruption here is nothing like the structure in the States. But just like in life, there are good and bad people. You'll need to judge them on their actions, trust your gut, and not immediately assume the worst just because someone is in the military or on the police force."

She worried her lower lip, her eyes misting. "You're not upset?"

The timid sound of her voice made him stroke her face and brush a kiss across her forehead. "No, babe. Nothing's changed between us." He dropped his gaze to her mouth before he covered her lips with his own. Passion exploded between them as he deepened the kiss. Tangling his tongue with hers, he enjoyed her for as long as he could. His team waited. Their time was dwindling, and they needed to move out immediately.

Breaking their kiss, he dropped his forehead to hers. "We need to go. You sure you got everything you want?"

She nodded against him.

"There's a high possibility we're not coming back here. Take another sweep just to be sure."

With a shake of her head, she picked up her backpack. "No, I'm positive. We didn't have much. Just memories and the shop." Quick fingers braided her hair once more.

Her bag was much fuller with a select few articles of clothing her aunt had made. His heart broke for her, because he understood that she had lost everything once already and was afraid she would soon lose him, too. That wouldn't happen. He wouldn't let it.

They needed to go. One last check below showed the streets

relatively clear. Blood mixed with the dirt below from a few random and unnecessary killings, but the majority of the cartel and police were gone. Mari's state of anxiety only increased because of it.

They waited a few more minutes while the sun inched toward the horizon. The faint sounds of someone crying carried through the stagnant air as they snuck out the back door of the shop. She pulled ahead of him a half step as he looked to the shadows, knowing one of his team would be there.

Movement drew his eye, and a smile split his face. The relief at seeing who stood before him robbed him of words, and Trevor's expression read the same.

He felt air displace by his side, and he swore. *Shit, I should have warned her.* He watched in horror as the blade headed straight for Trevor. And missed. Jerking to the side, Trevor narrowly avoided a knife in his throat.

Chris whirled around and wrapped his arms around Mari. "He's my brother. It's okay." Her body trembled, and when he leaned back he could see that her features were pulled tight with fear, which quickly morphed into anger.

Her fist pounded into his chest. "You knew? Did you know he'd be here, and you didn't warn me?" Panic flickered in her eyes at what she'd almost done.

CHAPTER 31

CHRIS

Relief and overwhelming happiness flooded Chris at being reunited with Liam, Hawk, and Trev, who had all been on his team. Crowded in Aunt Linda's apartment, they stayed out of sight. For a while, they would be safe. He trusted them with his life, but the tense body pressed to his side let him know Mari was very uncomfortable with the turn of events. There were things that would need to be discussed and planned before they could move out.

Mari's agitated wringing of her hands brought his focus back to her. "Babe, these guys are my brothers, my team." He nodded to each one as he introduced her. "You've already acquainted yourself with Trev." Her face flamed, and Trev chuckled. "The big bastard is Hawk. He's a sharpshooter. And that's Liam." He waved at Liam, who leaned against the doorframe.

Chris sensed her worry, and he knew where it stemmed from. They knew more about him than she did. Her discomfort was palpable. Dropping his arm lower around Mari, he tugged her closer. "And this gorgeous woman is Mari."

Hawk chuckled. "You sure you want to be with him, sweetheart?" His lips twitched. "He's a moody bastard. I, on the other hand, could rock your world."

Mari whipped out a knife and repeatedly flipped it in the air and caught it. "Not interested."

Chris's friends burst out laughing, and Hawk shook his head. "It's a pleasure to meet you, Mari. I was just messing with you. You'll fit right in with us." With a wink at her, he dropped his joking manner, and his features turned serious as he zeroed in on Chris. "Where've you been, and what the hell's going on?"

Chris groaned, giving Mari a gentle squeeze before he launched into how he'd woken in a freaking tree without any memory of how he'd got there—or any recollection of his past, for that matter—how Mari saved him, and what had happened as they made their way back. "We have two loose ends. I can't leave here until they're taken care of."

"What are they?" Liam's Irish accent thickened as his gaze sharpened on Chris.

"Hannah is still here. We were sent to rescue the Secretary of Defense, Henry, his security, and her. I'm assuming you got Henry out?" At their nods, anger climbed his spine. "I'm pretty sure she's a spy. There is no other way to explain why she's here."

"Jack is on that," Trev volunteered. "Rich came through with some surveillance pictures. She was in them, along with a partial view of your face by the side of a building."

Thank fuck that Rich Stevens, their CIA contact, had sent his brothers when he did. *We'll need all the manpower we can get to do what will come next.* With Jack, their military brother, on Hannah's trail, he set her from his mind. Jack would get to the bottom of Hannah's deception. He met Liam's gaze, as he knew this was personal for him, too. "Juan Carlos is after Mari. That's the reason he pulled the majority of his efforts from retrieving Liv."

Fury sparked to life in Liam's green eyes. The threat of the cartel wasn't new to him. Liv's former husband was Alejandro, or Alex, Juan Carlos's other son. "It's decided, then. We're ending this now."

Chris grinned. He knew he could count on them. Mari's body was rigid next to him, and he pressed a kiss to her temple. "This will be over soon, and we'll all fly back to the States. No more trekking through the Darien Gap to cross the border." He didn't miss the shiver that coursed through her. She flashed him a smile before returning her watchful gaze to his buddies.

Yeah, we have a few things to talk about. All in good time.

Hawk peered out the window, periodically keeping watch on the activity in the street below.

"How long have you guys been here?" Chris asked.

"About five days," Trev replied, his gaze darting back and forth from Chris to Mari. "We've been on Hannah's trail, hoping she'd lead us to you, but Jack took over, and we split up, thinking it'd be better to fan out."

Liam pushed away from the doorframe. "What's the plan for Juan Carlos?" The steely determination to his features matched Chris's.

"We took care of several of the coca farm operations."

Trev laughed. "Yeah, we caught that when cartel guys were running around like chickens with their heads cut off. Damn." He shook his head. "It was a good sign. We assumed it was you. We heard one of the explosions from here. The harbor."

"That was the first one. I'm sure that seriously pissed them off." Chris dropped his arm and laced his fingers with Mari's. "We need to survey Juan Carlos's home, figure out the best way to shake him out of there, and take out as many of the members of the organization as possible."

Liam grinned. "Let's get started, then." He angled his wrist and checked his watch. "We should get a move on. I'll message Jack and let him know, so if he can join us, he will."

Chris stood and tugged Mari along with him. They made their way over to a corner of the room, as much out of hearing distance as possible. He faced her and tucked a loose strand of hair behind her ear. "You doing okay?"

She nodded, but he didn't miss the caged panic that swam through her pretty brown eyes. "You have more of your memory back?" At his nod, she clasped her shaking hands together. "Then you—"

"Mari." *Yeah, we need to have that discussion, but another one takes priority.* With his team there, he needed to make sure she would be onboard with them and avoid flinging knives into their necks. "About my team. You understand not all those in authority are on the take."

"This is what I know, Chris. Intimately. The cartels are law here." Her voice shook, rising in volume.

"I agree with you. Juan Carlos has to die, babe. But you need to understand that people in authority there are just that— they're people. There are good ones, and a few bad. The evil ones are not the majority."

The stubborn set to her lips drew a small smile from him. "We're not where you come from. This is Colombia. And here, money talks, and the ones that have it are the cartels."

"Look, I don't disagree with you about how things are here. Even though not everyone in power is bad, it's impossible for that to be the case. I just ask that you keep an open mind about my team—please don't kill them—and for when we're in the States, okay?"

A tremor wracked Mari. She looked at him, her lower lip trembling. "You're taking me with you?"

"Fuck yeah, I am."

CHAPTER 32

CHRIS

In the dark of the night, Chris snuck into the Ramirez compound, while Hawk provided coverage in a large tree, should Chris need it. He set explosive charges and was back with the rest of his team in no time at all. Another day had passed. It was midnight, and they would strike soon. The moon cast enough light for them to move about.

Mari didn't know where Juan Carlos's bedroom was, but Chris guessed it would be on the ground floor. *Good, it'll be easier to escape should the need arise.*

Refusing to be excluded, Mari was in on the plan with them. She had wicked aim with a knife, so he wasn't terribly worried for the time being. He knew that would change when the cartel guys came at them and got too close to her. Then, he would be on shaky ground.

Soon, all hell would break loose.

Liam took off toward the east side of the house. Chris and

Mari moved to the west, Hawk remained in a tree that granted him a view of most of the house and property, and Trev took the front on a path for the door.

They sprinted to get into position before too many people saw them. Hawk took down seven, from what Chris could tell, as they neared the house. The consistent sound of gunfire and a few yells from the cartel guys sounded an alarm to the rest, who were inside.

Trev's gun was going off like crazy, and so was Liam's. Chris had shot four men, and Mari, three. There were more by the front of the house.

Chris slammed against the side of the house on one side of a window. Lights were turning on inside. On the other side of the window frame, he met Mari's eyes. Smashing the butt of his gun through the bars encasing the window, he broke the glass and tossed in tear gas. He planned to flush as many of them out as he could.

Explosions filled the night as the bombs he'd set went off in consecutive order. Angry voices shouted, screams permeated the air, and machine guns spewed bullets. They returned fire. Trev had brought a barrage of weapons.

Mari let knives fly before she changed her gun's magazine. Chris averted his eyes and focused back on the fight. They needed to get inside. Juan Carlos had to have an alternate escape route.

They held their positions, firing at the guards who swarmed from around the corner and in front of them. An explosion shook the ground, and the house shuddered from its blast. Chris grinned at Mari's smirk. Trev set more explosives at the door and signaled for how much time they'd have as he put enough distance between the bomb and himself. It was where Chris and Mari would enter—the area would be relatively clear.

The next explosion was deafening, and debris rained down around them.

Trev took his position at the entrance once more as Chris and Mari slipped through. Hawk eliminated any cartel members as they appeared. Trev and Liam handled the rest. The back of the house wasn't secure, which had bothered all of them when they devised their strategy. Liam planned to head to the back after tossing tear gas through every window he passed.

It was time. Gas mask in place, Chris picked his way across the rubble left over from the explosion at the front entrance, keeping Mari in his peripheral vision as they searched inside. Then came the part he didn't like—he went in one direction and she in another. They had to find the escape route Juan Carlos took. They couldn't let him get away.

The pop of bullets being fired echoed throughout the house. He was drenched in sweat. *Fuck, I hate having her in this.* He and his brothers had turned her into a walking weapon with the ammo, extra guns, grenades, and knives they'd strapped to her body. None of them wanted to see any harm to come to her, especially since they'd seen how much she meant to him. And she did.

With hand signals, Chris motioned for her to move to the back left. They suspected Juan Carlos's private wing was located there. What better place for a built-in escape route?

Smoke billowed around them, making the gas masks a godsend. Even so, fighting in that kind of soup wasn't easy. Several of the canisters had already emptied, and the thick fog took some time to dissipate.

They waded through with care. Though still in the air, the tear gas had lessened and became easier to see in. On his right, Mari shot off a few rounds, laying waste to the three men that'd rounded the corner. With his heart in his throat for her, he forced himself to concentrate on clearing the next passage.

Bullets flew around them. He grunted, taking the brunt in his bulletproof vest. Even with the protection, the hits stung, promising a colorful display of bruises when they finally got out of this hellhole.

Knives whipped past the side of his face, finding their intended targets' necks in their path. With a tug, Chris pulled the pin on a grenade and tossed it around the corner. As he covered Mari, they raced back a ways and huddled against the opposite wall, his body shielding hers. The blast shook them. Debris exploded several feet away. Not wasting any time, they took off in a run, guns extended, and raced to where the blast occurred. Bodies lay strewn about the destroyed hallway in a horrific display.

Their destination loomed like a beacon at the end of the demolished wing. They passed several open bedrooms, their doors and walls shredded, exposing them to view. The last bedroom in the hallway was their target, and it was unmistakable, with the gold-inlaid paneling and heavy brocade.

It was empty of people.

But there wouldn't be as many cartel members guarding it if there hadn't been occupants. Stepping over what used to be the threshold, Chris went to the closet while Mari lifted the paintings from the wall and tossed them to the ground. Shoving clothes aside, Chris checked the back walls, the ceiling, and the floor for a secret passage. There wasn't anything.

He met up with Mari in the enormous, spa-like, gold-and-marble bathroom. She looked inside the cabinets and under the sinks, while he turned to the linen closet. Something about the depth nagged at him, and he ran his fingers along the sides, the shelving, and the trim, until he found a small depression. Pressing on it, he stepped back as the interior released and swung open with a soft pop.

Mari was immediately at his side, and they passed through.

Chris took the lead. The dimly lit cement passageway was empty. He whipped off his gas mask and secured it on a clip on his belt, and Mari did the same.

"We need to go faster," Mari growled.

Inside, Chris grinned as they jogged down the tunnel. "If we sprint, we run a greater risk of running into a situation we can't get out of."

The faint sound of voices echoed up ahead, and Chris whipped his arm out, halting Mari. With his lips pressed together, he flashed her a warning look before moving toward the noise in measured steps.

The tunnel slanted down at a slow decline. Frantic shouting became clearer, and Chris counted five distinct voices. He had to assume there would be more. An engine roared to life, and he swore under his breath. With his jaw clenched, he took a risk and rounded the last bend in the passage, with Mari on his heels.

The hallway gave way to a large, garage-like room that boasted two vehicles, more lights, shelves of supplies, and several freestanding cabinets off to the side. They dashed for cover behind those.

Seven men stood around two black Hummers, yelling instructions at one another. The doors were wide open, and two slipped in. *Fuck!* He took out the two at the back right of the closest vehicle. Mari launched several knives, and two found their marks. The noise escalated between the gunfire and shouting cartel members. The Hummer farthest from them started its engine. A thug in black hopped inside, joining what was probably a full entourage. Windows down, men leaned out and rained bullets in their wake as the vehicle lurched forward and away.

Chris and Mari faced off with the two men who remained, and who stood between them and the other Hummer. A barrage of ammunition shredded their cover, and both of them dropped to the ground. Chris rolled out from behind the destroyed steel cabinet, firing as he moved, with his gaze locked on the men. He got off two bullets, which landed dead center in each of their foreheads. The men fell to their knees, one after the other, their guns clattering to the cement floor as they crumpled in heaps.

After regaining his feet, Chris rushed the SUV, leading with his gun as he peered inside. It was empty, so he got behind the wheel and started the engine. Mari rounded the other side of the vehicle and, after catching his all clear, hopped in. He gunned the Hummer, and they barreled down the tunnel as she closed her door.

Cinderblocks flew by the windows in a blur of gray, interspersed with flashes of light from the wall sconces. No men lined the exit, and there were no traps. They travelled about a mile without seeing the other Hummer. Mari's energy practically vibrated in the air. He got it. This needed to end. Not only for them, but for Liv and Liam, too.

They shot through the hidden escape, smashing the bushes planted in front just as the other vehicle must have done. Off in the distance, a cloud of dirt outed the SUV they sought. Chris floored the Hummer, pushing it harder than he had in the tunnel. The high speed over the bumpy road shook them inside the cab, and Mari grabbed the oh-shit handle.

"He has to die." Her voice raged with steely conviction. Chris grunted. There were orders he had to follow and a mission he'd finally remembered the instructions for, should they find themselves in the thick of things before they were officially sent. "Take the unit down—eliminate Juan Carlos," Rich had said. His instructions had been clear.

Mari turned in her seat and pleaded with him, her eyes wild. "If you turn him over to the authorities, he'll be out in a matter of hours at the most. He owns this town and everyone in his far-reaching territory."

"Hey babe, keep your head in the game."

They'd been made. Men leaned out of the other Hummer's windows, and one popped through the sunroof to man the machine gun there.

Dammit! A handheld missile launcher appeared through the rear window, and Chris swerved off-road. The blast sailed to the right of their SUV and detonated several feet past them in a narrow miss. The explosion rained debris high into the air, which fell with thuds all around and on them.

Mari returned fire, her body way too vulnerable to being hit for his taste. He maneuvered them back onto the dirt path, fighting the steering the entire way. Keeping them on course, he too extended his arm and got off as many shots as he could. The man who fired at them from the back of the Hummer tumbled out as they bumped over rough terrain, falling dead in a heap on the road. They ensured it when they bumped over his lifeless body.

Shots pinged off the bulletproof armor of their car and windshield. They closed the distance even more. The target's driver was having some sort of issue as the Hummer swerved, making it difficult for the men to get off a good shot. That worked just fine for them.

In a burst of speed, Chris rammed the back bumper then swung around, slamming into the right quarter panel. He fired off several more shots, effectively taking out the man in the back right of the vehicle. That left Juan Carlos, who was no doubt in the middle of the backseat, and potentially only three additional men, including the driver.

Mari hoisted herself halfway out the window so her butt sat on the door, and with one hand, she maintained a death grip on the oh-shit handle. She fired her gun and took out the man in the passenger seat.

"Get in!" Chris yelled to her so he could brake then crowd the other side of the Hummer. They had two more, for sure, to overpower.

As they swerved around the left rear panel, Mari leaned out the window and traded shots with one of their guards.

"Hold on!" Chris shouted as he yanked the wheel and slammed into the rear quarter panel. The Hummer lurched, hit a bump and spun off the road. He braked and turned to follow. The enemies' SUV tore through the brush and smaller trees, out of control until it crashed into a huge tree trunk.

Chris slammed on the brakes, they skidded to a halt, and he threw the vehicle into park. He and Mari leapt out and rushed the vehicle as the men poured out of it, blood dripping from their faces and hands. The driver didn't emerge, but the passenger-side door opened, along with the back doors. They had two to take down before they could get to Juan Carlos.

Mari jerked back, swearing, and Chris spared her a glance while firing. She kept moving around the SUV, and he refocused on the gun that was directly in front of him. Pain blossomed across his shoulder as he took a bullet. Diving, he fired as he tumbled, hitting the man's legs.

The guy shooting at him screamed, and the sound mixed with Mari's cries as he dropped to his knees. Jumping to his feet, Chris fired off three bullets and ended him, his need to get to Mari all-consuming.

Leaving the driver for later, he raced around the SUV to see Mari being punched in the face. He cursed as he emptied his clip into the back of the man's skull.

Chris caught her as she slipped down the side of the car. Setting her gently on the dirt, he promised everything would be okay, and that he'd be right back.

He ejected his empty cartridge then slammed another loaded one home. His body jerked back, and fire spread along his thigh. *Another bullet.* It had come from inside the car. *Fuck.*

Because the vehicle had bulletproof windows, Chris would only have one close entry point on the side. Reaching his hand around the threshold to the open door, he fired off several shots. A grunt sounded, followed by a gurgling moan, and he took advantage as he leapt in front of the opening while firing. One of Juan Carlos's men, armed with two guns, aimed them at him, blood pouring from his shaking arm. Chris got off shot after shot, ignoring the burning in his stomach as bullets punched into his vest.

Three to the forehead and two to the throat. *Dead.* Chris shifted his gun to the driver and buried a bullet in the back of the driver's head to be sure he was dead, although he lay motionless over the steering wheel. After a quick scan within the vehicle he allowed himself to focus on Mari.

Dropping to her side, he lifted a hand and gently touched the side of her swollen face. "They're all dead."

A small cry escaped her puffy lips before she clamped them together.

"Juan Carlos is in the backseat. We got him." He brushed the loose hairs from her face as she lifted her chin to meet his gaze.

"Oh." A shaky hand reached out, stopping just before she touched one of the bullet wounds on his arm. Tears leaked from her eyes, and she looked him over, pausing on the blood on his leg.

"I'm fine. Just have to clean and bandage them."

She let him help her up before leaning into the car. She just stood there, unmoving and staring at the lifeless body of Juan Carlos. Before he could stop her, she launched herself inside and buried her knife in him over and over again until he pulled her away. *Shit.* "He's already dead, can't get any more so."

He held her loosely in his arms, both of them staring at the lifeless drug lord. That man had been the root of too many problems for his team members, and for Mari. With another quick glance at the man who looked like his sons, Chris turned Mari in his arms.

"I can't believe it's over," she whispered in a hoarse voice.

"Almost. We need to check in with the team, make sure they're all okay."

She nodded and went with him back to the SUV they'd ridden in on. Chris dropped to his seat and tore off a strip of his shirt, which Mari took from his hands and proceeded to wrap around his leg. She pulled her shirt free from her pants and ripped a section off for his shoulder as he put a call in to Liam.

Pure relief washed over him at the sound of his buddy's voice and the all clear from his team. They were to meet back at Mari's aunt's apartment, where they could clean up and rendezvous with Jack, if he'd wrapped up the situation with Hannah.

CHRIS

Water poured down on them from the tiny shower in Mari's aunt's home. Chris shook his head as she tried to wash him first. With gentle fingers, he lathered her hair with shampoo, massaging her scalp. The luxury of the shower, no matter how primitive with its exposed wires, was a welcome change.

He moved so she could stand under the trickle of water, and he helped to rinse her hair. With a washcloth, he soaped her body in slow, sensuous strokes. Her breath came in pants. He wanted to make love to her—and he would, when they were home safely.

After she was rinsed, she took the cloth from him, held it under the water, then lathered it with soap and proceeded to give him the same treatment. When she finished, she returned to his wounds and cleaned them with infinite care.

The bullets had both gone clean through, missing any vital

arteries. The one in his shoulder was a flesh wound only, a mere scratch. They were painful, but he would heal. It could have been much worse. They were lucky.

Mari's face was swollen on one side, her left eye so puffy she could only open it a slit. The sight of it caused rage to bubble up in him all over again, and he wished the guy who was hitting her was alive once more and within reach so he could kill him all over again.

"I'm fine. Stop looking at me like you're ready to murder someone." She smiled. "I'll heal."

He grunted, not trusting what would come out of his mouth. He shut the water off then leaned out and grabbed a towel, which he wrapped around her. After doing the same for himself, they stepped from the shower stall into the equally small bathroom. He put a clean pair of briefs on and watched as Mari pulled on the clothes she'd brought inside. The tight, colorful top clung to her, and the bright skirt flowed around her toned legs. The clothes suited her, and he dropped a kiss across her forehead. As she worked on her tangled, wet hair with a brush, he slipped from the bathroom.

"Well, fuck." Trev thumped his good shoulder. "Look at you, dripping blood all over the floor." He forced Chris to sit as he got to work on first aid.

Hawk leaned against the wall, keeping an eye on the street. His six-foot-three frame looked strange in the small room—they all did. None of them were under six feet tall, and they were all stacked with muscle. The whole team was present—Trev, Hawk, and Liam. Only Jack was missing.

"Where the hell is Jack?" Chris whacked Trev on the side of the head as he patted his freshly bandaged leg.

Trev shifted to patch up Chris's shoulder, a frown marring his brother's usually easygoing features. "Don't really know. We've been trying to reach him on the satellite phone. The last contact we had was before we planned to decimate Juan Carlos's house. It is, by the way. We leveled it."

Thrusting his fingers through his short, wet hair, Chris ground his teeth. "Does Jack know she's a spy? She has to be. Nothing else makes sense."

Trev shifted back on his heels, repacked the supplies, and jammed them into his bag. Liam shoved off the doorframe to the kitchen to answer Chris. "Yeah. Whatever's going on, Jack'll get to the bottom of it. He knows we plan to head out tonight. The last transmission was really hard to understand through the static, but from what I got, he took off with Hannah and the jet. It should be back by now—he said he was sending it back. If not, we'll wait."

For how long? Jack needs to know what they'd done. Word would spread quickly of Juan Carlos's demise, and the balance of power would shift. It wouldn't bode well for whomever rose up and assumed control, no matter who it was. They had to leave as quickly and as quietly as possible, because finding themselves in another battle wasn't the plan.

The sound of the door opening drew Chris's gaze. Mari stepped from the bathroom and was breathtaking, even with the swelling on the left side of her face. She wrung her hands, and his brows rose from the clear sign of nerves. It was time they had that talk.

He stood, clasped her hand in his, and pulled her through the room to the back balcony. He indicated that she should take a seat at the small, rickety table in the equally cramped outdoor space then lowered himself into a chair as well, taking the weight off his throbbing leg.

Mari cleared her throat, breaking the silence before he could. "I have to confess something to you."

He paused, locked into the seriousness of her eyes.

"I'm not your wife."

Right. He'd realized that the moment his memory fully returned. He sat across from her in silence, counting down as her nervousness morphed into anger.

"You knew, didn't you? Why didn't you tell me? You said you remembered more, but not about *that.* For how long?" She huffed, crossing her arms across her chest as her voice rose. "You lied. You… you made love to me, and you knew we weren't really married."

Brows raised, he grinned. "When we were intimate, I only had the information about our relationship from what you'd told me. Those feelings were real. You're the one who claimed to be my wife." He continued to grin at her as her jaw dropped. All fun aside, he didn't want her to launch across the table and start pummeling him. That wouldn't serve either of them in the condition they were in. "Mari, I didn't remember until we saw Hannah in town. That's when I figured out you weren't who you claimed."

The anger drained from her face as quickly as it had first arrived, and she relaxed her arms and clasped her hands in her lap instead. "Then you're leaving soon."

"That depends." He studied her features, watching as hope bloomed over her fragile expression. "What did you expected to gain from saying you were my wife?"

She cleared her throat, and her tongue darted out to wet her lips. "At first, protection. If you thought I was your wife, you'd have a stake in my survival. Later, I was afraid if you knew the truth, you would change. You would become an enemy, instead of the man I was getting to know and coming to count on. I've been honest with you about my feelings. When I saw your military clothes and dog tags, I just couldn't risk it. Taking your identification and lying about us was a gamble, but when you didn't have your memory, the lie became easy, even safe."

"I can understand your fears." He really could. With Mateo

and Juan Carlos breathing down her neck, threatening to take her away, and controlling her life, he understood the helplessness that drove her and her worry that he would change into someone who would take advantage of her, or even turn her over to them, as they were the ruling power in the region.

Mari reached across the round table and clasped his forearm. "Everything I told you about running, about my fears of the military and cartels, and about you… It was real. I didn't lie about what you mean to me."

"Come here."

Mari moved around the table and faced him, fear clouding her eyes. He pulled her close, seated her on his uninjured leg, and wrapped his arms around her. Her small frame fit against him, and he rested his chin on her head. *This woman.* He'd come to care for her and to love her—he needed her too. There wasn't a single bone in his body that doubted her words. "Come home with me."

She pushed against his chest and sat up so she could see his face. Easing his hold on her, he dropped his grip to her waist and played with the long strands of hair that cascaded down her back.

"You'll still take me away from Colombia? And…"

"Yes, I will. Even if you don't want to stay with me or be in a relationship with me, I'll help you get on your feet in the States. You have a choice, Mari. Your life is your own."

Tears welled in her eyes, spilling over in rapid succession. Joy spread over her face, and the smile she gave him was blinding. "I want nothing more than to be with you."

EPILOGUE

MARI

Mari smoothed her hand over her sweater and turned to the side in the full-length mirror. Her curves had filled out since they'd been out of the jungle for so many months. A small smile played along the edges of her mouth, and her eyes sparkled back at her. Her hair hung down her back in long, loose curls. With a final look at her appearance, she turned and slipped on the new boots, which she'd bought the last time she and Chris had visited Liv and Liam.

Liv and Liam's home in Maine was beautiful. While she wasn't entirely used to the climate, she could picture herself living there with Chris.

They were going on a date. Chris was picking her up in five minutes. Heat flushed her cheeks, and butterflies fluttered in abandon in her stomach at the mere thought of him. *I love that man.*

They'd been in California for the past few months. Chris

had set her up in his place, deciding to bunk with his brother so she could have some space to decide what she wanted. He'd made it clear he wanted her. *That's what I want, too.* Even after she'd confessed how much she wanted to be with him, he insisted that she take some time to decompress and that they slowly get to know each other better.

She glanced around the very masculine apartment, noticing the few feminine touches she'd added and how their styles complemented each other. They did, too—they fit together. She'd tried to tell him that she didn't want to be without him, because she'd grown so used to having him around twenty-four-seven, but he insisted. It was a good thing. He'd courted her, taking her out a few times a week to dinner, to see the museums, to an art fair, and on more than one weekend trip to visit Liam and Liv.

While in Maine they even ran into Jack and Hannah. That'd been interesting. Not one of them—her, Liv, or Hannah—had a typical, or simple, beginning relationship with their guys. Complicated. It seemed as though they excelled at it. But Liv… In no time at all, she and Liv had grown close. They had something in common, the Ramirez brothers and the hell that family put them through.

The doorbell rang, and she rolled her eyes. *It's his place.* Ringing the doorbell was sweet but unnecessary. Opening the door, she grinned as every nerve ending in her body seemed to come alive at the sight of him. He flashed a crooked grin before he bent down to brush a too-short kiss across her lips. After she stepped outside, he shut and locked the door behind her.

The drive to her new favorite restaurant was short, and before she knew it they were seated. The experience was in tune with nature and delivered a retreat-like atmosphere. The laid-back waterfront patio boasted soft lighting and breathtaking views of the lake. They could watch the boats go by, and at night they sat underneath strands of twinkling lights strung around the outdoor dining area. It was quaint and romantic.

Heads had turned as they'd walked by the other diners, and her heart swelled with the knowledge that he didn't even notice the women lusting after him with their eyes. He only had eyes for her.

Chris held out her chair for her. As he pushed her closer to the table, he leaned down and whispered, "I have a surprise for you."

Craning her neck around to see him, she grinned. "What?"

The waiter came over right away, and they placed their drink order. As soon as they were alone again, he pulled a folded piece of paper from his pocket. Spreading it out between them, she gasped. In the flickering light of the candle, she fixed her gaze on the small-scale blueprint.

Tearing her gaze from the plans, she searched his face. "Is this…?"

"They're the tentative plans for our house on the property adjacent to Liv's."

When Liv had decided to stay in Maine, by Liam, rather than return to New York, she'd bought property that neighbored his. She didn't live there anymore—her home was with Liam on his property. There was a small cottage, which the guys sometimes used when they were there and where she and Chris had stayed. *He's building us a home.* Tears welled in her eyes and threatened to overflow.

"Hey." He leaned across the table, cupped her cheek, and brushed away a rogue tear. "If this isn't what you want, we can make changes."

She chocked back a sob with laughter. Never in her wildest dreams did she think she would end up with someone like Chris. He was someone who made her heart race and butterflies erupt in her stomach from a simple look or touch.

"No." She caressed the back of his hand, which still rested along her cheek. "It's perfect. It's everything we'd talked and dreamed about. I'm just so happy."

He picked up his chair and moved it to her side of the table. Draping an arm around her, he drew her close. They sipped the drinks that the waiter quietly dropped off. With the alluring view of the boats sailing along the water, they planned their future.

It lay ahead of them as fate had intended—wild, untamed, and filled with promise.

If you enjoyed reading EYE OF THE STORM as much as I did writing it, I hope you'll consider leaving a review.

The Gray Ghost series will continue with Book 3, Beneath the Surface. Join Amy's Newsletter if you don't want to miss it!

Follow Amy McKinley here:

www.facebook.com/amymckinleyauthor/
Newsletter | http://eepurl.com/b_Dc91
www.twitter.com/AmyMcKinley7
https://goodreads.com/author/show/14257449.Amy_McKinley
www.instagram.com/amymckinleyauthor/
https://pinterest.com/amymckinley7/

You can also find her at
www.AmyMcKinley.com

ACKNOWLEDGMENTS

Special thanks to everyone who played a part in this incredible journey.

To my husband, two daughters, and two sons for their encouragement, support, and belief in me.

To Kristin Kisska, who was instrumental in the process with her mystery writing background and assistance with the tagline.

Emily Albright, Victoria Van Tiem, and Kristin Kisska—fantastic writers whose friendship, brainstorming, and support I cherish. I'm lucky to be involved with such an amazing group of authors.

Maryellen Newton, my incredibly talented friend, who provides unwavering support and beta reads every one of my books. Love our weekly coffee times!

Maria Vickers, for her phenomenal brainstorming in figuring out the story's setting.

Jackie V Booknerd—my incredible assistant. Jackie, Natasha, Lynn, Amanda, and Cassie, my crazy-fun street team, whose encouragement and help with promoting this series are seriously appreciated.

Taylor Anhalt, my brilliant and talented editor. To the Red Adept team, Sara, Kate, and Irene, for making the task of editing so easy.

Christopher John, owner of CJC Photography, and Alex Neff, cover model, for such a fantastic picture.

T.E. Black Designs, who did the cover design and formatting, you are a dream to work with and each projects' end results exceed my expectations. Carol Eastman, for your wonderful blurb assistance.

Special thanks to all the bloggers who have encouraged and helped me along the way, Itsy Bitsy Book Promotions, Lip Services, and my readers—who continue to make my dream a reality.

Thank you.

ABOUT THE AUTHOR

Amy McKinley is the author of the Five Fates Series and Gray Ghost Novels. Her romance books have strong heroines, sexy alphas, and just the right amount of heat, danger, and always an HEA. She lives in Illinois with her husband, two daughters, two sons, and three mischievous cats.

You can find her at www.amymckinley.com